The Illuminator Rising

The Voyages of the *Legend*, Book 3

By Alina Sayre

Other books in The Voyages of the Legend series:
Book 1: The Illuminator's Gift
Book 2: The Illuminator's Test
Stay tuned for Book 4!

The Illuminator Rising

Text copyright © 2016 by Alina Sayre

Cover design copyright 2016 by Jenny Zemanek at Seedlings Design Studio

Map created by Brian Garabrant

ISBN: 1533448582

ISBN-13: 978-1533448583

Praise for The Illuminator Rising

"…a thrilling read…[Sayre] has a flair for being able to capture the interest of a reader and hold onto it."
-*Readers' Favorite*, 5-star review

"Painted in dazzling and exciting settings that inspire imagination, it is not just the illuminator coming into her own and rising, but the entire epic saga."
- Angela Wallace, award-winning author of the *Elemental Magic* series

"The characters are so memorable…I definitely shed some tears, but I also had smiles, chills, and laughs…Please see to it that the middle graders in your life get their hands on *The Voyages of the Legend*."
- Lloyd Russell, book reviewer at *The Book Sage*

Praise for the award-winning first novel
The Illuminator's Gift

"A strong first novel…refreshing."
- *The Wooden Horse: Toys for Growing*

"[*The Illuminator's Gift*] is a fabulous read that had me turning the pages...I predict you'll soon be hearing a lot more about this talented author."
- A. R. Silverberry, award-winning author of *Wyndano's Cloak*

"*The Illuminator's Gift* is a fabulous read! This book makes for an excellent read-aloud. The author's word choice is magnificent; her palette of words creates a detailed painting in the reader's mind."
- Nicole Raychev, elementary school teacher

"I got blindsided.... I was cheering, crying, gasping, crying, shaking, and, you guessed it, crying. It's rare that a book does that to me.... Alina gets high marks for the 1st 2/3 and off-the-chart marks for the last 1/3."
- Lloyd Russell, book reviewer at *The Book Sage*

"The storytelling reminds me of a C.S. Lewis-type fantasy story.... After I started I could not put it down."
- Jeff Landis, pastor

"...written with an imagination and poetic elegance reminiscent of C.S. Lewis's *Chronicles of Narnia* and Tolkien's *Lord of the Rings*."
- Angela Wallace, award-winning author of the *Elemental Magic* series

"...magical...the book is a real page turner."
- *Readers' Favorite*, 5-star review

Dedication

To all the writing teachers who helped me find my voice
and to my writing students, who remind me to ask good questions.

Contents

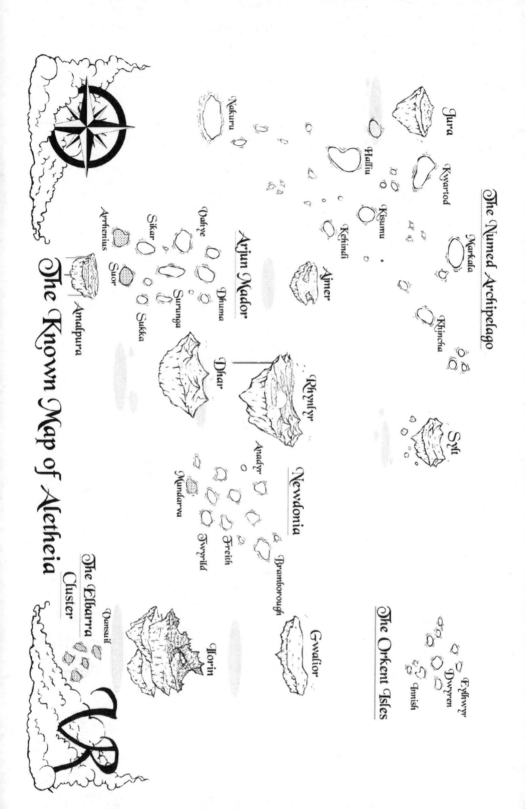

The Known Map of Aletheia

The Numed Archipelago

Jura
Kyarlod
Haffiu
Nakuru
Kisumu
Markala
Kehindi
Ajmer
Rhincha
Syft

Arjun Mador
Arrhenius
Sikar
Vahye
Suor
Surunga
Dhuma
Sukka
Amalpura
Dhar
Rhynlyr

Newdonia
Anady
Mundarva
Freith
Twyrlla
Bramborough
Gwalior

The Elbarra
Cluster
Vansuil
Ilorin

The Orkent Isles
Eyllwyr
Dwyren
Innish

Chapter 1
A Vision of Fire

Red pooled on the palette like a lake of blood. A drop of yellow splashed in, intense as the hot core of a bonfire. Swirled together, they created a brilliant orange like a sunrise at sea.

Humming under her breath, Ellianea Reid added the orange to her painting, pulling the color into two sharp spikes of flame. She added flecks of yellow and white for depth, then dropped her paintbrush in a glass of water and sat back to examine the results. In the foreground of the painting, a turquoise-blue lagoon lapped against a rocky beach. Beyond it stood the silhouettes of twin mountain peaks, their feet scored with dark caves. But from the tips of the mountains, blasts of fire spewed straight into the sky. Ellie stopped humming and frowned. *Fire-breathing mountains? Rua, are you sure you know what you're doing? This vision doesn't make any sense.*

Ellie mentally reviewed the message they'd received from survivors of the Vestigia Roi nearly two months ago. The crew of the *Legend* had been trying to solve the riddle since they left the island of Innish, but every attempt had ended in frustration.

Where the fire meets the sky
Between tall peaks your ship must fly.

Where the ocean swallows sand
Upon black rock your ship must land.
Where the sea roars into caves
Make salute, your lives to save.

Ellie sighed. When she'd seen this vision, containing all the elements named in the message, she'd thought Rua might finally be giving her the key to solve the riddle. But her painting looked like no place she'd ever seen, and a fire-spewing mountain was as fanciful as some of the stories she'd heard on Innish.

"Having any luck?"

Ellie turned to see Vivian, the ship's translator and librarian, standing behind her. Vivian could read eighteen languages, and she held a stack of books on codes and ciphers against her hip, making room for her expanding belly as the baby inside her grew. Ellie and Vivian spent almost every day in the ship's library together, trying strategy after strategy to solve the riddle. The other crewmembers tried to help, but Vivian's language skills and Ellie's gift of Sight were their best hopes. Ellie only wished her Sight would show her something useful once in a while.

"No. I thought I was on to something with this one, but it's just another dead end."

"That doesn't look like a dead end to me," said Vivian, examining the painting.

"How can it be anything else? I mean, fire-breathing mountains? There's no such thing."

"Now, hold on a minute," said Vivian. "I've never seen a fire mountain myself, but I once read an account of them in my studies at the Mundarva Library. They may be only a myth, but who knows? Perhaps they do exist somewhere in Aletheia. Jude has traveled a lot with the fleet. Let's go ask him."

"Do you think we should bother him about this? He's busy, and it seems like a silly question."

"If there's even a chance it could help us solve the riddle, no question is silly. Come on. If we don't ask, we'll never know."

On the weather deck of the *Legend,* the wind blasted Ellie's face and the hard, bright light shocked her eyes. Up on the quarterdeck, her twin brother Connor, now captain of the *Legend,* commanded the helm and shouted orders to Jariel and Finn, who were fifty feet up in the rigging. Jariel, who had trained for nautical service at the Vestigian Academy and wasn't afraid of anything, climbed without a harness, like a monkey in a tree. Finn, an Innish storyteller and the newest member of the crew, had a rope securing him to the wooden yard. Still, Ellie thought that for having been a sailor only two months, he navigated the rigging gracefully. He and Jariel unwrapped the bindings of a mended topsail.

"And…hoist sail!" shouted Connor.

The enormous, shapeless piece of cloth gradually stretched into a tight square as Kai, Owen, and Alyce hauled on the lines from below. Kai's powerful muscles easily trimmed his side of the sail. He had been a sailor in the fleet before he lost his eye, and then he'd become elite security for the Vestigian Council. Even though he was now first mate of the *Legend* and no longer Ellie's personal bodyguard, she was glad he was still watching out for this crew.

On the other end of the sail, Owen and Alyce were not having such an easy time.

"Pull, Owen! You're not helping!" shouted Alyce.

"I *am* pulling!" Owen grunted, his face red from the effort. His knowledge of chemicals and electricity had saved the *Legend* during a battle and a lightning storm, but the ten-year-old boy's arms weren't much thicker than the line he was handling. His yellow dog, Sunny, stood behind him, barking.

When they finally got the line cleated off, Alyce and Owen came for a drink from the water pail.

"We really need a mechanical way to trim those sails," said Owen. He opened his shirt pocket to check on his bluestripe ribbon snake, Moby. "I'll work on inventing something."

Alyce looked up at the repaired sail. "My patch looks good, though. I'd say I'm a natural sailmaker."

"Natural for a landlubber, maybe," said Connor from above them, rolling his eyes. "Don't get cocky. Any sailmaker's work can fall apart."

Alyce sniffed. "I have as much experience being a sailmaker as you have being a captain."

Ellie noticed Connor's ears turning red. "Back to work. Deck needs scrubbing."

"Yes, *Captain*." Alyce turned on her heel and stalked off.

Ellie called up to Connor. "Have you seen Jude?"

Connor jerked his thumb behind him. "Up here. He's doing some woodwork."

Ellie and Vivian climbed the stairs to the quarterdeck. Jude, Vivian's husband and the *Legend's* second mate, doctor, and carpenter, was kneeling in the far corner, half-hidden behind some barrels and spare lumber. He was hammering in a new section of railing while Alyce's six-year-old sister Aimee followed him, sanding down the rough wood. Suddenly she let out a wail and dropped her sandpaper.

"Owww!" She held out her thumb to Jude. "It hurts!"

Jude set down his hammer. "Looks like you have a splinter there."

"Make it better?"

Concentrating closely, Jude pinched the splinter between two fingers and pulled. Aimee whimpered, and he dabbed at her thumb with his handkerchief.

"There. All better."

She held out her thumb again. "Kiss it? Mama said kisses make things all better."

Alyce and Aimee's mother had died just a few months ago in the attack on Rhynlyr. Jude kissed Aimee's thumb. "How's that? Better?"

"Uh-huh." Aimee kissed her thumb again herself.

"Good." Jude looked up and saw Ellie and Vivian. "Thanks for being such a good helper, Aimee. Why don't you go see what Sunny is doing?"

"Okay!" Aimee hugged Jude and ran off down the stairs.

Vivian smiled as Jude stood up, tucking his handkerchief back in his pocket. "You're going to make such a good daddy." She stood on tiptoe to kiss his cheek.

Jude smiled thoughtfully, his hand brushing her belly. "I hope so. How's the work on the riddle going?"

Ellie held up her painting. "Vivian said I should show you this."

Jude took the painting and looked at it closely. "*Hakaran.* Interesting."

"They have a name?"

Jude considered the burning mountains. "The Numbani, people from the Numed Archipelago, call them hakaran, 'fire mountains,' because of the lava they spew out. In the Common Tongue they're called *volcanoes.*"

"But…I thought they weren't real."

"Just because you haven't seen one doesn't mean they're not real," said Jude with a wink. "As far as I know, they exist only in the Numed Archipelago. I saw one on a medical mission to the outer Numed on one of my first assignments with the fleet."

"I told you we should ask him," Vivian nudged Ellie's shoulder.

Ellie stared at the painting. "So…if hakaran are real…"

"*Where the fire meets the sky…*" Vivian quoted from memory.

"I think…we need to find one. Maybe two," Ellie said slowly.

"Finally, a clue! Well done, Ellie!" Vivian spun Ellie around.

Ellie laughed and sat down on a crate. "Well, it was more Jude's doing than mine. Jude and Rua."

Jude scratched his head. "I hate to be the bearer of bad news, but...there are more than two hakaran in the Numed Archipelago. There could be dozens, hundreds, for all I know."

Ellie's face fell. "How will we know which are the right ones?"

"I say we start with a look at the ship's maps," said Vivian. "Connor, do we have any maps of the Numed Archipelago?"

"Sure," said Connor. "Owen, watch the helm."

They headed into the captain's cabin. Kai, Jariel, Finn, and Alyce came in as Connor selected some maps from the pigeonholes on the wall.

"So you're telling me that all this time we've been charting a course for the Haven of Jura, but now we're looking for a mythical land formation called a volcano?" Connor said, weighting down the corners of a Numed map.

"I guess it's not mythical. Jude says he's seen one," said Ellie.

"And Jura was only a guess in the first place," said Kai. "When we sailed past the Haven of Sylt and saw it burning, we knew it was only too likely that Draaken's forces had also overtaken Jura. Now that the Enemy has flying ships, it seems he's trying to systematically destroy all Vestigian outposts."

"Isn't that what he's always been trying to do?" said Jariel, leaning her chin on her hand, revealing the fractal scar branching down her right arm and the compass-shaped burn in her left palm. Her near-fatal encounter with lightning had given her a more serious side. "Isn't his nasty idea of Khum Lagor only accomplished when everybody else is conquered or dead?"

"Yes," said Kai. "But now he's making a determined effort to bring Khum Lagor into reality, and soon."

"He probably thinks that Lagorite prophecy guarantees him victory—'For the victory of Draaken / the child of visions is key,'" Vivian quoted. "Even though he failed to capture Ellie on Rhynlyr."

"I'd like to see him try again," grumbled Connor.

"But doesn't the Vestigian prophecy say that all the islands will rejoin under the One Kingdom, and then Ishua will return and triumph?" said Alyce. "Only one of those prophecies can come true."

"Yes, and Draaken is working hard to make sure it's his," said Kai. "It seems he is mobilizing his forces to crush the Vestigia Roi once and for all."

"Well, we're not doing any good by sitting here talking," said Connor. "Let's start looking for a volcano."

Their search results proved disappointing. Dozens of hakaran were marked on the larger islands of the Numed Archipelago, and there could be dozens more on the unmarked smaller islands.

"There are so many," said Ellie. "How do we choose where to go?"

"Pick a random island with a hakara and scout to see if it has any of the other elements of the riddle?" suggested Vivian.

"But that kind of search could take us *years*," groaned Connor. "Draaken will have won the war by then."

"Without more information, it seems we have no choice," said Jude. "We have to start somewhere."

"In the meanwhile, Ellie and I will keep working on the riddle," said Vivian. "Besides, when we start scouting islands, we can ask questions of the locals. Maybe they can give us more clues."

Ellie stared at the map, not feeling Vivian's optimism. Even now that they knew they were looking for volcanoes, this search felt like a wild goose chase. How were they ever supposed to find the right ones? Even if they did, how could they be sure that the Vestigia Roi were still hiding there? What if the ten people aboard the *Legend* were really the only Vestigians left in Aletheia?

That night, Ellie dreamed she was standing alone on the *Legend's* deck. The ship's *lumena* shone out brightly into the darkness, but below there was no light at all. If there were any islands in that dark ocean, not a soul was awake.

"It's so dark," she said aloud.

"Lonely, isn't it? Feels like there's no one else left in the world." Ellie looked up and saw Ishua standing beside her, leaning on his crutches. His shaggy curls fell into his eyes, and his callused hands were stained with deck varnish.

"Yes, exactly," she said softly. "How did you know?"

Ishua looked at her. His deep brown eyes held bottomless, mysterious joy, but also deep sorrow.

"You think I don't know what it is to be lonely?" He looked out again into the night. "Everyone who leads is lonely sometimes. Everyone who carries the responsibility for guiding others. Everyone who follows the pull of the Song, even when it means they must follow it alone. It can feel like sailing over an empty sea at night, awake like the last star left in the sky."

"Sometimes I'd rather be on the ground with a few other lights around me," Ellie sighed.

"Yes," said Ishua.

In silence, they stared out into the darkness together. Ellie pictured all the faces aboard the *Legend*—Connor, Jariel, Jude, Vivian, Alyce, Aimee, Owen, Kai, and Finn. They were all trying to be brave, all trying to do their part to reunite the One Kingdom. But the efforts of one ship's crew seemed insignificant compared to the force of Draaken's power and hatred.

"Can't you do something about all this?" she said to Ishua. "I mean, you're so powerful and strong, and we're so small in this big world. Why don't you just fight back against Draaken yourself?"

Ishua remained silent, gazing out into the night. Ellie felt tears prick her eyes. This task was unfair. How was a crew of ten people supposed to win a war, not knowing if they had any allies left alive? How was she, a thirteen-year-old who'd discovered her powers of Sight less than a year ago, supposed to know the right way to go, let alone guide others?

"Ishua, this is your Kingdom, isn't it? Then shouldn't you tell us what we have to do to save it?"

Ishua still stared out to sea, intent on something in the distance. Anger suddenly surged up in Ellie. She gripped the ship's railing with both hands.

"We are outnumbered and alone in a war that's too big for us. If you're not going to defeat Draaken for us or even tell us what to do next, then at least give us the strength to fight!"

Now Ishua looked at her, a smile twitching at the corners of his mouth. His eyes traveled back to the ship's bow. Battling frustration, Ellie followed his gaze. From the *Legend's* glowing lumena, tiny flecks of light, like snowflakes or stars, began to drift out into the night. Delicate golden threads followed them. The stars fell to earth like bright raindrops, their tails shimmering behind them. Some disappeared into the darkness, but others landed and bloomed into flowers of light on distant islands. Ellie watched in wonder. The world was dark no longer. A garden of light was springing up all around them.

"What does it mean?" she asked, bewildered.

"It means you're asking the right questions," said Ishua with a secretive smile.

The next morning, Connor announced that they would begin their search for a volcano on a small island south of Markala. He estimated they'd reach it about sundown, and he named Kai the leader of the scouting mission. Kai chose Finn to go with him, and they prepared to leave at first light the following day.

They located the island just after supper, and Connor shut off the *Legend's* stern propeller to hold their position until morning. The crew relaxed on deck as the sun set in a fanfare of saffron clouds.

Sunny lay on his back, his tongue lolling as Aimee rubbed his furry belly.

"He's saying, 'this is the best day of my life,'" she giggled.

Jude and Vivian sat together on the quarterdeck, talking quietly. Finn was plucking out the melody of the Song on his harp, and Alyce was standing next to him, singing along. Watching them together, Ellie felt a strange, sharp pain. She turned away, focusing instead on the sunset, which had turned blue and silver in her changed vision.

As she looked north, she glimpsed two spots in the distance. She blinked hard, trying to clear away dust in her eyes, but the spots stayed. The one on the left was orange, while the other was such a dark brown it was almost black. Ellie squinted at them for a moment, then visualized the image of a microscope. The orange and brown spots jumped closer, and Ellie could see that they were ships. Flying ships. They were some distance apart, but it looked like the orange one was chasing the other.

Quietly Ellie walked up to Jariel, who was sitting on a barrel and practicing her sailor's knotwork. "Can you come…check something for me?"

Jariel frowned. "Are you okay, Ellie? Are you…seeing something?"

Ellie nodded. "I think so. But I want you to confirm it before I say anything to the crew."

Jariel slipped off her barrel. At the railing, she extended her spyglass and peered in the direction Ellie indicated.

"I see something," Jariel said. "In this light, it's hard to tell what it is. But I do see lights, so my guess is it's a ship with lanterns."

"Two ships," Ellie said softly.

"Then you can see better than I can," said Jariel, collapsing the spyglass. "You're not imagining anything. Want me to tell the others?"

Ellie nodded, and the lookout cupped a hand to her mouth. "Ship ahoy!"

The whole crew came running. Alyce stopped singing, and Ellie's vision snapped back to normal. Connor already had his spyglass out.

"Two flying ships, Captain," Jariel reported. "Ellie saw them."

"Does that mean we've finally found other Vestigians?" asked Finn eagerly.

"It could mean a lot of things," said Connor. "Now the Enemy has flying ships too."

"The two ships aren't working together," Ellie said. "It looks like one is chasing the other."

"Then at least one is unfriendly."

"If the other one is Vestigian, though, we have to help them," said Jariel. "That was part of our Vow of Dedication."

"And if we find Vestigians, they might be able to lead us to the others," said Vivian.

"Use caution, though," said Kai. "If those are full-size, armed Vestigian ships and even one is hostile, we could be in for trouble."

"Then we'd better get ready for trouble," said Connor. "To the hold! Arm for battle!"

Chapter 2
Sky Battle

The *Legend* had no cannons, but Kai and Jude moved the two large ballistae to the deck, and Owen supplied them with explosive vials of his own making. Most of the crewmembers had their own weapons of choice, but the Innish had also outfitted all of them with knives and short, sturdy bows. Ellie tested the band of her slingshot. She didn't think she'd ever get over the knot of dread that settled in her stomach before a battle.

Connor, his tiger claws already on the knuckles of his left hand, estimated that the *Legend* would converge with the other ships about thirty minutes after nightfall. He'd ordered all the exterior lanterns extinguished, and Jariel was at the helm. The rest of the crew was gathered belowdecks. A lantern illuminated a large map on the table.

"I want those ships identified before we decide on a final strategy," said Connor, tracing a line between one rock that represented the *Legend* and two other rocks representing the strange ships. "If they're Vestigian, we can't fire on them. But we also can't afford to be taken by surprise."

"Why not sail above them to get a better view?" said Ellie.

"That would also give us an advantage if we do fire on them," said Kai, checking the mechanism on his crossbow. "And some protection: their cannons can't fire straight up."

"We could blow up their lumenai, like we did in the battle after Rhynlyr," said Owen, slipping a dart into his blowpipe.

Connor shook his head. "Even if the ships are hostile, I want to try to capture them if we can. If we ever do find the rest of the Vestigia Roi, they'll need the ships. And with the Havens under attack, we have no access to more lumenai anytime soon."

"All right," said Owen. "So we sail in from above and scout. Then what?"

"If it's true that the two ships aren't working together, I think we should strengthen our firepower by teaming up with one of them, at least until the first ship is taken," said Connor. "Then we can decide if the second ship is a friend or foe. If it comes down to a negotiation afterwards, we might need you to translate, Vivian. We don't know who's on board or what language they speak."

"I'm glad there's *something* I can do," Vivian said ruefully. "I'm afraid I'm rather useless at fighting these days."

"You can stay belowdecks with Aimee and Sunny," said Connor. "Keep an eye on the Song Book, too."

Jariel's head appeared through the hatch. "We're approaching the target, Captain," she said softly. Connor nodded toward the deck. The crew stood up, loosening knives and checking bowstrings, and headed toward the stairs. Halfway up, Ellie turned and saw Jude, last in line, stop to kiss Vivian goodbye. For the first time, Ellie thought that she looked small and lonely, standing with Aimee and Sunny at the bottom of the stairs.

The *Legend* had gained altitude and was now close enough to look down on the other ships. Connor peered through his spyglass. Ellie hummed under her breath, trying to use her Sight. The ship that had looked dark brown was actually splotched with black, like wet mud thrown against tree bark. Pulling the vision closer, she saw the hunched, twisted shapes of enemy *urken* moving on deck. The name *Defiance* was written on the hull. The other ship, surrounded by a rusty orange haze and called the *Venture*, was swarming with dark-skinned people, probably Numbani people native to this archipelago. Flecks of light danced around a tall man who seemed to be giving orders. She reported back to Connor.

"Well, we're not allying with urken," Connor said. "We don't know if we can trust the Numbani, but we'll team up with them, at least to start."

As if in confirmation, a series of *booms* sounded from the *Venture*. The Numbani had fired their cannons at the urken ship.

Connor nodded. "All missiles to port. We'll broadside the *Defiance*. Don't destroy the lumena, but keep the urken busy. Fire on my signal."

As the urken returned fire on the Numbani, the *Legend* sailed into place over the *Defiance*. Ellie readied her slingshot, aiming for a monster with a round head and a jagged sword.

Both the *Venture* and the *Defiance* were reloading for a second cannon volley. But before they could finish, Connor yelled, "Fire!"

Arrows, blow darts, stones, and explosive ballista bolts rained down on the urken. Shrieks and howls rose from below. The crews of both the *Defiance* and the *Venture* looked around in confusion, searching for the source of the unexpected missiles. By the time they spotted the shadowy *Legend* overhead, the crew had reloaded.

"Fire!"

The urken were disorganized and distracted. Some tried to fire their cannons upward, but the mechanisms didn't extend that far. The Numbani took advantage of the distraction and fired again. Holes gaped in the side of the *Defiance*.

But the urken were not going down without a fight. One lit an arrow on fire and shot at the *Legend,* catching the ship just below the railing. Others fired more arrows. Tiny flames began to lick the sides of the *Legend.*

"Ellie, Owen, get water!" Connor shouted. They ran belowdecks for buckets.

When Ellie returned to the deck, extinguishing some of the flames with a hissing sound, she saw the urken fire on the *Venture* again. Wood splintered as some of the cannonballs found their marks. But the next round of Numbani fire cracked *Defiance*'s foremast. With a deep groan, the enormous wooden pole crashed down across the deck, bringing down its network of lines and sails on top of the urken. Chaos followed, and the Numbani prepared to board. Dozens of grappling hooks bit into *Defiance*'s railing, and scores of strong arms pulled the two ships together. Panicking, the urken fired wildly at their attackers. Some of the dark-skinned crew fell, but the rest pressed on. When the first wave of Numbani set foot on *Defiance's* deck, Connor held up his hand.

"Hold your fire!" he commanded the *Legend's* crew.

Ellie watched as the Numbani fought fiercely. Their weapons looked improvised: pitchforks, sickles, long knives, wooden spears. But they swarmed over the urken like a gale at sea. Ellie hoped that these fierce people would be their allies and not their enemies. She wouldn't want to be on the receiving end of such anger.

Nervously, she began to hum from the Song, looking for any other information they might need. She went cold when she saw what looked like a white butterfly lazily fluttering near the *Legend's* foremast. A *helkath*—a creature of the Enemy whose poisonous bite could drain a person of hope. Ellie ran down the stairs and carefully sighted down her slingshot. One well-aimed rock crushed the helkath against the mast. The creature dropped to the deck, its eight legs curling inward as it shriveled up. Pulling out her handkerchief, Ellie quickly tossed the dead thing overboard, but not quickly enough to prevent it from leaving a faint scorch mark on the *Legend's* deck. With a shudder, she turned back to the quarterdeck—then stopped.

"Owen, look out!"

He ducked, but it was too late. The helkath that had attached itself to the back of his neck dropped dead, its poison already injected. Ellie stopped singing and ran to him. Owen rubbed his neck.

"What happened? It feels cold," he muttered.

"Oh no," Ellie said, glancing from the dead helkath shriveling beside Owen to the tiny purple mark beginning to spread on the back of his neck. "Jude! Help!"

Jude ran over. He tossed the dead helkath overboard, then sighed when he saw the mark on Owen's neck. "It's helkath poison. There's nothing we can do to reverse it. I'll treat Owen as best I can after the battle. For now, get him belowdecks. He'll only put himself in danger up here."

Ellie quickly put her arm around Owen and helped him down the stairs. He didn't struggle, but he hung on Ellie's arm like dead weight.

When she hurried back on deck, fierce shouts of victory rose from the conquering Numbani. The urken wailed in despair. Ellie's shoulders relaxed. They'd won.

Then the first grappling hook caught the *Legend's* railing.

"Captain!" shouted Kai, severing the rope with one slash of his knife. "They're trying to board us!"

"Draw hand weapons!" shouted Connor. "Cut their lines!"

The *Legend's* crew hastily changed strategies, swapping out their long-distance weapons for knives, swords, and axes. But the seven people on deck couldn't cut the ropes fast enough. The Numbani were coming after the *Legend* with the same ferocity they had used on the urken.

Dark faces began to swarm over the *Legend's* railing, teeth bared and weapons bristling. Metal clashed on metal. Jariel courageously chopped an invader's pitchfork handle in half, Connor swiped with his tiger claws, and Jude positioned himself over the door to the hatch, quarterstaff at the ready. But the Numbani, though they had the advantage of numbers, did not move to kill. They simply surrounded the crew of the *Legend* and closed in from all sides, pressing in until the defenders stood back to back in the center of the deck.

"Haka ka mundu nwangi!" The command came from a short soldier wearing a straw hat. The defined bones of his face gave him a sharp, angry look. He jabbed a finger at Jariel's short sword, then pointed at the deck. Jariel gripped her sword hilt with both hands and swung. The soldier dodged swiftly and stabbed at her with his javelin. Jariel dropped and rolled, but the soldier's aim followed her. When Jariel came up, the javelin was an inch from her forehead. But the blade did not strike.

The soldier's hat had flown off, and long hair tumbled down his back. Ellie's eyes widened. *He* was actually a *she*.

"Haka ka mundu nwangi!" the female soldier shouted.

Connor let out his breath. "I think she wants us to lay down our weapons," he said. He glanced around at his crew, then pulled the tiger claws off his left hand, letting them fall to the deck. "Do as she says."

There was a clatter of metal on wood as the crew obeyed orders. The commander prodded Connor with the butt of her javelin.

"Haruku!" She pointed at Connor, then at the deck. There was no choice. Connor slowly sat down, folding his hands on top of his head. The others followed. Jeers came from the Numbani crew.

Ellie sat there in disbelief. The very people they had tried to help were now their captors. What would happen to them now?

There was a creak as the hatch door opened. Vivian appeared abovedecks, brandishing a frying pan.

"Laoko!" shouted the commander. Two guards detached from the rest of the mass and headed for Vivian. Jude tried to scramble to his feet, but a Numbani soldier struck him on the side of the head with a club. He slumped forward.

"Jude!" Vivian shrieked. She knocked out one of the guards with her frying pan before the other one pinned her arms down. She stomped on his foot, and it took two more guards to force her to sit down with the others. When she reached for the unconscious Jude, one of the guards held a javelin point under her chin. Vivian took a deep breath and turned her palms upward in a gesture of surrender.

The commander shouted something at Vivian. The words sounded clipped and angry.

"What is she saying?" Connor muttered.

Vivian kept her expression smooth, but Ellie could see the tense lines around her eyes. "I don't know," she murmured. "I've never heard this dialect before."

The commander continued to yell, jabbing her finger or her javelin into the faces of various crewmembers. There was fire in her eyes, but still she made no effort to kill the captives. As Ellie looked around, she noticed that while many of the Numbani were huge, muscular men, the commander was not the only woman among them. Some of the soldiers were boys and girls not much older than herself. This was no army, drilled and trained for war. This was a band of misfit fighters. But why? What did they want?

"Ishua, help us," Kai muttered under his breath.

A new wave of Numbani soldiers began to wash over the railings. They leaped onto the *Legend's* deck, clutching long knives in their teeth or brandishing swords plundered from the dead urken. Leading them was a man taller than most. His sleeveless tunic revealed powerful arms, and he carried a long-handled hammer with two heads. There was a rustle of feathers as a black-winged falcon spiraled around his head and settled on his shoulder. The man's eyes narrowed when he saw the captured crew.

"Iblis no ku'a mapepo?" he said to the female commander.

She gestured at them. "Mapepo no. Bindamu ay. Ku'a bindamu?"

Ellie saw Vivian's eyes widen. "Mapepo no," she said in a clear voice. "We are *not* the demon spawn who sailed the other ship." Ellie frowned. Hadn't Vivian said she'd never heard this dialect before?

The tall man strode forward and stood over her. He crossed his arms menacingly. "No mapepo, iblis ay?"

Vivian shook her head energetically. "Mabharia Vestigia Roi ay, watume Adona Roi e Ishua. Mapepo kuharihiwa nyum. Ay kusada."

The leader raised his eyebrows. "Kisiwa nyum kuharihiwa?" He nodded at the commander. "Haka nwangi."

The Numbani soldiers lowered their weapons. Ellie breathed a sigh of relief. As the leader and the commander conversed in their own language, Vivian reached for Jude, who was just regaining consciousness.

"Are you all right?" she whispered.

"I think so." He sat up and rubbed his head. There was blood matted in his hair. "What are you doing up here?"

"I heard silence on the deck. When none of you came down, I thought you might be in trouble."

Jude sighed, touching her face. "You shouldn't have put yourself in danger."

"How did you speak to them?" Ellie asked Vivian. "I thought you didn't know this dialect."

Vivian frowned. "That's the strange thing. I don't. It was like…"

But the leader and the commander had finished their conversation. "Kukubala no mapepo. Ek kujua Vestigia Roi. E iblis Ishua?"

"I have told them that we are not urken, and they seem to believe us, but they want to know more about Ishua and the Vestigia Roi," Vivian explained hurriedly. Taking a deep breath, she began to tell the story of Ishua and the One Kingdom in the strange new language she found she could speak. When Ellie heard the word *Draaken*, angry hisses broke out among the Numbani, and the word *urken* drew loud shouts and wails.

When Vivian had finished, the female commander told the Numbani crew's story. Every so often she paused to discuss a point with the tall leader, and Vivian hastily translated for the *Legend's* crew. The leader's name was Makundo, and his first mate, who had captured the *Legend,* was Korrina. Their people had been peaceful farmers, goatherds, and fishermen on a small island called Janaki. Makundo had had a small patch of land, where he and his wife and two children had kept chickens and raised crops of beans. Occasionally he was hired as an extra man aboard a fishing boat. Korrina was a family friend who fished with him. They were out fishing when the flying death came: ships that sailed in the sky and rained down fire on their land and homes. What the fires did not destroy, the yellow-eyed demon spawn did. Makundo's fields were wiped out by an explosion, and his wife and children were killed by urken. Taking up any weapons they could find, Makundo, Korrina, and the other survivors had fought back, managing to climb a ladder and capture one of the flying ships. With their island home destroyed, the misfit crew of men, women, and children had made it their mission to track down and kill the monsters that had brought the flying death to Janaki. When they had seen the *Legend,* they had believed it to be crewed by more demon spawn, which was why they had attacked.

Vivian answered by explaining that flying ships had originally belonged only to the humans of the Vestigia Roi. The urken had stolen their ships when they destroyed the Vestigians' home island. Makundo said it seemed that they had a common mission: to destroy the world's remaining urken.

"But our purpose is much bigger than that," Vivian explained in the Janaki dialect, pausing occasionally to translate for her crew. "The urken are only the tools of Draaken. He is using them to conquer all the

31

islands. But he is not the true ruler. We seek to stop his destruction and bring back the true king, Adona Roi."

The conversation went on for some time. But at last Makundo held up his hand.

"Haki ay. Ku'a mapepo, utawala ujumbe Ishua."

Vivian exhaled with a smile. "They believe us. They want to fight the urken and sail under Ishua!" The crew cheered, and Ellie gave a sigh of relief. Tonight they had set out to fight enemies, and instead they had gained new allies. Whether or not the rest of the Vestigia Roi was alive, the crew of the *Legend* was no longer alone in the war against Draaken.

Dawn was only a few hours off when the Janakim returned to the *Venture*. Both crews had agreed to take some rest for what remained of the night and view the damage to their ships tomorrow.

Kai volunteered to keep watch over the *Legend*, and the rest of the crew dragged themselves belowdecks. Alyce ran to find Aimee in the galley. Ellie glimpsed Sunny sitting watchfully in the doorway of the kitchen. Alyce came out carrying her sleeping sister. Aimee was six and no longer small, but Alyce held her on her hip as gently as if she'd been an infant.

"She was asleep in the pantry," Alyce murmured, a tired smile softening her features.

Exhausted as everyone was, Jude insisted on performing a medical check before anyone went to bed. The purple helkath bite on Owen's neck was now the size of a plum, and Jude bound it with a lumpy poultice of black borrage root and made Owen drink a foul-smelling tea made from the same herb.

"Why do I have to drink this?" said Owen, looking down into the dark liquid. "If I'm going to die anyway, I'd rather enjoy what's left of my life."

"A helkath bite won't kill you," said Ellie quickly. "You're going to be fine. You just have to take extra good care of yourself for the next—how long, Jude?"

"Two weeks, more or less," said Jude, kneeling down in front of Owen. His forehead was lined with worry. "And Owen, you will drink this tea or I will pour it down your throat. That's not a suggestion."

Owen sniffed the tea, wrinkled his nose, and took a sip.

Jude methodically attended to the rest of the crew one by one. The damage had been mild, and they carried mostly scratches and bruises. When Jude had finished with Vivian, she turned to him.

"Now you," she said.

"Me? But I'm—"

"No arguing. I saw the way they hit you. Sit."

Jude sat down in the infirmary's rocking chair. His head wound wasn't deep, but it took Vivian a while to clean the blood out of his matted hair. While she worked, Ellie glanced out the open door to the dining room, where Owen was sitting with his cup of tea.

"Are you sure he's going to be okay, Jude? Owen, I mean?"

Jude frowned. "The helkath bite itself won't cause him any permanent harm. The poison will naturally work itself out in a few weeks. It's what he might do in the meanwhile that worries me. He'll feel hopeless, and it will alter his judgment. He'll be more vulnerable to—whatever Draaken may throw at us. We'll have to keep close watch on him over the next few weeks, remind him why he's sailing with us and why our mission is important." He sighed and rubbed his forehead. "I wish I could have prevented the bite in the first place."

"It was my fault," said Ellie. "I saw the helkath, but I couldn't reach Owen in time."

"It's neither of your fault. You both did the best you could," said Vivian. "Now all we can do is take good care of Owen. You can't keep harm from coming to everyone."

Jude squeezed her hand. "But I want to. I want to keep you—all of you—safe."

Vivian kissed his forehead. "Someone I know likes to remind me that nowhere in the universe is truly safe, except the City of Adona Roi. He alone knows our futures. So let's leave the worrying to him and focus on the mission before us."

Chapter 3
Gifts

A clanging ship's bell woke Ellie the next morning. The *Legend* didn't have one, so it took her a moment to remember where she was. Oh yes. The battle. The Janakim. Ellie, Jariel, Alyce, and Aimee tumbled out of the bunkbeds in their dormitory, dressed hastily, and hurried up on deck. The *Legend* and the *Venture* were lashed together with ropes, and planks of wood ran between them like bridges. Makundo and Korrina were already there, along with Kai and Connor, while the rest straggled up. Makundo seemed to be arguing with Kai, their voices getting louder as each tried in vain to make the other understand.

When Vivian appeared, finishing a braid in her hair, Makundo shouted at her. At first she blinked, not understanding, then she translated for Kai.

"He thinks you are the captain and wants to know why you keep directing him to speak with your cabin boy."

Connor's face turned red. "I'm *not* Kai's cabin boy!"

A muscle twitched in Kai's jaw. "I keep trying to tell him that Connor's the captain, but I can't get him to understand."

Vivian said a few words in Janaki, and Makundo looked at Connor. His eyebrows rose and he laughed, showing white teeth. Connor crossed

35

his arms and threw out his chest, scowling. "I don't see what's so funny. I trained under a captain in the field *and* at Nautical House at the Academy. I sailed this ship through a waterspout and came out alive. Oh yeah, and I rescued you and your crew from an urken attack. I have just as much right to be a captain as you do."

Vivian translated, and Makundo's face sobered. He said a few words in Janaki, directing them to Connor this time. Vivian smiled.

"He wants to know what the plans are for today, Captain."

Connor's arms stayed crossed, but his scowl eased.

"I've already had a look at the *Defiance*," said Kai. "It's not sailing anywhere with that broken mast. If we want to keep it, we're going to have to tow it. Strange—I found some big, curved sections of mirror in the hold."

"That is strange," said Connor. "But I say we keep the ship and tow it. When we find a safe place to land, we can think about the mast. For now, let's focus our efforts on the *Venture*. I don't think the *Legend* needs much repair." Vivian translated the message, and Makundo communicated it to his crew.

Connor directed the *Legend's* crew over to the *Venture*. Vivian would stay behind to watch the helm.

"I'll get some food ready for you in the meanwhile," she offered. "It's about all I can do."

Owen groaned aloud. Even though everyone knew Vivian was a better translator than cook, Jariel smacked his arm.

"Owen! That was rude! You should apologize!" she hissed.

Owen just shrugged, his expression blank.

Vivian smiled cheerfully, letting the insult roll off. "I was just going to make sandwiches. Even I can't burn, melt, or putrefy sandwiches, right?"

Ellie's job aboard the *Venture* was to coat dry, brittle ropes with tar to protect them from the weather. It was hot and messy work. She had to dip each rope into a bucket of warm black tar, one slow coil at a time. The ropes were heavy, and tar kept slopping onto her. Her arms were black and sticky to the elbow.

"Ellie? Can I talk to you for a minute?"

Ellie looked up to see Alyce standing there. She was wearing her sailmaker's palm, a strip of leather that protected her hand from the thick needles she used for sail repair. She also carried a strip of oilcloth to repair the next sail. But she looked perfectly, disgustingly clean. Ellie used her shoulder to wipe sweat out of her eyes.

"Fine. But you'd better actually be working on something. If not, you can help me with this."

Alyce sat down on a crate. She made a few stitches on the sailcloth, then sat there, idly fiddling with the end of the needle.

"You have...dreams sometimes, don't you, Ellie? You know... dreams that mean something?"

"Like dreams of Ishua? Yes. Sometimes."

Alyce kept bobbing the needle in and out of the cloth. "I remember—during your lessons with Zarifah at the Academy—she talked about dreams of Ishua, that any Vestigian could get them, but they don't happen very often."

Ellie felt a pang as she thought of her sharp-tongued but wise teacher, who had been killed in the attack on Rhynlyr. "I remember her saying that."

"Well...I think I had one. Last night."

Ellie looked up. "You dreamed of Ishua?"

Alyce looked frightened. "Shh! Yes—I mean, at least I think so. You can't tell anyone, Ellie. I just need some advice, and you're the only one who knows what I'm talking about."

"I can't promise not to tell anyone until I know what the dream was about. And anyway, my dreams of Ishua are usually nice ones. What are you so afraid of?"

"Well...I dreamed I was back at choir practice at the Academy," said Alyce, her voice little more than a whisper. "All my old choirmates were there, and we were working with the sheet music for Canto Two, Movement Four of the Song. I remember it clearly. I could see the pencil marks I'd made on my music. But instead of one of the Academy professors directing us, there was a man on crutches. I'd never seen him before. But then he looked straight at me. Don't ask me how, but I knew it was Ishua. He—he smiled at me." Alyce had completely forgotten about her sewing. She was staring up at the rigging. "He was nothing like I'd ever seen in any of the statues or stained-glass windows at the Academy. He was dressed like a worker from the fields, and he had messy hair that fell in his eyes—no starry armor or glittering sword anywhere. But his face—it was so kind. I'd never seen him before, but with one look, I felt like he knew all about me. And that he liked me, even though he knew all the bad things I'd ever done."

Ellie smiled. "Sounds like Ishua, all right. That's a nice dream. What are you so worried about?"

Alyce's face clouded over. "But that's not all. At the front of the choir, Ishua began to sing, and it was music I'd never heard before. It had a rhythm sort of like Canto Twelve of the Song, but the notes were all different, and it felt faster, more exciting and dramatic. And right then, the music sheets we were practicing from...they caught on *fire*. Canto Two, Movement Four of the Song. I remember that the paper wasn't hot in my hands, and it didn't turn to ashes, but it burned like a candle. And...and it was like the new music had set the old on fire." Alyce's eyes were wide with fear. "It seems so *wrong*, Ellie. The Song is the most sacred music we have. And it came from Ishua in the first place, so why would he ever set it on fire? It seems like something Draaken would suggest. I feel dirty for even *dreaming* such a thing." Alyce hid her face in her hands.

"Do you remember the music Ishua was singing?" Ellie asked.

Alyce nodded, looking down at her feet.

"Can you sing some of it?"

Alyce looked up. "Are you sure that's a good idea? Maybe we should just forget about the whole thing."

"Just try it. I want to test something."

Alyce took a deep breath and began to hum. It was a melody Ellie had never heard before, swift and energetic like eager flames leaping up. And like a blast of heat from that fire, a change struck Ellie's vision. All around her, she saw the working Janakim marked with silver VR tattoos and carrying swords made of light. Far to the east, in the direction of Rhynlyr, a star glimmered in the daytime, growing brighter and lighting up the sky like a second sun. When Alyce stopped singing, Ellie felt all the breath rush out of her lungs. She sat down hard on the deck. Alyce was staring at her, white-faced.

"Are you okay, Ellie? Did you...see something?"

Ellie nodded slowly.

"But...only the Song makes you see your visions! What I heard in my dream...how can something that's not part of the Song make you see?"

Ellie rubbed her forehead, smearing streaks of tar on her skin. "I don't know. Unless it *is* part of the Song."

"But that's not possible! I *know* all the music of the Song, and I've never heard this music before."

"And yet it made me see," said Ellie, confused. "If it really was Ishua in your dream and that music really did come from him, then it seems like he's trying to tell us something. We should tell the others about it. Maybe they'll have some ideas."

"No! We can't do that," said Alyce.

"Why not? They might be able to help us understand what it means."

"But..." Alyce licked her lips. "What if this music *isn't* from Ishua? I mean, what if it was a dream from Draaken? Does that mean I'm a traitor? Will they have to maroon me on the next island we pass? What about Aimee? I'm a singer, not a seer. I never wanted this." She crossed her arms tightly.

Ellie sat down next to her. "Whatever it means, you're no traitor, and the crew of the *Legend* would never maroon you anywhere. We're family, remember? The others will help us figure out what to do."

"At least can we wait a few days, then?" Alyce looked desperate. "I...I'd like some time to think about it."

"Sure." Ellie looked at her bucket of tar, which was hardening as it cooled. "In the meanwhile, help me stir this tar, and then I'll help you hang that sail."

Two days later, every muscle in Ellie's body ached as she descended the stairs into the *Legend*'s dining room, followed by most of the crew. They'd repaired the worst of the damage to the *Venture*, and Makundo and his crew had helped repair the *Legend*'s minor injuries as well. They'd be ready to set sail in the morning—though where to, Ellie had no idea.

As the crew entered the dining room, Vivian was sitting at the dining table with Makundo. On the tabletop was Ellie's painting. Vivian looked up.

"Listen to this! You won't believe it!"

The crew wearily gathered around. Ellie sat down on a bench.

"When Makundo was down here working, he saw your painting, Ellie." Vivian leaned forward, her eyes shining. "He says he's seen a pair of volcanoes that looks like this!"

Ellie darted a glance at Makundo, his brown eyes deep and difficult to read. She turned back to Vivian. "Is he sure? We don't even know if this painting is a real place."

Vivian exchanged a few words with Makundo in his language. "He says these volcanoes are on a small, uninhabited island south of Kwartod and west of Kisumu. He's only seen them from sea level, but he thinks he can find them again from the air."

Kai rolled his neck. "It's a slim chance."

"But a chance," said Jariel. "And if he's right, it could save us weeks or months of random searching."

"I'd say it's worth a try," said Connor. "Owen, go get the Numed map from my cabin, and we'll chart a course immediately."

"Go get it yourself," said Owen without emotion.

Connor's jaw tightened and he began to say something, but Ellie took hold of his elbow.

"Remember," she said softly.

"I'll get the map," said Finn, excusing himself.

Connor glared at Owen across the table. "Helkath bite or not, you need some manners."

Finn returned with the map, and Vivian translated between Connor and Makundo as they charted a course.

"Well, at least we know where we're headed next," Connor said when they were finished. "It looks like about a four-day voyage."

Makundo said something else in Janaki.

"Of course," Vivian said. "Makundo says his crew is very crowded aboard the *Venture*. Some of them are sleeping on the weather deck. He wonders if we could take a few aboard the *Legend* for the rest of the voyage. Do we have room?"

"I don't see why not, if they're willing to work," said Connor. "We have four bunks in the extra dormitory, plus the floor. And we could use some extra help, especially with Owen out of commission."

Vivian translated, and Makundo replied.

"He thanks you, and says they will be under Korrina's supervision. She will see that they work hard and cause no trouble." Vivian paused as Makundo said something else. "He also wants to know if I can teach them some of our language when they are not working."

"Sure," said Connor, stifling a yawn. "With a few extra hands on deck, everyone will have more free time."

That night, after a supper of Vivian's unbearably spicy and burned stew, Korrina and another Janaki family of five came aboard. They said little, but showed their gratitude with sharp, quick nods.

At sunrise, the *Legend* and the *Venture* set sail for the island with the two volcanoes. Between the extra weight of the disabled *Defiance* and the inexperienced Janaki crew, progress was slow. But the Janakim aboard the *Legend* were hardworking and quick to learn. All six of them hauled lines and scrubbed decks energetically. Many hands made the work lighter, and Vivian had most of the afternoon free for language lessons in the library. Ellie sat in for a while, and Kai dropped in at one point to make sure no one was causing trouble. The three Janaki children giggled and whispered when they were supposed to be listening, and the parents seemed to be having trouble understanding even basic phrases. But Korrina, her straw hat jammed on her head again, was picking up the Common Tongue rapidly. Within the first hour, she could say "hello," "goodbye," "yes," "no," "thank you," and "my name is Korrina." When Vivian praised her progress, though, Korrina scowled and rattled off something in her own language. Vivian raised her eyebrows.

"What did she say?" frowned Kai, leaning against the doorpost.

"That she'd rather be practicing with her javelin," said Vivian. "In some rather...colorful language."

Kai glared. "Show some respect," he said, jerking his chin at Korrina. "Vivian's working hard to teach you."

Korrina glared right back at him, her dark eyes glittering. "Kukubala! Mapepo e silaha ay."

Kai looked at Vivian, but she coughed. "I'm not going to translate that one."

Kai crossed his arms and leaned back against the wall, glowering. With a satisfied smirk, Korrina turned back to her lessons.

Mid-afternoon, Ellie slipped away from the language lesson and took her sketchbook up on deck. Connor was taking readings with the sextant and Jariel was up in the rigging, but Sunny and Aimee were sitting near the bow of the ship, looking at each other, both being surprisingly still and quiet. Ellie took the opportunity to sketch them. She was noticing how much the feathery ends of Aimee's hair looked like the fringe on the dog's ears when the little girl spoke.

"He says it smells like smoke."

"Smoke? Who says?" said Ellie.

"Him." Aimee rubbed Sunny's head. He lifted his nose and licked her hand.

Ellie sniffed the air. "I don't smell anything."

"That's 'cause dogs can smell better than people."

Ellie frowned. "Then how do you know what he's smelling?"

"He told me."

"*Sunny* told you?"

"Yep."

"Really." Ellie couldn't keep a note of sarcasm out of her voice. Had Aimee suddenly gone out of her mind?

The little girl looked at her and smiled, showing her pearly baby teeth. "Sunny says lots of things. He's funny."

Ellie didn't know what to say. "What is *Sunny* saying now?"

Aimee cocked her head and was quiet for a moment, looking into Sunny's eyes. He leaned forward and slimed her face with a wet kiss.

Aimee giggled. "He says he wants his tummy rubbed." The dog lay down and immediately rolled onto his back.

That was something Aimee could have made up. But the smoke? Ellie watched the girl and the dog play for a while. She wasn't sure what to think. She wanted to ask the others—which reminded her about Alyce's dream. Ellie had forgotten it with all the activity going on. Tonight she'd bring it up, and Aimee's strange behavior too. Maybe someone would have some answers.

That evening, Finn entertained the crew with a ballad he'd made up about their battle against the *Defiance*. Kai was away on deck, watching the helm, but everyone else was gathered in the dining room. Vivian leaned her head on Jude's shoulder, Jariel tapped out the rhythm, and Aimee and Sunny were curled up together on the floor, taking turns snoring. Even Korrina seemed to listen with interest.

Finn paced the room as he sang the story, accompanying himself on his harp, Tangwystl. Sometimes he moved closer to the audience for intensity; sometimes he backed away to show space and time passing.

The fire-flaming bolts
came down like roaring rain
The terror-tranced urken wailed
but more rain came down again.

Ellie watched Finn's movements, fascinated. She tried to sketch him as he played, but she kept getting distracted by the story. When Finn caught her eyes and grinned, she felt a shiver that was warm and cold at the same time.

When he finished his ballad, Finn took a bow. The crew applauded him heartily, then began to disperse for bed.

"Wait," Ellie said. She looked at Alyce. "Before you go, we need to talk to you about something."

"Not yet!" Alyce said, panic in her eyes.

"It's time. We have to tell them," Ellie urged.

"Tell us what?" said Jariel. The crew hovered around, listening. Alyce chewed on her lip.

"Are you going to, or shall I?" said Ellie.

"You."

Taking a deep breath, Ellie told them about Alyce's dream and the vision it had caused. She asked Alyce to sing the music. Though the crew had been sleepy at first, they sat up straight when Alyce began to sing.

"That sounds like quite a dream," Jude remarked when they finished.

"Strange," said Finn.

"And that's not the only strange thing that's been going on around here," said Ellie. "Think about it—Vivian, three days ago, you said you'd never even heard the Janaki language, and then you suddenly started speaking it fluently. And today, Aimee told me something Sunny said, like she could actually understand him."

"Aimee could have been making it up," said Alyce. "She has a good imagination, and she doesn't always understand the difference between truth and pretend."

"But Aimee told me Sunny smelled smoke, when neither she nor I could smell any. It just didn't seem like the sort of thing she'd make up if she were playing a game."

"Smoke," muttered Connor. "I wonder if that could be from the volcano cluster we're heading toward. Wind's in the right direction, though it's still a long way away."

Vivian traced thoughtful circles on the tabletop with her finger. "I wonder if Rua could be at work here."

"Or Draaken." Alyce shuddered.

"Possibly. We know that he has the power to reach into dreams," said Vivian. "But I've never heard of Draaken having the power to give gifts like these. Even if he could, why would he give us gifts that strengthen us against him? That makes no sense."

Give us the strength to fight! Ellie remembered her dream the other night. Maybe this was Ishua giving them what they needed to fight back against Draaken?

"Perhaps we'll understand more as time goes by," said Jude. "In the meanwhile, I prescribe some rest for all of us."

"And no more dreams," said Alyce.

The next day, Makundo transferred to the *Legend* to learn some steering maneuvers and flag signals from Connor. He smiled as Korrina showed him the new Common Tongue phrases she had learned, including the Vestigian salute and password. He seemed disturbed, though, that his falcon had flown off and had not returned.

When Makundo returned the following day, however, the falcon swooped out of the sky and landed on his shoulder, screeching loudly. Smiling, Makundo spoke to it in Janaki and tried to stroke its head, but it just ruffled its feathers and screeched again.

"She says there's a forest on fire," came a voice from near Makundo's elbow. Aimee was standing there, her hands clasped behind her back, looking fixedly up at the falcon. "She says the big stone trees make lots of smoke."

Ellie looked at the little girl. If Aimee was playing a game, it was time for it to stop. "This is serious, Aimee. No more pretending."

"I'm *not* pretending," said Aimee, as if it were obvious. "I can hear her talking, just like I heard Sunny. She says her name is Zira."

Owen, leaning against the mizzenmast, raised his eyebrows. "And you're going to listen to a bird?"

Ignoring him, Jude knelt down in front of Aimee. "Does the falcon have anything else to say? How far away is...the burning forest?"

Aimee looked curiously up at Zira. The bird fixed her with its piercing golden eyes.

"She says we'll reach it when the moon is over our heads."

"The volcano range," murmured Vivian. "We must be only a few hours away." Makundo looked confused, and she translated for him. He responded in Janaki.

"Makundo recommends we stop here for the night and move forward at dawn," said Vivian. "He says the passage is dangerous and should only be attempted in daylight."

"You're not even worried that Aimee might be lying?" Owen put in.

Alyce glared, putting an arm around Aimee's shoulders. "Aimee is not a liar. I believe her."

"The message does correspond pretty well with our map, Owen," said Connor. "And Aimee's a generally truthful person. Even if she's a little bit off, we only lose a few hours."

"Fine, then. Listen to her, not me." Owen's expressionless face frightened Ellie.

Connor crossed his arms. "Owen, don't be like that; it's just—"

Suddenly Owen took a running start toward the *Legend*'s railing. Ellie grabbed at him, but missed. He was going to jump!

"Owen, *no!*" Ellie screamed.

As Owen leaped, Kai tackled him from the side, taking him down and pinning him to the deck. Owen tried to wriggle away, but Kai held him fast.

"Let me *go!*" Owen shouted.

"Not if you're going to try another stunt like that," Kai growled.

Jude ran up. "Owen, what were you *thinking*? You could've—" he glanced over the side of the deck. There was nothing but empty air between them and the ocean thousands of feet below. Jude exchanged a look with Kai. "We can't let him up here anymore. It's too dangerous."

"There's a small storage room beside the galley," said Kai. "No windows. And it has a lock."

"I hate to do it." Jude looked at Owen sadly. The boy's eyes were wild. "But I see no other choice. We have to keep him safe until the helkath poison leaves him."

Kai took Owen's wrists and ankles in each of his burly hands and slung the boy over his shoulders. Kai was not rough, but Owen screamed all the way down the stairs. Jude followed. The rest of the crew stood silently on the deck. Vivian wiped her eyes. Aimee held tight to Alyce's hand.

"That was horrible," Ellie whispered.

"I just hope the poison goes away and we get the real Owen back soon," said Jariel.

Ellie had first watch at the helm that night. Other than the loss of sleep, she didn't mind. She liked the quiet deck, where she could watch the unfamiliar stars shift positions and the clouds turn silver under the crescent moon. Even the surface of the distant ocean shimmered. Ellie didn't sing or try any visions, but occasionally she thought she saw a burst of light in the distance, like a sputtering torch. Could that be the volcano range? Were they really going to find the other survivors of the Vestigia Roi tomorrow? Even though Rhynlyr was lost, maybe forever, finding the Vestigia Roi again would be almost like coming home.

The door to the captain's cabin opened, and Connor came up the stairs, carrying his telescope on a tripod.

"You're up late," Ellie said.

"Can't sleep. Thought I'd have a look at the stars." The moonlight turned Connor's blue eyes silver, like the clouds. He angled the scope upward until he found what he was looking for. "Here. Look at this." He positioned Ellie in front of the eyepiece.

She peered at a tiny dot of distant light. "What's it called?"

"Etella, the brightest star in the Hwim constellation." Connor took another look, then adjusted the telescope to see other stars. After a while he straightened up and sighed. "Nice to know the stars are right where they're supposed to be. You can always count on them. Looking through the telescope reminds me of that." He glanced at Ellie. "*You* don't need a telescope, though. You can see anything, anytime you want."

Ellie smiled. "That's not how my Sight works, and you know it."

"Yeah, but…" Connor ran his hands over his hair. "You can see so many things. With your gift, people respect you, trust the things you say."

Ellie frowned. "People trust the things you say too."

"Do they?" Connor let out his breath. "Sometimes I feel like I made a mistake, accepting this captaincy. It feels like people look at me, and all they see is a little boy playing make-believe on a ship."

"What do you mean? Our whole crew listens to you—even grown-ups like Kai and Vivian and Jude. We trust you to be our captain."

"Not Makundo. Did you hear him laughing at me the other day? He didn't even believe that I *was* the captain. Even when people do obey my orders, I wonder if they're laughing behind my back." Connor touched the smooth wood of the helm. "I love this ship. I feel more at home here than anywhere else I've ever lived. And I'm trying my best to be a good captain. Sometimes I just wish I were...gifted, like you. Maybe then people would actually take me seriously."

"But people do take you seriously. And you *are* gifted," said Ellie.

"Not like you, I'm not. You're the special one in this family."

"That's not true. Look at you! You're thirteen, and you already steer this whole crew the same way you steer the *Legend.* You look at a person and know what they're good at; you know how to make them listen and work as part of the team. You're a leader, and that's just as much a gift as my Sight is."

Connor was quiet a moment, staring up at the stars. "You think so?"

"Of course I do." There was a long pause. "Now, are you going to bed, or are you going to take the rest of my watch? I feel like I could sleep for days."

"Think I'll stay out a while longer. You get some sleep, Ellie. And...thanks."

She hugged him. "'Night."

Chapter 4
Home?

First thing the next morning, the crews of the *Legend* and *Venture* prepared to make a water landing at the island of the twin volcanoes. Maps and charts were unrolled on the table before them.

"If all these islands have hakaran on them, this lagoon will be the only place large enough to land all our ships together." Connor tapped a medium-sized blank space in the midst of several small islands.

Makundo pointed at the surrounding islands and said something in Janaki. Vivian translated.

"He says that we need to take careful stock of conditions before going in. If a volcano erupts, it can spew not only fire, but thick clouds of ash as well. Those would make it impossible to see, and they might also clog our propellers." She paused as Makundo added something else. "Oh, and he says volcanic eruptions can also cause undersea earthquakes, which create huge waves. One of those could swamp our ships under forty feet of water."

"So nothing could possibly go wrong," said Connor sarcastically.

"Don't be gloomy," said Jariel. "What do we do if conditions are favorable?"

Vivian translated, and Makundo made a tall arc with one hand.

"We have to fly high over the tops of the volcanoes to avoid the heat?" Finn guessed. Vivian translated, and Makundo nodded.

"Makes sense. With all the oil in our decks and sails to protect them from weather, too much heat would blow us up like a firestar," said Connor.

"Thank you for that comforting image," muttered Jariel.

"If we come in at that height, though, we'll have to make a pretty steep landing, judging by the size of this bay," said Kai.

"Then let's not waste any more daylight," said Connor. "Everyone remember the flag signals?"

Vivian translated and Makundo nodded.

"Good. Then let's get to work." He threw the Vestigian salute, tapping two fingers to his left shoulder, then to his forehead. "To the One Kingdom!"

Even the Janakim knew the answer. "May it be found."

The *Legend* sailed forward, towing the *Defiance* and flying blue flags to signal clear sailing. The *Venture* followed. After about an hour, the sky began to grow hazy, and Ellie caught a bitter, sulfurous smell on the air. "There's that smoke Aimee said Sunny was talking about."

Connor didn't look up from his compass as he adjusted the helm. "That kid's sharp as a knife. I knew she wasn't faking it."

The crew peered tensely ahead from their positions on deck. Jariel was keeping watch from a few yards up in the rigging. Jude and Alyce stood to starboard, Kai and Finn to port, with two Janakim on either side, ready to adjust the sails at a moment's notice. Vivian sat on a crate by the helm, holding Aimee and a copy of the riddle in her lap. They could only hope that the meaning of the last four lines would become clear when they saw the island—if it was the right one.

Hulking gray volcanoes appeared out of the mist, not only on the island in front of them, but rising up from other islands as well. Some of their sides were streaked with dribbles of orange lava. Ellie gaped at the huge, imposing fire mountains. Makundo's falcon hadn't been far wrong. They did look like a forest of stone trees on fire. Patches of turquoise ocean were faintly visible between them.

Connor glanced at Makundo's ship. The Janaki captain was sweeping a blue flag in an upward motion.

"We need more height," muttered Connor, pushing the *Legend's* brass altitude lever forward. Ellie's stomach dropped as the ship rapidly ascended. The volcano's heat chased them upward, and Ellie unbuttoned her nautical coat.

Progress was slow as they sailed carefully forward. Connor's hands were constantly busy between the helm and the altitude lever. The sail crews tugged and sweated over the lines, now increasing the ship's speed, now slowing her down. Ellie hummed softly, watching for visions. As had lately been the case, they were more confusing than helpful. The haze around the *Venture* had brightened from rusty orange to saffron yellow. She saw her shipmates wearing golden circlets, each emblazoned with a single flame. But from the *Legend's* hatch, she saw a billow of black smoke seeping out. Ellie frowned and stopped singing. The smoke disappeared.

"Connor, I think—" she began.

"Lagoon ahoy, Captain!" shouted Jariel.

Connor looked over the *Legend's* side, his eyebrows puckered the way they did when he was thinking hard.

Ellie tried again. "Connor—"

"Empty the sails! Halt the ship!" he called. The rigging crew raced to obey orders. Connor hurriedly pulled back on a lever, and the ship's rear propeller stopped whirring.

This was a bad time. Ellie decided to go check on the black smoke herself. She ducked through the hatch.

Belowdecks, the ship was deserted and quiet. On instinct, Ellie pulled off her boots and padded noiselessly across the wooden floor. She peeked inside the Oratory, where the ship's waterfall cascaded in colorful patterns under the glass-studded ceiling. Nothing amiss there. She checked the other rooms with similar results. Then she stopped in front of the door to the storage room where Owen was being held. Inside, she could hear Owen talking aloud. It sounded as if he were talking with someone, but Ellie couldn't hear the other side. She put her ear to the door.

"…they never listen to me; they're always telling me what to do."

A pause.

"You're right. Nobody appreciates me. I'm the smartest one on this ship. But what do they do? Lock me up like a bug in a cage."

Another pause.

"Well, at least I know *you* appreciate me."

Frightened, Ellie knocked on the door. "Owen? Are you all right?"

The conversation stopped. "Go away."

Ellie crouched down to peer through the keyhole. The windowless room was dark, since no one trusted Owen with a candle. "I just thought I heard you talking with someone."

"I said, go AWAY!" Owen's voice became a roar so terrifying that Ellie ran for the stairs. The voice wasn't his. Something else was in there—something that felt big and dark. Ellie grabbed her boots and ran back up to the deck. She needed help.

Just as she cleared the hatch, Connor yanked back on the altitude lever. The *Legend* dropped almost straight down, and Ellie went sprawling.

"Ellie! Are you all right?" Vivian started to get up, concerned, though her own face was a sickly shade of green.

"Fine," Ellie groaned, pushing herself upright. Her ears popped. "What…?"

"We're beginning our descent." Vivian gripped the side of the crate with one hand, sucking in a deep breath.

The twin volcano peaks loomed up before them. The *Legend* was cutting a course between them in order to land on the lagoon directly on the other side of the island. If the Vestigia Roi was actually here, the fleet had certainly chosen an inhospitable place for a hideout. The island was an alien landscape of tumbled black rock, broken only occasionally by scrubby trees with red flowers. Directly ahead, a giant heap of boulders was rushing up to meet them.

"Up ship, Captain!" yelled Jariel. Connor pushed on the altitude lever, but the ship didn't respond. The boulders loomed nearer.

"Up ship!" repeated Jariel frantically.

"I'm…trying! The lumena must be nearly out of power!" Connor shoved the altitude lever all the way forward, but still nothing happened. At the last minute, he grabbed the helm and twisted it sharply to port. The boulders passed by to their right, like tall heads looking over the ship's railing with displeasure. The nearest one caught the tip of the starboard wing sail and bumped the side of the disabled *Defiance*. Ellie cringed as she heard wood snap and fabric tear. There were shouts from the *Venture* behind them as the tallest boulder scraped against the ship's hull. Suddenly the rocky ground dropped out from beneath them, and they were sailing over a turquoise-blue lagoon. Hazy sunlight sparkled on its surface.

With the altitude lever no longer responding, Connor quickly directed the crew to haul in the sails. Riding the turbulent air currents, the *Legend* bumped and bounced downward until it hit the water with a plume of salty spray.

"Nice landing," said Alyce sarcastically, releasing her white-knuckle grip on a rope.

"Considering the difficulty of the approach, you managed it very well, Connor," said Kai. Connor sighed and wiped his forehead with his sleeve.

Suddenly Vivian vomited over the side of the ship. "And I made it all that time, too," she groaned. "This baby does not like sea landings."

Jude was by her side with a dry cloth. "Just sit down, breathe deeply, and it will pass." He helped her sit down. "Are you all right?"

She squeezed his hand, her face pale. "I'd be fine if I had a glass of water."

Jude started to head belowdecks. Suddenly Ellie remembered Owen's strange conversation.

"Jude!" She hurried up to him and quietly described what she'd heard.

He frowned. "That does sound suspicious. I'll go check on him."

"Don't go in alone! It sounded like there was...something in there with him. He was different. He sounded angry."

Jude's frown deepened. "All right. I'll take Kai in with me when we land. But first I'll listen for any more conversations." He disappeared belowdecks.

The *Venture* splashed into the lagoon beside them. If the *Legend's* landing had been rough, the other ship had it much worse. One of the *Venture's* wing sails was completely crushed, and she had a long scrape along her side. Janaki sailors crowded to the rails, vomiting over the sides. Ellie patted Vivian's shoulder. "See? You're not the only one."

"What does the riddle say next?" said Connor, holding onto the helm for balance as his legs adjusted to the roll of the sea.

Ellie recited from memory:

> *Where the fire meets the sky*
> *Between tall peaks your ship must fly.*
> *Where the ocean swallows sand*
> *Upon black rock your ship must land*
> *Where the sea roars into caves*
> *Make salute, your lives to save.*

"So...we need to make landing on the island?" said Connor.

Ellie looked nervously up at the twin volcanoes. The island's sharp, jagged coastline cut the lagoon's edge to foamy white ribbons. "I guess so."

"Not here, silly." Connor shook his head. "We'll look for a safe beach where we can land."

Jude returned to the deck, his expression dark. The weary rigging crews folded in the *Legend's* wing sails, a fine, salty mist spraying their faces as the ship bobbed in the lagoon's gentle swells. The air was warm and humid, and Ellie took off her coat and rolled up the long sleeves of her nautical uniform.

Jariel waved their blue flag, and the *Venture* followed the *Legend*. They began to sail around the island, past sheer black cliffs that dropped straight down a hundred feet or more into the sea. Only an experienced climber with full gear could ever hope to scale those walls. Even if Kai could manage them, they'd never get Vivian or Aimee to the top.

At last, Jariel sang out. "A beach, Captain!"

Connor lifted his spyglass. Ellie hummed from the Song, but she could see no light on the island. The land mass shuddered and throbbed as if it contained a giant, beating heart, but all she could see was the shell of black rock. Why, oh why couldn't her Sight show her fewer falling islands and more of what she wanted to see right now?

"Keep an eye out for underwater rocks as we approach," Connor ordered.

Ellie stole a glance over the railing. As it got shallower, the water was clear almost to the bottom. Rocks were hard to see against the dark sand below, but schools of brightly colored fish were easily visible as they darted under the surface.

"Rock to port!" shouted Jariel suddenly.

Connor immediately yanked the helm to starboard. He saved the prow, but the rest of the ship was not so lucky. There was an awful grinding sound as the rock scraped along the *Legend's* hull.

"That'll be a leak," said Connor grimly. "Jude and Kai—go below and bail. And you'd better let Owen out, or he'll be swimming." Connor spun the wheel. "I hate to risk the propellers, but we're going to have to beach the *Legend*. We leave her out in the lagoon, and she'll sink in twenty minutes."

Jude and Kai hurried below. Jude returned a few minutes later with Owen. The boy had dark purple circles under his eyes, as if he hadn't slept.

"It's good to see you in the sunlight, Owen," said Vivian.

Owen grunted.

"Owen, we need your help!" shouted Connor. "Go below and help bail!"

Owen didn't answer.

"Owen, I gave you an order!"

In response, the boy crossed his arms and sat down on deck. "Who made you the boss?"

"I'm the *captain*!" Connor retorted, flushing.

"Well, I think you're nothing but a big bully."

Connor's face grew dangerously still. Ellie grabbed his arm. "I'll help bail, Connor."

Connor didn't take his eyes from Owen's face. "I'll deal with you later."

As Ellie headed for the hatch, Owen's eyes followed her movements. His stare was somehow both vacant and intense. Ellie hurried belowdecks.

At last the *Legend* ground to a halt, her keel crunching against a crescent-shaped beach with black sand. Ellie, Kai, and Jude returned abovedecks. Jariel immediately kicked off her boots, grabbed a rope, and slid off the ship, splashing into seawater up to her knees.

"It's *warm*!" she shouted up. "And the gash in the hull is above the waterline."

Connor glanced up at the sky. "Still plenty of daylight. We should send out a scouting party before it gets dark. I'll go. Jariel, Ellie, and Kai, come with me. The rest of you, stay with the ship. We'll be back within three hours. Jude is captain in my absence. Vivian, can you pass the message on to Makundo and his crew?"

Vivian nodded.

"Right." Connor nodded to Ellie and Kai. "Pack light—just a weapon and a day's ration of food and water each."

Five minutes later, Ellie was carefully climbing down a rope, trying not to let the rough fibers slide by too quickly and burn her hands. She'd tucked her boots and Jariel's into their knapsacks and carried one over each shoulder. Her feet touched the clear, turquoise-blue water and slipped in happily. It *was* warm! The bottom was rocky and sharp, though. Gingerly she handed a knapsack to Jariel, who was looking around, dazzled.

"Have you ever *seen* anything like this place? All these colors! I'm going to catch Owen one of those big yellow fish—" she pointed—"or a sea turtle. That'll make him feel better."

"I feel like catching Owen something else," Connor grumbled, dropping into the water with a splash that got Ellie wet. She dipped her fingers in the water and splashed him lightly back. Jariel gave him another, much wetter splash.

"Hey!" he reached down to take revenge, but Kai landed right beside him.

"Not now," he warned, his one eye scanning the cliffs that rose steeply from the beach. "We don't know what waits for us here."

"If anything," Ellie murmured to herself.

"Watch out for spineflowers under the water," Kai called, already heading for the beach. Step on one, and it'll make your foot numb for a day."

Ellie, Connor, and Jariel followed him, their eyes now on the water to avoid the dark purple spineflowers.

To the west, the beach continued around the island as a narrow path. To the east, it seemed to stop at the base of the cliffs.

"The waves don't sound normal in that direction," Ellie said, looking east. "There's a…hollow sound, like an echo."

"Then let's go find out where the echo's coming from," said Connor.

Leaving their shoes in their packs, they crossed the rough beach barefoot. The black sand looked powdery and soft, but it felt more like broken glass on Ellie's feet. The air was warm and damp, and her face was soon slick with sweat. She pulled her hair into a tail with a leather strap, glad to have it off her neck.

As they reached the eastern tip of the crescent, Ellie saw what had been causing the echo. Waves from the lagoon rolled into natural caves at the base of the black cliff. Right now the tide was low, and the waves were only tiny ripples. But Ellie could imagine that at high tide, these sea caves would be deadly. A person caught inside would be smashed by the force of the waves—if they didn't suffocate first.

She stopped.

Caves.

Ellie turned to Jariel, her eyes wide. "Are you thinking what I'm thinking?"

Jariel looked at her blankly. "Um…dangerous place to be when the tide comes in?"

An ankle-high wave rolled past them, into the first cave. The hollow space made it sound like the roar of a giant animal.

Ellie shook her head. "No! The final piece of the riddle! *Where the sea roars into caves...*"

Jariel's face lit up. "You found it, Ellie! The last piece!"

Ellie laughed. "Not quite. We still haven't found the Vestigia Roi."

Connor led the way into the first cave. It was just a shallow scoop in the rock, barely tall enough for Kai to stand up. Though it was shady and cool inside, the enclosed space made Ellie uneasy.

"Keep an eye on that tide," said Kai. "It's already turned. We need to be back on the ship in no more than an hour. We don't know if any of that beach stays above the waterline."

The second cave was much like the first, shallow and featureless. By the time they reached the third, the waves were halfway to Ellie's knees, and she was starting to feel the pull of the current.

"If there's nothing in this cave, I think we should turn around and come back later," she said as Connor stepped inside.

"Wow! Look at this!" The cave made his voice sound loud and booming.

Ellie followed him, with Jariel and Kai behind her. This cave had a low ceiling, but it was deep, its rear wall shadowed in gloom. Connor was already back there. Ellie could dimly see his white shirt and his hands, pale as they groped along the black stone wall.

"There's an opening here!" he called. "It's like a vertical tunnel—and I feel something with my foot—"

"Connor, be careful," Ellie warned, pulling out her slingshot and a smooth stone. "We don't know what's back there. An animal might..."

"They're stairs!" Connor crowed, interrupting. "Bumpy ones, but definitely stairs. There's a whole flight of them. And they go up so far..." His voice faded as he climbed up the enclosed stairway.

"Connor, wait!" Ellie hurried to catch up. But as she set foot on the first step, Connor's chatter turned to yells. Ellie looked up and saw her brother struggling with large figures holding torches. The flames threw crazy shadows against the walls of the stairway, and Ellie couldn't tell how many attackers there were. One of them grabbed Connor. Connor threw his weight downward, trying to wriggle away, and Ellie fired her slingshot. Her hasty shot missed the attacker's head, but hit the arm holding Connor. The attacker let go and Connor jerked away, throwing himself down the stairs. He crashed into Ellie's legs, knocking her backward just as a bolt of pain seared through her left arm. Ellie cried out and splashed into the water. The cave amplified her cry to a howl. Through a haze, she glimpsed Kai running up the stairs, shouting, "To the One Kingdom! To the One Kingdom!"

"Ellie! Ellie, are you okay?" Jariel's hysterical voice broke into Ellie's consciousness. A hand touched her arm, and Ellie felt a shock of pain, sharp as broken glass.

"Don't touch it! You'll make it worse!" barked Connor.

Biting her lip to hold in the pain, Ellie looked down. A rough, homemade arrow stuck out from her upper arm. The sight made her stomach churn.

Kai ran back down the stairs, followed by two white-faced young sentries carrying torches. Their tattered clothes might once have been the gray tunics and sky-blue cloaks of Rhynlyr guards. One had a ripped sleeve that revealed a VR tattoo in the crook of his left arm.

Kai crouched in the water beside Ellie, examining the arrow. "Just her arm, thank Ishua." He glared at the guard. "What were you thinking, you careless lout?"

The guard, his bow still in his hand, fell to his knees, trembling. "Forgive me, Seer Ellianea! I did not recognize you in the darkness! Cursed be my bow and this hand, if I've…"

"It's all right," said Ellie shakily. Her arm burned and the pain was spidering out in all directions, but it wasn't going to kill her. "I'm okay. And I shot at you first."

"But why the blazes didn't you say something—identify yourselves?" growled Connor at the guards.

"It's not as if we get many visitors here," said the second guard dryly. "The only other party we've met was a small detachment of urken. We have to act quickly to keep the Vestigia Roi safe."

Ellie sighed and leaned against Jariel. She was soaked in seawater and her thoughts were clouding with pain, but there was a comforting sense of relief at the edges of her mind. They'd found the Vestigia Roi. They were home at last.

"I'll deal with you later," said Kai to the sentries. "The tide's coming in fast. I must take the news to our waiting crewmembers, but Ellie can't walk all that way, nor hoist herself back aboard our ship. Someone has to accompany her to the Vestigia Roi."

"I'll stay with her," said Connor and Jariel in unison.

Kai nodded, then fixed the kneeling sentry with a sharp glare. "I will bring the rest of the Vestigians here at the next low tide. In the meanwhile, look after these three as you value your life. If any more harm comes to them, I will find you, and there will be a reckoning."

The first sentry, who looked only a few years older than Connor, gulped and nodded. Kai touched Ellie's good shoulder reassuringly, then hurried out of the cave. Connor and Jariel helped Ellie stand. She cried out when Connor bumped the shaft of the arrow.

"I'm Ravago. I'll get you to a healer as soon as possible," the first sentry promised, trying to lead the way up the stairs backward with his bow in one hand and his torch in the other. "Supplies of everything are short, but everyone will be glad to have our seer Ellianea returned."

"No thanks to you," grumbled Connor. The sentry sheepishly turned around and led them up the passageway.

The stairway narrowed as they climbed, and Connor had to follow Ellie as she leaned on Jariel. The roar of the waves grew faint behind them, and the air began to get stuffy. Ellie's lungs began to constrict. She hated being in places where she felt trapped, especially underground. She tightened her grip on Jariel's shoulder.

"Does your arm hurt?" said Jariel, her eyes filled with concern.

"Yes—but this tunnel bothers me more," said Ellie, fighting to keep her breathing calm.

Jariel held tighter to Ellie's waist. "You can do this. Remember when you made it through that tunnel under Miss Sylvia's orphanage? Focus on how much your arm hurts instead. It'll distract you."

The suggestion wasn't hard to follow. Every step jarred the arrow, aggravating the wound, and Ellie felt throbbing heat spreading through her whole arm. Blood stained her sleeve, and some of it had dried, leaving the fabric stiff and sticky. She felt shaky. She wondered if bleeding to death hurt, or if it just felt like falling asleep. Every step felt heavier and slower.

She was ready to collapse with exhaustion when the stairs finally opened into a large tunnel of the same black rock. Daylight trickled in through high, narrow holes in the walls. More passages branched off in other directions.

Ellie's knees felt weak, and Connor supported her other side as they followed the sentries forward. Along the passageways, dull-eyed Vestigians watched them from the mouths of small caves they passed. Ellie's heart twisted to match the pain in her arm. She had hoped that finding the Vestigia Roi again would feel like returning to a safe, familiar place. But these sallow-faced refugees were nothing like the strong, laughing Vestigians she had known on Rhynlyr. These people looked more like stray dogs—pitiful, hungry, and sick. The attack on Rhynlyr seemed to have destroyed more than the Dome and the Academy—it had broken the Vestigians' spirits as well.

Ellie remembered only parts of what followed. There was a dim room, and an old woman bending over her, and something that scorched her arm like a bolt of lightning. Then there was nothing but blackness.

Chapter 5
Mharra

When Ellie woke up, she was lying on a thin blanket on the ground. They were in what looked like a low cave. Two old women moved among bodies crowded together on blankets. There was a sound of coughing.

As she regained awareness, Ellie noticed that the arrow had been removed, and her arm was wrapped in a bandage and bound in a sling. The wound felt stiff and sore, but it no longer burned so intensely. Jariel was curled up beside her on the blanket, snoring softly. Ellie turned her head and saw Connor sitting with his back against the wall.

"You're awake," he said softly.

Ellie nodded. "How long was I asleep?"

"Don't know. A couple hours, probably. It's hard to tell time when you can't see outside."

"Are the others here?"

Connor nodded. "That fool sentry who shot you, Ravago, came back to tell me. He said living space is short, and we'd all been assigned a cave together. He told me how to get there."

Ellie raised her eyebrows. "One room for all of us. That'll be interesting." Using her good arm, she pushed herself to a sitting position. Her head spun for a moment, but otherwise she felt all right. "I'd like to go see them."

"Can you walk?"

"I think so."

At the movement, Jariel stirred and smacked her lips. "Morning, Ellie. How do you feel?"

"Better, thanks."

"I just had the nicest dream. There was a table of Rhynlyr strawberries," Jariel smiled. "Big as your fist and sweet as honey. Someone kept putting bowls of them in front of me..."

"Stop! You're making me hungry." Connor steadied Ellie as she got to her feet. "Lean on me. We'll go find the others."

Ellie thanked the old woman in charge, and they left the infirmary. The window holes were dark, and the only light came from lanterns, but an air current moved through the passageway. The underground settlement seemed full to overflowing. They passed a long line of people waiting for supper. A few children played, but most stood as silently as their parents, watching the newcomers with listless eyes. Ellie didn't recognize anyone until they turned another corner. A woman sat in front of a cave, watching a little yellow-haired girl play with a rag doll.

"Laralyn! Gresha!" Jariel cried.

"My dears! How wonderful to see you." Their former host mother hugged them all. "We saw the rest of your crew earlier. We're so glad you made it here safely. So many...so many didn't make it off Rhynlyr that terrible night."

Gresha hugged Jariel around the knees. She squealed with delight as Jariel picked her up.

"You've gotten so big, Gresha!"

"Big giwl," Gresha said proudly.

"Is Deniev all right?" asked Connor.

"Oh yes, he's fine. Food's scarce, but we're supposed to stay hidden, so he's fishing in one of the covered caves nearby. But you're looking for your friends, I imagine. They're just down this passageway."

The children thanked Laralyn and continued to another cave mouth some twenty yards away. Out front, Finn was strumming his harp softly.

"Hullo! You're alive!" he called. "Are you all right, Ellie? Kai told us you'd been wounded."

Ellie glanced at her bandaged arm. "I'll live. How are all of you? And the Janakim?"

Finn nodded. "We're fine. A couple of Vestigian guards came and showed us where to hide the ships. There's a sheltered cove on the other side of the island, and they've already got about two dozen other ships there. They brought us back here at low tide."

Connor craned his neck inside the cave, dimly lit by a single lantern. "So all ten of us are going to be crammed in here together?"

"Looks like it," said Finn. "The Janakim got two other caves, but they're even more cramped."

Jude stepped out of the cave. "Shhh, others are sleeping. Ellie, Kai told me what happened. I want to take a look at your arm."

Inside the cave, blankets crowded the floor, and some of the crewmembers were stretched out, asleep. Owen was lying down, but his wide-open eyes instantly found Ellie and followed her. She shivered. It was like being watched by a stranger.

Jude sat Ellie down beside the lantern and unwrapped her bandage, frowning at the dirty cloth. "If this is what they're using for bandages, they're going to have an epidemic on their hands." He tipped a bottle of clear liquid onto a clean, soft cloth and dabbed at the ugly red wound. It burned, and Ellie sucked in a breath.

Jude's eyes were gentle. "I know it hurts, but I want to make sure you're safe from infection."

"We already know how that can go," Ellie whispered, remembering the days of Jude's delirious fever.

Jude nodded grimly. "I'll see if they need help at the infirmary tomorrow. From the looks of things, they don't have proper supplies or enough people with medical training." He wound a clean white bandage around Ellie's arm and readjusted her sling.

Ellie glanced over at Owen, his eyes still fixed on her. "What about him? How is his helkath bite looking?"

Jude shook his head. "The bite itself is healing. But his other symptoms…this isn't like any helkath bite I've ever seen. If there are any other healers here, I'll ask their advice tomorrow."

In the morning, the crew of the *Legend* was rolling up their blankets when the sentry Ravago appeared at the mouth of their cave. He cleared his throat awkwardly.

"The…the Council would like to see you, and the other crew you came with."

"When?" said Kai.

"Er…now. As soon as you're ready."

Grumbling, Kai went to get the Janakim while the others finished getting ready. Ravago shyly spoke to Ellie. "How…how's your arm?"

She looked down at her sling. "Better. I have to wear this sling for at least a week, but it hurts less than yesterday."

Ravago's face was scarlet. "I'm so, so sorry. What a fool I am."

Ellie shook her head uncomfortably. "It's okay. It was an accident. Any of us could have done it."

"Any of us who shoot before thinking, that is," said Connor, appearing beside Ellie and crossing his arms. Ravago looked like he wished the floor would swallow him whole.

Kai returned with Makundo, Korrina, and their crew. Ravago straightened up, looking relieved for the diversion.

"Follow me," he said. They wound their way through the labyrinth of passageways. At last they stopped at a doorway where two more sentries stood guard. Ravago gave the Vestigian salute.

"To the One Kingdom!"

The door guards returned the salute. "May it be found."

They all entered a large cavern. Scattered lanterns and wall torches lit the room dimly. Along one wall was a clump of rough camp stoves, on which a few red-faced women were already preparing tonight's supper. A few tables were scattered throughout the cavern. Around one was seated a group of five people, their faces illuminated by a pair of lanterns. Two of the people were strangers to Ellie: a short, bald man and a plump woman with a seemingly permanent frown between her eyebrows. After a moment, Ellie recognized the third man as Tobin, the councilmember from Occupational House on Rhynlyr, but Ellie was shocked at how much he'd aged in just a few months. The old man's forehead was deeply creased with wrinkles, and he had dark circles under his eyes. But more than the signs of aging, he looked ill—very ill. He had a fit of rattling, wheezing coughs that left him gasping for breath, and his eyes were bright with fever. Beside him sat two girls. The elder, with a round face and a crown of gently curling golden hair, offered Tobin a handkerchief; the younger, with sharp, pointed features and quick dark eyes, helped him lean forward to get a breath of air. Though the girls' nautical uniforms were old and worn, Ellie at once recognized Katha and Meggie, the daughters of Consul Radburne—the man who had betrayed Rhynlyr into the hands of Draaken.

Ravago went down on one knee as he approached the councilmembers. "The crews of the ships *Legend* and *Venture,* your honors," he said. The two crews inclined their heads respectfully, and the Council returned the nods.

"Welcome to the island of Mharra. We rejoice to...see you all alive," said Councilman Tobin, pulling in each breath with effort. "Not least you, Ellianea, our...Seer. You bring...hope for the Vestigia Roi. And hope is our...rarest commodity in these days." Vivian translated for the Janakim.

Ellie saw bitter recognition flare in Connor's eyes as he looked at Katha and Meggie. Before he could blurt out something embarrassing, Ellie spoke up.

"Are you...all that's left of the Council? What happened to the others?"

Tobin had a fit of coughing. The woman nodded at the bald man. "You tell them, Serle."

Serle spoke up. "We know for certain that Provost Amra and Admiral Wollerin were killed in Draaken's invasion of Rhynlyr. As for Consul Radburne, the traitor—" Ellie saw Meggie flinch at the word— "his whereabouts remain unknown. Councilman Tobin has appointed

Councilwoman Phylla and myself as Acting Councilmembers to help lead the Vestigia Roi until a proper election can be held."

"And *you?*" Connor said, his voice dripping with disdain for Meggie and Katha. "Are you councilmembers too?"

Katha sniffed, tossing her blonde curls. "No. Councilman Tobin is our godfather, the guardian our parents appointed for us. We are here to assist him through his illness."

"Which, if I may say so, your honor, sounds serious," Jude put in. "I do not know what medical help you have already sought, but I would be glad to perform an examination."

Councilman Tobin shook his head. "It's what…everyone has down here. Underground fever, they're calling it. Seems to be no way to prevent it—or cure it." A series of coughs shook his shoulders. Meggie offered him a clean handkerchief.

"Still, with your permission, I'd like to examine you to learn more," said Jude, frowning. "Especially if the illness is widespread, it is essential to identify and quarantine the cause."

"Very well," said Tobin, waving his hand. "Later."

"Where is Lady Lilia?" asked Vivian. "We followed her message here."

"Lilia left two days ago on a mission to the Haven of Jura," said Councilman Serle. "We have heard that several Havens were taken over by flying ships under the control of Lagorite forces."

"May she return soon," said Councilwoman Phylla. "These caves are cramped and full of sickness, and we need a safe place to move."

"Not to mention the lack of food," Meggie said quietly.

"That's at least one thing we can deal with while we wait for her," said Connor. "Have hunting parties been organized?"

"We cannot risk being seen from the air!" said Councilwoman Phylla. "That is the entire purpose of this hiding place. A few men have ventured out, but to send an entire party would be foolhardy."

"But trained hunters know how to stalk prey without being seen," said Connor. "May I have your permission to organize a hunting party?"

Councilman Serle narrowed his eyes. "Who exactly are you? Why should we trust you?"

Ellie watched Connor's ears turn red. "I'm Connor Reid, captain of the *Legend*. And I know some fine hunters who could handle the mission easily."

"Such as?"

"Me, for one," said Kai, crossing his arms. The burly, one-eyed man looked both impressive and intimidating.

"Very well," said Serle, backing down. "Coordinate a hunting party, by all means. But remember that secrecy is of the essence. The forces of the Enemy are searching for us, and we cannot offer them any clues."

"Do any others among you have skills to volunteer?" asked Phylla. "There are so many needs down here, and precious few resources."

"As I said earlier, I am a doctor," Jude spoke up. "I'd be happy to serve in that capacity."

"Thank Ishua," Meggie murmured.

"My training is in linguistics," said Vivian. "I served as translator of the Song Book on Rhynlyr. Is there anywhere I might be of service?"

"We have no one to teach the young children," said Phylla. "Since we don't know how long we'll be here, it is important to keep up their education. Would you be willing to do that?"

75

Vivian nodded. "I've never taught little children before, but I'll do my best."

"We have some old books that might be useful to you," Phylla added. "Ravago can show you where they're being kept."

Vivian's eyes lit up. "Of course."

One by one, the crewmembers volunteered their skills, except for Aimee, who was too young to work. A group of Janakim, including Makundo and Korrina, would help with hunting, as would Kai and Finn. Connor and Jariel would go with another group of Janakim to repair the damaged ships in the harbor.

"As for you, Ellie—" Councilman Tobin coughed. "Would you assist us in our…Council meetings again? When your… injury is healed. Your Sight would be…most helpful to us."

Ellie hesitated. She remembered the tangled webs of power that had nearly snared her on Rhynlyr, pulling her away from her friends and from Ishua—and pushing her into dangers that had almost claimed her life. But she glanced around the table. Tobin was clearly pushed to the limits of his strength. She didn't know Serle or Phylla, but they seemed inexperienced at best. And Katha and Meggie—if they were anything like the snobbish, calculating girls she remembered from Rhynlyr, she didn't trust them within a mile of Council power, whether or not they were acting members. With one more glance at Katha's self-satisfied face, Ellie knew what she had to do.

"I'd be honored to help the Council in any way I can. But I'd like Alyce to be included as well. I need the Song for my visions to work, and she's an experienced singer." Alyce threw Ellie a grateful glance. She'd had an important choir position on Rhynlyr, but had done little besides cook cloud trout and mend sails since they left.

"And what of the boy?" Councilwoman Phylla said, gesturing to Owen. His eyes roved hungrily around the cavern.

"Owen was bitten by a helkath about a week ago," said Jude. "Yet his symptoms are strange, and they seem to be getting worse. Is there anyone here who has experience with the poisons of the Enemy?"

Councilman Serle looked at Owen sadly. "If only we did. But many of our brave healers were lost as they tended the wounded on Rhynlyr, and more have succumbed to the underground fever here. If you do not have the medical knowledge to help him, no one here does. Perhaps it is Adona Roi's will that Owen's illness runs its course. Perhaps he may learn valuable lessons from the experience."

Ellie felt a surge of anger. She had seen the blankness in her friend's eyes, even seen Owen try to jump off the *Legend*. Her friend was in there somewhere, but he was suffering. How could Councilman Serle dismiss Owen so easily? And to blame it on Adona Roi, too!

Jude also looked like he was having trouble controlling his feelings. "We are very sorry there is no one here to help our friend. Permission to depart for our work crews?"

"Granted," said Councilman Tobin. "Ellie...report for duty as soon as...you are able."

The two crews gathered back in the cave assigned to the *Legend*. Kai, Finn, Makundo, Korinna, and the hunting detachment of the Janakim checked their weapons.

"We'll head out immediately, to make full use of the daylight," said Kai.

"And so will we." Connor nodded at Jariel and the Janakim in their crew. Among them was the family who had sailed on the *Legend* and taken lessons with Vivian. "Hopefully you'll be able to help us understand each other."

"I'm headed to the library," said Vivian. "Who wants to come with me?"

"Since I don't start work with the Council for a few days, I will," Ellie volunteered. "I can't do much lifting, but maybe I can help in other ways."

"Aimee and I will, too," said Alyce. "I can't go to the Council without Ellie."

"What about Owen?" Ellie asked.

"We'll take him with us," said Vivian.

"You'll have to keep an eye on him," said Jude, quickly taking stock of the supplies in his medical satchel. "He's unpredictable these days."

"We will," Ellie promised.

"Then I'll walk with you on my way to the infirmary," said Jude.

The crews dispersed, and Ravago led the library group to the cave where the books were being stored. Jude left them at the door, and Ellie and the others stepped inside. By the light of Ravago's lantern, they saw jumbled heaps of books on the wet cave floor. In places, the stacks were taller than Ellie. Vivian made a strangled sound. She grabbed a volume sitting on the edge of a puddle, dabbing its leather cover dry with her sleeve.

"This is outrageous! These are precious volumes rescued from the Academy library, no doubt. What was the point of saving them if they're being left to rot here?" Her eyes quickly swept the room.

"Ravago, I know you have other duties, so I will simply ask you for two lanterns. We'll do the rest."

Ravago ran off, and came back a few minutes later with the requested lights. With an awkward bow, he left them.

"Right," said Vivian grimly. "We have our work cut out for us. And no bookshelves. Not even much wood for bookshelves. Owen, could you invent another way to keep these books off the floor?"

"Why should I care?" Owen's eyes glinted, and they kept returning to Ellie. She looked away uncomfortably.

"Well. In that case, let's begin by cataloguing what we have. Oh, if this is really all that's left of the Academy library…" Vivian sighed sadly.

"I'm surprised they saved anything," said Alyce. "We escaped with just the clothes on our backs, remember? And…not everyone escaped." She put her arm around Aimee, doubtless thinking about their mother, who had perished in the attack.

"You're right," said Vivian. "I'm sorry. We'll do our best with what we have. Owen, would you like to help?"

"Wouldn't you like that," he sneered.

"You don't have to, but there's no need to be nasty. Girls, you look for Common Tongue titles and stack them against the left wall in alphabetical order. Here are some pencils; keep a list as you go. I'll tackle the foreign-language titles."

The task was daunting. Even in the Common Tongue, Ellie had trouble reading some of the book titles, so Alyce had to help her. Aimee split her time between stacking books and petting Sunny, who had sprawled across the entrance to the cave. About an hour in, the dog yelped, and the workers turned to see Owen sneaking out the door.

"Where are you going?" said Aimee.

"Just needed a breath of fresh air. Is that a crime?" Owen snapped.

Ellie's heart twisted. She could hear the lie in his voice. The real Owen would never tell a lie—but he'd never be so rude, either. What kind of a helkath bite *was* this?

"Owen, please sit down. You're going to stay here with us today," said Vivian. Her voice was kind, but brooked no argument. Owen sat down against the wall and sulked.

They worked all day, with only a break for a midday meal. The soup served in the vast cavern hall was watery and bland. By the end of the day, Ellie felt ravenously hungry, her arrow wound was sore, and her uninjured right arm ached from lifting books. Still, she felt accomplished: all the books were now neatly stacked and organized on top of an oiled piece of sailcloth they'd found. At least they'd stay dry until Vivian figured out some bookshelves.

Vivian, however, looked pale and exhausted.

"Are you all right?" Ellie asked as they returned to the cavern hall for supper.

Vivian took a deep breath. "To tell you the truth, I don't feel very well. I think I overdid it today. Maybe I'll take the day off tomorrow."

In the dining hall they met up with the others. Connor and Jariel were smeared with tar from their repair work on the ships. Finn dramatically told the story of how Kai had shot a bird out of the air, mid-flight. Jude stopped in for a hasty bowl of stew, but then had to go back to the infirmary. And always Owen's eyes roved around the room, taking in everything and everyone in it. But they always returned to rest on Ellie. She shuddered.

Chapter 6
The Underground Fever

That night, Ellie dreamed she was falling. Her stomach lurched and she clawed frantically at the air as the ocean rushed up to meet her. The churning gray water was swirling into a whirlpool, like a mouth gaping to swallow her whole. At the bottom she saw yellow eyes and a glint of dark scales.

The current of the whirlpool caught her and sucked her into a tight spiral. She lost all sight of the world around her. But now she saw that the walls of wind and water around her were made of the fine golden strands of the Song. She saw as well as heard it whirling around her—choppy phrases from different cantos, and from tunes she didn't recognize. There were words, too, but they were spinning so fast that Ellie couldn't even tell if they were Knerusse graphemes or Common letters.

Among the golden strands, she caught other fleeting images—a mirror in the desert, a dead coral branch returning to life. Last she saw an island, its surface blackened by fire and infested with urken, with the stump of a great tree in the center. *Rhynlyr.* But from the nest of charred wood, a tiny shoot of green was rising. And all around Ellie, the Song's music turned to wailing.

Ellie gasped and woke herself up. Her heart was racing, and she touched the hard floor of the cave to make sure she wasn't really falling toward the ocean. In the dimness around her, she could hear the soft breathing of her shipmates. She walked out to the mouth of the cave.

To her surprise, Finn was sitting there, silhouetted against a single lantern in the passageway. He was strumming soft chords on his harp.

"You all right?" he whispered.

Ellie rubbed her eyes with her good hand. "I think so. Just a bad dream. No, not bad exactly—just strange. I didn't understand it."

"Tangwystl helps me when I can't sleep," he said. "If you go back to bed, maybe she'll help you too."

After a moment, Ellie went inside and lay back down on her blanket, listening to the faint, soothing notes of the harp. Finn was right. Within a few minutes, Ellie was asleep.

In the morning, Vivian wasn't feeling well. But she waved away Jude's concern.

"I'm all right," she insisted. "Just tired, that's all."

"Alyce and I aren't going anywhere today," Ellie volunteered. "My arm's still pretty useless. If you tell us what to do, we can look after Vivian."

"She's right. Ellie and Alyce are excellent nurses," said Vivian.

"All right," Jude said cautiously. "Vivian just needs to rest and drink plenty of fluids today. There's always a big kettle of hot water in the dining hall. Come fetch me if anything changes. I'll be in the infirmary."

"What about Owen?" Alyce asked.

Jude glanced at the boy, sitting against the dim wall of the cave, knees hunched up to his chest. He was mumbling to himself. Jude sighed.

"I'll prepare another dose of black borrage root, and you can give it to him in tea later. I wish I knew what else to do for him, but that's the only helkath remedy I know. Other than that...just keep him in sight. Anything else you need for today?"

"That's all, Doctor. Now go. The Vestigians need you." Vivian kissed Jude's cheek and playfully shooed him out the door.

Ellie, Vivian, Alyce, Aimee, and Owen passed a quiet day. Two lanterns burned in the cave, sustained by the slow burn of *ujuba* berry oil. Vivian napped for a while, then asked for a book she'd seen in the cave yesterday. Alyce and Aimee ran errands for tea and books, only getting lost in the winding tunnels once or twice. Ellie drew in her sketchbook, resting her injured arm and glancing up at Owen occasionally. In spite of the quiet cave and the dim light, he didn't nap even once, though he had dark purple circles under his eyes. Sunny curled up beside him, but Owen pushed the dog's nose away whenever he moved to rest it on his master's knee.

Mid-afternoon, Ellie was just considering a nap when Vivian shifted and muttered something to herself. She pulled a pencil from behind her ear and began to copy something out of her book onto a scrap of paper.

"What is it?" said Ellie.

"I don't know," Vivian murmured. "I had a dream about this book while I was napping earlier. I just found this...what looks like a poem inside. I'm not sure why, but it seems important."

Ellie and Alyce both craned their necks to see the paper. Vivian chuckled.

"Good luck reading those. They're Knerusse runes. I'll translate them tomorrow. For now, silly as it sounds, I feel I could sleep again."

"It's not silly. You're sick," said Alyce.

"Well in that case, good night," Vivian smiled, tucking the paper with the runes under her pillow.

Jude wasn't back by suppertime, so Ellie and Aimee went to the great cavern to stand in line for food while Alyce stayed with Vivian and Owen. The line was long, and to keep Aimee from getting cranky, Ellie tried to distract her by playing a game.

"I see...a little girl with yellow hair."

"Gresha!" Aimee squeaked with pleasure.

"That was an easy one. I see a man with no hair at all."

As Aimee searched for him, Ellie saw two other people she recognized. "Doctor Steele! Miss Amalia!" she cried. Aimee held their place in line as Ellie ran to hug her old teachers. Dr. Steele looked thinner, and Miss Amalia had holes in the knees of her paint-splotched pants, but they were alive and unharmed. They were happy to see Ellie too, and wanted to hear all about her adventures.

Thanks to the work of the hunting crew, tonight's soup was a little thicker than yesterday's, but as Ellie balanced three bowls with her one good arm, she still saw a few fish bones and nutshells floating around. Nothing was being thrown away as the cooks worked to stretch their supplies. How long would it be before this underground colony wasted away from hunger, sickness, hopelessness? Wouldn't that be exactly what Draaken wanted for them?

It was late, and the crew of the *Legend* was preparing for bed when Jude finally came in the cave door.

"Jude!" Aimee squealed, running to hug him around the knees. He tousled her hair wearily.

"Hello darling," said Vivian, looking up. She frowned. "What kept you so long? You look wretched."

Jude sat down on the edge of her blanket and kissed her forehead. "I feel wretched, actually. The infirmary is overflowing with patients, and not nearly enough medicine or trained staff to go around. And the underground fever is raging unchecked. Councilman Tobin let me examine him tonight, and he has an advanced case. He said he had a few days of fever and cough soon after he arrived here, then he seemed to recover. But two weeks ago it returned with a vengeance. That makes me think it's a spore-based illness—which means no matter how light a patient's first brush with it, it can return anytime, as long as the spores remain alive in the patient's body. For Tobin, it seems to have gotten into his lungs. With his advanced age…"

"He'll make it, though, won't he?" asked Ellie worriedly.

Jude's face looked sad. "Only time will tell. What we really need is a remedy to kill the spores—then we'd have a chance." He sighed heavily. "I hardly feel deserving to be called a healer when there's so little I can do."

Vivian brushed the hair away from his forehead, tracing the worried lines there with her thumb. "My poor darling. And you obviously overworked yourself trying to do it all anyway."

"I only wish I could save everyone. But how are you feeling?"

"Better. Ellie, Alyce, and Aimee took good care of me. And Owen was quiet all day."

"I'm glad. Some good news is just what I needed. Good news, and sleep."

The next morning, Vivian woke shivering, even with a blanket pulled all the way up to her chin. Then she grew too warm and pushed it off. Jude had a pail of cool water beside him and kept replacing the wet cloths on Vivian's neck and forehead. He looked as if he'd been up half the night.

"I'm staying here today," Jude informed Vivian calmly.

"No," she argued, her face pale and damp. "The people in the infirmary...the underground fever..."

Jude frowned. "Exactly. I'm not taking any chances. Ellie, Alyce, Aimee—you can have the day off. You deserve a rest. I'll keep an eye on Owen here."

"If you're sure you don't mind," Ellie said, picking up her sketchbook. To tell the truth, she was happy to have a day out of the dim, stuffy cave. In spite of the window slits that let natural light into the passageways, the enclosed spaces were starting to get to her. She longed for light and air.

"Can we show you something, Ellie?" Alyce exchanged a grin with Aimee. "We found it while we were running errands yesterday."

"I was actually planning to go outside. I know the Council doesn't like it, but I'll stifle if I stay underground much longer."

"Trust me. I think you'll like this," said Alyce. "Do you think she'll like it, Aimee?"

Aimee covered her mouth with her hands to hold in an escaping giggle. Her brown eyes danced with laughter. "Mm-hmm."

Ellie soon became confused as branches split off the main tunnel, but Alyce and Aimee knew their way. Aimee led them, running down passageways as if she'd lived underground all her life. Finally they turned a corner and stopped.

"We're here!" Aimee crowed.

A dark hole opened in the rock floor. Ellie could see the first few steps of a staircase.

"Um...down there?" Ellie asked.

"Yep!" Aimee was already pattering down the stairs.

"Um...Alyce...remember what I said about feeling stifled underground..." Ellie mumbled, backing away from the hole.

"It's all right," said Alyce, smiling from two steps down. "You'll like this."

"You're...sure?"

Alyce nodded. "Trust me."

Swallowing hard, Ellie clenched her fists and followed her.

They descended just a few feet before the stairs turned a sharp corner, and the three girls burst out into full daylight. Ellie squinted and blinked, gulping in deep breaths of fresh air. As her eyes adjusted, she saw that they stood on a ledge in a vertical shaft of rock. About fifteen feet below was a beautiful blue pool. The water, turquoise at its edges but sapphire at its deep heart, cast luminous reflections on the walls. A few vines hung down from the circular opening overhead, through which Ellie could see the cloud-chased blue sky.

"This is...glorious," Ellie breathed.

"There's a rope ladder," said Alyce, pointing to the structure hanging below their feet. "Want to try it?"

"Is it safe?"

"Oh yes. We asked one of the sentries yesterday. They said these holes are called *onotes,* and the water down there is actually fresh, coming up from springs inside the island. The Council has set aside some onotes for drinking water, but not this one. The sentries built the ladder for fun."

Ellie looked down. "I'd love to, but…my arm. I don't think I can manage the ladder yet. But you go ahead. I'll sit here and watch."

Alyce and Aimee climbed down and were soon splashing and giggling in the water, their laughter bouncing off the sides of the rock shaft and disappearing into caves at the base of the onot. Ellie smiled and looked up into the sky, hugging her sketchbook to her chest. A breath of wind, warm from the tropical skies outside, stirred her hair, reminding her that Rua was everywhere, even here. *Someday we will get out of here. The Vestigia Roi won't stay hidden underground forever.*

When they returned to the cave several hours later, Vivian was asleep on a blanket. Jude had also fallen asleep sitting against the wall, his chin dropped to his chest.

"Where's Owen?" said Aimee aloud. Jude opened his eyes, then sprang to his feet.

"I—I'm sorry; I don't know what came over me," he blurted sleepily. "I shouldn't have fallen asleep. That was careless of me."

"You had to sleep sometime," said Ellie. "But do you know where Owen went?"

"No," said Jude. "We have to find him, and quickly. Aimee, can you stay here with Vivian? Go get Laralyn next door if she needs help." Aimee nodded solemnly.

"We should split up," said Alyce. "Ellie, can you find your way to the great cavern?"

Ellie nodded.

"Then you go that way. Jude, you know your way to the infirmary. I'll go to the right, where Aimee and I explored yesterday."

"Meet back here," said Jude. "If none of us has found him, we'll come up with another plan."

They split up. Ellie hurried down the passageway, calling Owen's name softly. Her heart pounded. Sick as he was, he might be capable of anything.

She turned a corner and found him standing at the top of the stairs that led out to the sea cave.

"Owen!" she called in relief.

He whirled. For a split second, his eyes gleamed yellow, and his pupils were vertical slits. Ellie's stomach clenched and she thought she was going to throw up. Then Owen's eyes returned to normal. The change had been so quick that she wondered if she'd imagined it.

"Leave me alone! Why do you always have to follow me everywhere?" Owen snapped.

"I was just worried about you. You shouldn't be alone," Ellie said, trying to make her voice sound calm and soothing. "Come on back to the cave. It'll be suppertime soon."

Owen bared his teeth at her furiously and took a step toward the stairs. The younger boy was a little smaller than Ellie, but he was at least as strong. How was she going to get him back to the cave?

At that moment, Finn came trotting up the stairs, his bow strapped across his back. He took the stairs two at a time, humming a tune, and Owen backed away from the music.

"Finn!" Ellie called, relieved. "Can you help me?"

"Sure." Finn looked back and forth between them. "What's going on?"

"None of your business," Owen growled.

"Jude fell asleep and Owen slipped out. We've been looking all over for him," Ellie explained. "We need to get him back to the cave."

"No trouble at all," said Finn. "Come on, old boy."

Owen scowled and made a sudden jerk as if to dart away, but Finn, taller than Owen by a head and shoulders, clapped a hand to Owen's shoulder and steered him away from the tunnel mouth.

"Suit yourself," Finn said. "Let's get back."

Ellie took Owen's other arm. He tried to wriggle away, but there was nowhere to run. Wedging Owen safely between them, Finn and Ellie delivered him safely back to the cave, where Alyce and Jude were already waiting.

"Thank Ishua. You found him," Jude sighed. "Time for some more black borrage root tea for you, young man." He marched Owen inside.

"Thanks," Ellie breathed, looking up at Finn. "You came at just the right time. Owen got so…angry. I wasn't sure how I was going to get him all the way back here by myself."

"Happy to help." Finn had a crooked smile that scrunched up the left side of his face and made his gray eyes twinkle. Ellie hadn't noticed that before.

"What were you doing back so early, anyway?"

"I slipped on a rock and strained my bowstring wrist while we were hunting. Kai sent me back inside for the rest of the day." Finn rubbed his right wrist and flexed the fingers. "Bother, really. But guess it put me in the right place at the right time."

"Yeah," said Ellie. She felt strangely lightheaded, her mind uselessly blank. "I…I guess it did."

Chapter 7
New Music

I n the morning, Jude knelt and kissed Vivian's forehead. "How are you feeling? Your fever's a little lower."

"All right," Vivian smiled, though Ellie thought it looked a bit forced. "You should go to the infirmary today. They need you."

Jude searched her face with concern. "Are you sure? If you're still ill, I'll stay."

"As long as Ellie and Alyce don't mind, they can stay with me. You go."

"It's all right, Jude. We'll look after her," said Ellie.

Jude nodded reluctantly. "Watch her temperature. If it rises again, come get me. Oh—and make sure Owen doesn't go anywhere. But I don't have to remind you of that."

Owen glowered from his corner.

"We'll be fine," said Alyce.

Aimee was restless in the dim, quiet cave, so Alyce took her over to play with Gresha. Owen seemed even more agitated than usual, and it was a relief when he finally curled up and took a nap.

"It's good to see him sleeping," Vivian whispered.

Ellie sat down on the edge of Vivian's blanket. "Yes."

"It seems he's always awake these days, his eyes roaming everywhere. This helkath bite has really given him a difficult time."

"I wonder if that's all it is," Ellie muttered, thinking of the frightening change she'd seen in his eyes yesterday. "How are you feeling?"

"Not very well, actually," said Vivian. "I didn't want to keep Jude away from his work, not when there are so many people who need him. But I feel...tired and weak. More than I should be. And last night, I had such dreams..." She squeezed her eyes shut. "Ellie—I want to ask you something. Please don't be frightened. But after last night's dream...will you promise me something?"

Ellie's stomach tightened. "What is it?"

Vivian pressed her lips together. "I always knew having a baby was dangerous, but I'm usually in good health, and I didn't think much about it. But last night...last night I dreamed...I didn't make it. It sounds so strange, dreaming about your own death. But I saw it so clearly, Jude and the baby all alone..."

"Vivian, don't talk like that," Ellie said urgently. "It was just a dream. You don't need to be thinking about those kinds of things."

"But I *am* thinking about them. And after I've been sick these past few days..." Vivian took Ellie's hand, her grip warm and damp. "You're so brave, Ellie, such a light for the rest of us, and I want my baby to have someone like you to look up to. Jude is a wonderful man and a splendid doctor, but he'll need help if—if anything happens to me. Promise you'll help them? Please?"

"Of course I'll help them, but so will you." Ellie wet her lips. "You're healthy and strong, and you're going to be a great mother."

Vivian's eyes were intense and bright. "Promise?"

Ellie sighed. "Okay. I promise."

Vivian squeezed her hand. "Thank you."

"You're welcome. But I think what you really need is some sleep. You have to get well soon so you can put that library to rights."

Vivian closed her eyes. "I do feel like I could sleep again. How ridiculous. A library to arrange, and here I am sleeping."

Ellie smiled. Vivian's breathing gradually grew deep and even. Ellie watched her friend with concern, then began to hum the new Song music from Alyce's dream.

Ellie's vision changed. Vivian slept on, looking serene and peaceful. Her skin looked faintly translucent, as if she were a glass vase filled with water that glowed just the slightest bit. There was a circlet of pearls in her hair, and she wore a rich gown patterned with roses. The hem of the dress was white, but the color gradually shifted, deepening to a rich red at her shoulders. As Ellie looked closer, she realized the roses on the dress were *growing*. She watched a single bud bloom into a flower, rising and intensifying from white to red. But over the round bump where the baby was, the rose design became a golden branch of coral. It, too, rose and grew. Ellie watched in fascination. What did it mean? Was it a sign for the baby's future?

When the coral's growth slowed, Ellie glanced over to where Owen slept. He had curled into a tight ball as if to shut out the music. But in his sleep, he looked just like his sweet old self—a small boy with lopsided glasses, his pet ribbon snake Moby curled around his arm. But covering him almost completely was a large, silken black cloak. The deep hood swallowed most of his head, and only an arm and a few bits of clothing peeked out from the engulfing black garment. Ellie noticed a subtle design, black on black, of serpents crawling around the edges.

Owen, the real Owen they all knew and loved, was not gone, not lost. But he was wrapped up in this cloak, whatever it meant.

So many signs. Ellie only wished she had the wisdom of Zarifah or Lady Lilia to interpret them all. She sighed, letting the music and the vision wash away from her, and padded over to where Owen slept, dressed once again in his wrinkled nautical uniform and frowning in his sleep. She laid a gentle hand on his shoulder, remembering the boy who had been her first friend on the *Legend*, who had helped her rescue Vivian from Mundarva, whose quick thinking had saved them all from the lightning storm. Ellie's eyes filled with tears. She was sitting right beside him, and yet it felt as if the real Owen were miles away.

"Adona Roi does *not* want you to stay sick like this, whatever the Council may say," she whispered to the sleeping boy. "The Good King wants you to be healthy and whole, collecting bugs and experimenting with potions again. Please come back, Owen. Please, Ishua, Adona Roi, Rua—please bring Owen back to us."

Ellie held her breath, not exactly sure what she was waiting for. Owen groaned softly and shifted in his sleep. A tiny breath of air stirred the lantern flames. But that was all.

To everyone's relief, Vivian was better in the morning. Her fever was gone, and she was able to sit up and take some broth.

"My arm's feeling much better," Ellie told Alyce. "I was thinking of joining the Council today, but Vivian still needs someone to look after her."

"I'll stay," said Alyce. "Aimee's trousers need mending. When Vivian's up and about again, I'll join you in the Council."

Ellie felt tiny in the vast space of the great cavern. As she approached the Council, Katha looked up and sniffed.

"So you finally decided to grace us with your presence?"

"Katha," Councilman Tobin chided gently. He looked even more frail than he had a few days ago. Ellie felt sorry for the old man. On Rhynlyr, he would probably have been retired, enjoying the twilight of his life in rest and peace. Instead, he was holed up in this underground prison, trying to keep the Vestigia Roi from going extinct while the underground fever ate him up from inside. "How is...your injury, Ellie?"

"Better, thank you," Ellie said. "I'd like to join you today, and help if I can."

"We are glad of your help," said Councilman Serle. "I have heard much of your gift, but never witnessed it personally."

Ellie nodded and sat down quietly. The Council was discussing plans for a new latrine.

"Better sanitation may help slow the spread of the underground fever," said Councilwoman Phylla. "Have you seen all those children in the infirmary? Something must be done."

"Jude Sterlen informed me that the underground fever comes from a spore that lives on this island." Councilman Tobin paused to draw a slow breath. "Until we discover a cure for the spores, the underground fever will continue, new latrine or no."

"But shouldn't we at least *try?*" argued the councilwoman. "It seems hardhearted to allow the sickness to continue to spread without even attempting a solution."

"But the solution, Councilwoman, is not..." Tobin coughed, "a change in infrastructure. That will not save us."

"There is another possibility that we have not yet discussed," said Councilman Serle. "What if it is not Adona Roi's will that we be saved? First we witnessed the destruction of Rhynlyr, and now this terrible plague." The councilman sighed. "Perhaps these are his judgments upon a people no longer faithful to him. After all, the Song ended hundreds of years ago. Perhaps it is Adona Roi's will that the Vestigia Roi ends too, and that we go to swell the ranks of those in his City."

Councilman Tobin began to speak, but his voice was lost in a fit of coughing. Before she knew what she was doing, Ellie spoke up.

"If I may speak, Councilman, I do not believe that is Adona Roi's will. A little over a week ago, my friend Alyce—she dreamed of new Song music. Even if the Good King could possibly wish for us to be destroyed—which I can't imagine he would—why would he speak to us now if he only wants us to die out?"

The Council stared at Ellie. The only sound was a cough from Councilman Tobin.

"*New* Song music? No matter how gifted you are, young lady, surely you know better than to joke about such a serious subject," scolded Councilwoman Phylla.

Ellie's cheeks flushed. "I'm not joking. Alyce is staying with our sick friend, or she'd tell you herself."

"We do not doubt her truthfulness," said Councilman Serle patiently. "People often dream of music. Phylla is saying that your friend cannot have dreamed new *Song* music."

"But it *was* the Song," said Ellie. "Alyce dreamed that Ishua was singing it, and Ishua does not lie. Besides, my Sight only works when I hear Song music, and this music makes me see visions."

"Impossible," scoffed Councilman Serle. "The last addition of music to the Song was made over three hundred years ago, when Oron Talmai pushed the Enemy back to his underwater lair. *That* was the rightful ending of the Song, when the Vestigia Roi came as close to achieving the One Kingdom as it ever will in Aletheia."

"As close to…what do you mean?" said Ellie. "Isn't the One Kingdom what the Vestigia Roi is always working toward? What about the prophecy? You know:

> *"When all the islands rejoin*
> *And Aletheia again is One Kingdom,*
> *The Captain of Winged Armies*
> *Will return to rule his own."*

"Ah—you are thinking of a *literal* rejoining," said Councilman Serle. "Such is not the belief of all Vestigians. After all, the prophecy uses figurative language, suggesting a philosophical rejoining in which representatives from each archipelago will join the Vestigia Roi. This has already taken place."

"Then why isn't Ishua here in Aletheia yet?" Ellie argued.

"Some—I include myself here—see the prophecy as predicting *our* return to *Ishua*—which will happen to each of us upon our death. Ishua has spoken his final words to us, and now we must simply wait for our joyful reunion beyond the Edge of the world."

A sudden flush of anger surged up in Ellie. "And just wait here for Draaken to find us? Or for the underground fever to destroy us?"

Councilman Serle frowned. "Now you go too far. Do not speak the name of the Enemy here. Whatever music your friend dreamed, it is

97

blasphemous even to suggest that it is part of the Song. I detect an unhealthy attachment in you to this world of broken islands. I suggest you work to rid yourself of this tendency. It suggests a greedy desire for personal power and ingratitude for Ishua's existing gifts."

"And what about the new gifts?" Ellie described Vivian's sudden language acquisition and Aimee's ability to communicate with animals.

Councilwoman Phylla gasped. "There is no record in the Song of someone suddenly speaking a foreign tongue, let alone communicating with beasts. I can only think that our Enemy—for I will not speak his name here—is not called the Deceiver for nothing. You must insist that your friends stop using these unnatural abilities."

"We ought to have examined the crew of the *Legend* more carefully before allowing them into our midst," said Councilman Serle. "That ought to be remedied."

"There is…no reason to…doubt this crew," said Tobin, his breathing labored. "They have all been…decorated with the Lumena Medal for…their courage and service to the…fleet. Whatever mystery is…taking place here, their…loyalty is sure."

"I'm not so certain," said Councilman Serle, narrowing his eyes. "In any case, we will have no more discussion of this…music. Our first responsibility is to protect what we still have, being thankful for this safe refuge and giving glory to Adona Roi for the perfection of the complete Song he has already given us."

"But we can't just ignore—" Ellie began desperately.

"Enough! Councilwoman Phylla, continue with your plans for the new latrine."

That evening, Ellie dragged herself wearily back to the cave. Alyce was finishing a knee patch on a pair of pants while Vivian sat in bed, scribbling on a scrap of paper.

"Where's everyone else?" Ellie asked.

"At supper," said Alyce. "They said they'd bring some back for us. You look about done in, Ellie. What happened?"

Ellie flopped down next to her on the floor. "Bad day at the Council." She explained what had happened. By the end of her story, Alyce was frowning and Vivian had put down her pencil to listen.

"I just don't understand," said Ellie. "Why don't they think Ishua could bring us new music? I mean, it's his Song after all. Can't he do what he wants with it?"

"It sounds to me like the Council is afraid," said Vivian. "I'm sure they feel responsible for keeping the Vestigia Roi safe. In the midst of danger and uncertainty, they're only trusting what's familiar."

"But is it working? How can they think they're keeping us safe when people are dying from fever and starvation?" Alyce argued.

"I mean, I know it must sound strange to them—new languages and talking to animals and everything," said Ellie. "But why couldn't Rua be sending us these gifts to help us? We're going to need all the help we can get if we're ever going to win this war."

"Speaking of which..." Vivian held up the paper she'd been writing on. "Today I translated those runes I copied out of the Knerusse book. Listen:

Come awake, O sleepers,
from the silence of night.
Dawn rises,

new life from fire!
Rise up, O golden ones,
keep time with the music.
Come follow the Kingdom
to its glorious day.

Ellie felt a shiver pass through her at the words. "What does it mean?"

Alyce took the paper from Vivian. She hummed a starting note, then began to sing, her eyes following the words on the paper. The quick, dramatic music of the new Song swept up the words, enfolding them as naturally as an oyster shell around a pearl. In Ellie's changed vision, she caught a quick glimpse of golden letters rising like sparks from a bonfire of music.

When Alyce finished, silence stretched out for a moment.

"But...*how?*" Alyce burst out. "If these words are so old, if they've been sitting in that book for ages, how can they possibly fit with this new music?"

"Maybe they've been waiting for it," Ellie mused.

Vivian's face glowed. "It *is* the Song; I know it. It makes me feel—" she raised her eyebrows and reached for the girls' hands, guiding them to her stomach. "Feel this! The baby hears it too!"

Ellie waited a moment, then felt a small, sharp kick in the palm of her hand. "It's dancing!"

Tears of joy glittered in Vivian's eyes. "Ishua *is* guiding us toward the One Kingdom! It really is coming!"

Ellie smiled weakly. "I only wish it were so easy to convince the Council."

Chapter 8
Sparks of Life

Three days later, Vivian was finally well enough to get up and return to the library, though she promised Jude she'd take it easier. She said she wanted to finish fixing it up so she could begin teaching classes there. Owen and Aimee went with her. Alyce and Ellie walked with them before heading to the Council.

They reported at the doorway of the great cavern, and Ravago showed them in, expressing his delight that Ellie's arm was healing and out of its sling. Ellie smiled, but barely heard him. She was too focused on the fear and doubt throbbing in her chest, right beneath where Vivian's translation of the new Song words was tucked in her shirt pocket.

The Council was seated around their table as usual, but Katha was absent. Councilwoman Phylla gestured for Ellie and Alyce to be seated.

"Where's Katha?" Ellie asked.

"Sleeping," said Meggie, rolling her eyes. "Getting up early is not my sister's strong point."

"She will…join us later," said Councilman Tobin. His pale skin had taken on a grayish tint.

As usual, the Council was debating the problems of overcrowding, hunger, and sickness below ground. Ellie kept quiet as Councilman Serle proposed sending a flying ship on a mission to get food and medicine from another island. Meggie, though not technically part of the Council, casually suggested disguising the ship as a sea vessel and sending it by water to avoid suspicion. But Councilwoman Phylla would not agree to either version of the plan, saying it was too dangerous. Their best safety was in hiding, she insisted. Meggie turned away to offer Councilman Tobin a drink of water, but Ellie noticed that the other girl's lips were pressed into a tight line, and her hands trembled with contained frustration.

From across the dim cavern, a blonde figure came gliding across the floor. Like everyone else here, Katha owned only the nautical uniform she'd worn in the escape from Rhynlyr, but she wore it as if it were a frilly pink ballgown, and her hair was perfectly dressed and curled.

"Katha, what's wrong with you? The morning's half gone," Meggie groaned.

Katha tossed her golden curls, glancing around the table. Her gaze chilled as it lit on Ellie. "Well. One doesn't simply arise from bed fully dressed and groomed. Besides, I've had an idea." She seated herself daintily on Councilman Tobin's other side, kissing his cheek. "Good morning, Godfather."

"Good morning. And what is…this idea you've had?"

Katha paused for dramatic effect. "A ball."

"A what?" Meggie raised her eyebrows. "Katha, be serious. We're here to talk about things that are actually important."

"But just imagine it! A big party, with food and lights and dancing. Everyone would love it. I know *I* would."

"It always comes back to you," Meggie snorted. "People are starving, and all you can think about is hosting a party?"

"It's not just for me!" Katha snapped back. "People are miserable down here. Nobody's had any fun for ages. They need a ball to lift their spirits. After all, on Rhynlyr we used to have dinners and parties to go to every night, and we were happy then, weren't we?"

"Well, we're not on Rhynlyr anymore," said Meggie. "Those days are gone."

"I don't see why they have to be," sniffed Katha with an injured air.

Meggie rolled her eyes.

"If you two are *quite* finished bickering, let's return to business," said Councilwoman Phylla, sounding annoyed. "We cannot risk sending out a ship, and yet the problem of overcrowding remains."

"Why not establish a second...colony on a nearby island?" rasped Councilman Tobin. "There are many small islands in this area. If we split...our numbers, there will be more...resources."

"But the requirements for a livable island are strict," sighed Councilman Serle. "Its volcanoes must be dormant, of course. And it must offer underground lava tubes or caves for concealment. It must also have enough food and fresh water to support life. Although our island here seems hostile, it is actually a rare find."

"What about setting up a floating colony on the ships in the harbor?" said Meggie. "The ships are there anyway."

Phylla shook her head. "Again, too dangerous. The ships are hidden from above by an overhang of rock, but it would not hide the noise of a colony. Besides, it would be very difficult to monitor people's comings and goings from such an exposed location. All it would take would be one careless swimmer to reveal our presence to the Enemy."

"But we must do *something*," Meggie urged. "Sickness and starvation threaten the people."

"And yet outside is the threat of the Enemy, who wishes for nothing more than to slaughter every man, woman, and child of the Vestigia Roi," shuddered Phylla. "It seems a hopeless choice."

Ellie's heart hammered as she exchanged a glance with Alyce. Was this her moment to speak? She heard herself clearing her throat.

"Begging your pardon, Councilwoman, but I do not believe the choice is hopeless—not yet, anyway," said Ellie. "Alyce here is the one who had the dream of the new Song music."

"I can sing it for you," Alyce offered.

"And now there's more." Ellie pulled Vivian's translation from her pocket and began to unfold it. "Another of my shipmates discovered these words, and they match perfectly with the new music—"

"Are we back here again? I thought I instructed you to put this unsuitable topic to rest," said Councilman Serle, his eyes flashing dangerously. "Have you no respect for the Council's decision?"

Ellie bit her lip. "I do not wish to be disrespectful, Councilman," she said quietly. "But when multiple Vestigians have received such strong messages in so short a time—wouldn't it at least be worth listening to what they've heard? It might—"

"Enough!" Councilman Serle pushed himself to his feet. "Will you all sit by and tolerate this blasphemy? I will not hesitate to admit that you are gifted, Ellie, but your gifts do not grant you permission to make disloyal claims about the One Kingdom, especially here in the last Vestigian outpost."

"We do not...know that it is...blasphemy," Councilman Tobin said slowly, each breath an effort.

"Whatever it is, it is diverting precious time away from more important matters," said Councilman Serle.

"Could it hurt to at least listen—" Meggie began.

Councilman Serle held up his hand. "I will not stand by and see the cherished traditions of the Vestigia Roi disregarded. I move that Ellie be dismissed from this Council, to return only when she is ready to conduct herself in a more respectful manner."

"I agree," said Councilwoman Phylla. "Why don't you take leave for the rest of the day, Ellie, you and your friend? Get some rest and clear your mind."

"This is...a mistake," rasped Tobin.

"You're overruled," said Councilman Serle. "Two against one. Ellie, you are dismissed."

Stung, Ellie rose from her seat, Alyce following her motion. She folded Vivian's translation back into her pocket, squared her shoulders, and walked out of the room with as much dignity as she could muster.

Ellie and Alyce walked back to the cave in silence. Inside, Ellie sat down with her back to the wall, leaning her forehead on her knees.

"What a disaster," she groaned.

"Not the best day I could have imagined," Alyce agreed, lighting a lantern before sitting down next to Ellie.

"I don't know which is worse—being called blasphemous and disrespectful, or that the Council won't even consider a new part of the

Song. It's not as if the words or music dishonor Ishua or the Vestigia Roi."

"And it's not as if life in these caves is going especially well," said Alyce. "The Council must be truly terrified if they're not even willing to *listen* to a new idea."

"So much fear," Ellie sighed, leaning her head back against the wall. "I can't help but think that that's exactly what Draaken wants us to be feeling. If we're too frightened to make a move, then he's already won." She sighed again. "Maybe if I'd just presented the idea in a better way…"

Alyce bumped her shoulder. "Don't give yourself so much credit. Their fear has nothing to do with you. We'll just have to find another way to get them to listen."

They heard the tramp of the returning hunting party in the passageway.

"They're back early," Ellie frowned.

A moment later, Kai, Korrina, Finn, and Makundo, with Zira sitting on his shoulder, stumbled into the cave. Korrina was leaning on Kai, her face drawn with pain.

"Move aside," Kai growled. He helped Korrina sit down on a blanket before lifting the edge of her shirt. A red gash opened at the base of her rib cage.

"Doesn't look deep," Kai said. Jude had left some rolled-up bandages in his satchel, and Kai began to bind the wound tightly. Korrina made a soft grunting sound, but did not cry out.

"What happened?" Alyce asked in shock.

"We surprised a wild boar," said Finn. "I tried to shoot it at a distance, but its hide was too thick. We trapped it in a shallow cave, but it panicked and turned on us. Korrina speared it, but it slashed her with its tusk. Makundo finished it off."

"It was my fault," grumbled Kai. "I was foolish to push it into a corner."

"We wouldn't have, if there were a normal amount of game on this island," said Finn, rubbing his forehead. "Pigeons, ground squirrels, the occasional hare…Mharra just doesn't have resources for this many people."

Korrina growled as Kai's rough hands tied off the bandage.

"Too tight?" Kai asked quickly.

Korrina tugged at the knot. "No. Too loose. Not stop blood."

Kai tightened the bandage. "Jude can examine you tonight and make sure you're all right."

"Fine. Blood stop. Hunt more tomorrow."

Makundo clicked his tongue and said something in the warm, rhythmic Janaki tongue. Korrina argued with him. Kai's head turned back and forth, following their gestures and facial expressions. Ellie felt uncomfortable. "We'll leave you alone for a while."

She, Alyce, and Finn stepped out into the passageway, meeting Connor and Jariel as they returned from ship repair duty. Connor wiped the back of his hand across his forehead, leaving a smear of tar behind.

"What a day," he mumbled.

"You can say that again," said Ellie.

Connor raised his eyebrows. "You too? We had a beast of a time finding a new mast for the *Defiance*. Had to traipse over half the island to find a tree big enough."

"Doesn't the Council forbid outside travel, except for hunters?" Ellie asked.

Connor shrugged. "No choice. Without a new mast, that ship's not going anywhere. We stayed under cover as much as possible and kept a lookout, but the sky and sea were clear."

"Well, not *exactly* clear," Jariel corrected. "Across the lagoon, Ellie, we saw something amazing. A tiny black rock was sticking out of the ocean and spewing lava. As the lava hit the water, it cooled off with a big pfff! of steam. Then the lava got hard and turned into more rock. One of the repair crew told us it was a young hakara forming a new island!" Jariel's eyes were shining. "Know what that means?"

Ellie could picture the clouds of white steam, the blue ocean, the orange flame, but Jariel finished the thought for her.

"It means Aletheia isn't lost! Draaken's busy pushing islands over the Edge or taking over the ones that are left, and sometimes it seems like he's going to get them all. But that hakara we saw today showed that new islands are also getting made. Draaken can't possibly destroy them all."

A shiver passed through Ellie. *New life rises from fire.*

"Good speech, General," Connor said drily. "But all I really want is a swim. I'm hot and sticky, and we couldn't get permission to swim in the lagoon. Too open to the sky."

Alyce looked at Ellie with a grin. "Should we show them?"

Minutes later, all five children stood barefoot on the ledge over the onot. Jariel pulled back one of the overhanging vines with a stick and tested its strength. She offered it to Ellie, her eyes twinkling. "You want to go first?"

Ellie shook her head, and Jariel swung out on the vine, dropping into the onot with a whoop and a splash. She surfaced in a cloud of bubbles, her red hair streaming.

"You gotta try that!"

Connor followed her, tucking his arms and legs into the shape of a cannonball. Finn flipped upside-down into a smooth dive. Alyce and Ellie took the ladder. There was a narrow beach of black sand, and Ellie left her sketchbook there before dipping her toes into the jewel-blue water. The pool was surprisingly temperate, cool without being too cold. She rolled up her pant legs and waded in up to her knees, amazed that she could still see her feet perfectly through the clear water.

"Come in deeper! The water's fine!" Jariel hollered, splashing a big wave at Connor. Even Alyce was giggling as she squirted water through her hands.

Ellie shook her head. "I can't swim."

The others looked up all at once. "What?" Jariel spluttered. "How is that possible?"

"Only Nautical House students learned at the Academy. And none of my adopted families ever taught me."

"Then it's time you learned," said Connor. "Nobody—and definitely no Vestigian—should grow up without knowing how to swim."

Ellie looked out into the deep water with panic. "What about my arm? I still can't move it all the way."

"Then today you can just float," said Jariel. "You hardly even have to move for that."

"Come on. I'll help you," said Finn, offering his hand. With a deep breath, Ellie followed him until the water was up to her shoulders. Then Connor bumped Finn out of the way.

"I'll take it from here," he grunted.

"First you have to lean back," said Jariel, coming up on Ellie's other side. Ellie tipped her head back, making sure her feet could still touch the ground. Jariel giggled.

"You can't keep your feet on the ground and swim at the same time! You have to let go. Here. Lean on me." Jariel slipped an arm behind Ellie's shoulders.

Connor, holding Ellie's good arm, snickered. "Relax, Ellie! You're stiff as a board."

"How am I supposed to relax? I'm about to drown," Ellie snapped.

"You're not going to drown," said Finn, calmly treading water a few paces away. "Do you remember your mother?"

Ellie paused, surprised. "Well...sort of. Mostly from my visions."

"Then imagine that the water is like her. She holds you up, supports you. Trust her, and she won't let you fall."

Ellie recalled the visions she'd seen of her mother, Kiria Reid—her long dark hair, her laughing blue eyes. Ellie's shoulders relaxed a bit, and her feet left the bottom of the pool.

"Good," said Jariel. "Now fill your lungs with air. You need air to float."

Ellie took a deep breath and drifted to the top of the water. "Am I doing it right?"

"You're doing brilliantly," Finn's voice came across the water.

"Actually, you look like a whale," said Connor.

Ellie let all the air out of her lungs and stood up. "Hey!"

"But whales float," teased Connor. "You were doing it right."

"Try again," said Jariel. "By yourself this time."

Now that she knew what it was supposed to feel like, Ellie was soon able to float on her own. The sky was like a blue eye watching kindly from above, and the water cast wavery reflections on the walls of the onot. From across the pool, Alyce began to sing.

Come awake, O sleepers
from the silence of night.
Dawn rises,
new life from fire!

Though no one else knew the words, they could follow the new Song melody. Jariel, Finn, and Connor hummed along, their voices echoing in the shaft like a whole choir. Ellie's vision shifted, and she watched the light-ripples on the wall fuse into a whirlpool of golden fibers that rose and rose until it fountained out through the hole in the ceiling.

Dawn rises.

Could anything stop the coming of day?

Could anyone stop Ishua's Song?

Ellie stood up and splashed brilliant droplets into the air. They glinted like sparks of fire.

Chapter 9
A Ball

llie didn't want to go back to the Council, but Alyce woke her up early the next morning.

"If you quit, they win," Alyce insisted. "Fear wins. Draaken wins. Those councilmembers may not be willing to let you sing yet, but if you're ever going to get a chance, you have to show up."

With a groan, Ellie rolled out of her blanket.

She and Alyce sat quietly through the Council's debates on ration plans and ventilation shafts and work crews. Councilman Tobin tried once or twice to suggest longer-term plans, but speaking cost him so much effort that he rarely tried. His voice was so faint and raspy that often Meggie or Katha had to repeat his words so the others could hear. Ellie only got involved when the councilmembers asked for a vision of the One Kingdom's movements. But after a few tries, they stopped asking. The golden lines kept pointing back to Rhynlyr.

As Ellie and Alyce left the cavern at the end of the day, Meggie trotted to catch up with them.

"I didn't have time to tell you yesterday, but I think it was really brave of you to stand up to the Council," she said in a hushed voice. "The acting councilmembers—they're good people and I think they really want the best for the Vestigia Roi, but they're just so afraid. They think our only hope of survival is to stay hidden and hope the Enemy won't find us. Which he will, of course, sooner or later."

Ellie looked at Meggie warily. She still remembered the frilly, giggly Meggie who'd acted so superior on Rhynlyr. Besides, this was the daughter of Consul Radburne, who'd betrayed Rhynlyr into the hands of the Enemy. Why should Ellie trust her? She changed the subject.

"That was a real lecture you gave your sister about her idea for a ball. I thought you two were very close."

"We are…well, were," Meggie said. "When you grow up with a life like ours—a father like ours—it pulls you together. We were a team against the world, Katha and I, especially after…after Mother died. We would always stick together at those fancy political suppers. Katha taught me how to dress my hair to make me look older, and I was good at thinking of things to say to boring officials. But Katha's still trying to live the life we had then. She misses the fine clothes, the glittering parties, and our beautiful house on Council Row. She doesn't realize that life is gone now. Here on Mharra, we're fighting for our lives and the survival of the Vestigia Roi."

"And what about you? Do you miss your old life?" Ellie asked suspiciously.

"Sometimes. It *was* nice having an easier life—pretty clothes, servants and tutors to wait on us, no worries about having enough to eat. And it was more peaceful before we knew our father was…a traitor." Meggie's voice tightened. "But I don't miss all the rules or the endless small talk. Sometimes I felt like a little dog on Father's leash, always being paraded around and shown off. Now, even though I only sit with the Council to look after Godfather Tobin, I can listen to the debates and sometimes even share my ideas. I may not be powerful or important, but I feel like I'm actually doing something useful." Meggie stopped suddenly, reddening. "I didn't exactly mean to say all that. It just came out."

Ellie paused at a split in the passageway. "It's all right. I'm glad you feel useful here," she told Meggie. "See you tomorrow."

Alyce headed for the library, and Ellie turned to follow her.

"Ellie?" Meggie touched her arm. "I...I know we weren't the best of friends on Rhynlyr. I wasn't always kind to you, and I'm sorry. Do you think...we can start again? Try being friends from the beginning?" Ellie's stare must have looked blank, because Meggie rushed on. "It's all right if you don't want to. You're an experienced sailor now, and you're brave and smart and everyone respects you. I don't really know why you'd even want to be friends with me now. But I'm different than I was, and I just thought..."

"Okay." Ellie nodded.

"Okay—let's be friends?"

"Being friends...takes time. But we can try again—from the beginning."

"Really?"

Ellie sighed. "I believe you. You do seem different. And...well, with the whole Vestigia Roi changing, this seems as good a time as any to start something new."

Meggie grinned, relief written all over her face. "Okay. See you tomorrow, Ellie." She waved and hurried back down the passage.

Ellie put her hands in her pockets and continued on toward the library. Surprises never seemed to end. If Meggie was truly sincere and the change in her was real, well...maybe Ellie would gain a friend.

In the library, Vivian was on her knees, stretching out a sheet of sailcloth. Aimee held the other end. Owen sat against the wall, his knees pulled up to his chest, with Sunny curled beside him.

"What are you working on?" Ellie asked, sizing up the situation.

"You'll see in a moment," said Vivian, her forehead puckered with concentration. "Now, hold your end tight, Aimee." Vivian nailed her end to a wooden support, then handed the hammer to Alyce. "Can you help Aimee nail the cloth to that other board?"

When both ends of the sailcloth were securely fastened, Alyce and Ellie lifted up the contraption. A cloth sling stretched between two wooden supports with wide bases. Vivian smiled.

"It's like a hammock—a book hammock. There's not enough wood here to build proper bookshelves, and I can't just leave these books sitting on the damp floor. So this has been Aimee's and my project today. Owen even helped a little in the morning." Vivian smiled at him, but he just scowled, watching Ellie from under his glowering eyebrows. Vivian sighed. "At least this will tidy the place up enough so I can start holding classes here. It seems like libraries are fated to be neglected, burned down, reduced, then dumped—and it seems like I'm fated to bring them back to life."

"New life from fire," Ellie murmured to herself. An idea was forming in her mind. "Vivian, are there any books here about Oron Talmai?"

"The seer who received Canto Twelve of the Song? I think I remember seeing a book of Vestigian history in here." Vivian ran her finger down a stack of books, finally pulling out a thick, red-bound volume. She riffled through the book until she held a page. "Here. Oron Talmai."

Ellie looked hopelessly at the marching lines of letters, all threatening to scramble themselves up and cause her hours of frustration. "I remember learning about him at the Academy, but there's still so much I don't know. Will you read this to me?"

"I can't at the moment. I need to finish shelving all these," Vivian gestured to the haphazard stacks of books around the room. "But why don't you take the book back to the cave with you? Perhaps someone can read it to you tonight."

After supper, Ellie held the book out to Jariel as they stood in the passage in front of the cave. "Can you read me a section from this book?"

Jariel flipped to the page Vivian had marked. She wrinkled up her nose. "It sure looks boring."

Ellie sighed. "I think it might help with Council stuff. It'd take me hours to read it alone. Please?"

Jariel sighed and sat down with her back to the cave wall, her long legs stretched in front of her.

"These are the doings of the great Vestigian seer and warrior, Oron Talmai," she began in a dry monotone. A few sentences in, Finn poked his head out of the cave.

"You're absolutely *murdering* that book. If you're going to tell a story, you have to do it right."

Jariel cocked an eyebrow. "Do *you* think you can do any better?" She held out the book.

Finn caught it up and scanned down the page. Then, with a pause for effect, he began to read, pacing back and forth, his shanachai voice rising and falling with dramatic expression. At times his voice even seemed to come from elsewhere: the cave door, the end of the passageway. Ellie watched him, spellbound, as his words and his gestures painted a vivid picture of the life of Oron Talmai: a courageous young seer who received the music that was to become Canto Twelve of the Song. The crew of the *Legend* trickled out into the passage to listen as Finn told of the resistance to Talmai's visions within the Vestigia Roi, even at a time when Draaken had a presence on most islands. Ellie couldn't resist a wry smile. Even three hundred years ago, it seemed people had been suspicious of new Song music.

Talmai's solution, though, was to gather the Vestigia Roi together for what they thought was a singing of one of the existing Song cantos. Instead, aided by his friend, the great singer Lady Sharaya, he substituted the new Song music he had received. Some people were angry when they realized his deception, but their anger soon turned to remorse and zeal. The music itself mobilized them. The Vestigian fleet rallied all its agents and sympathizers to rise together against Draaken's forces. Together they made a concerted attack that virtually wiped out Draaken's land presence, pushing him and his army back into the sea and securing peace for the next three hundred years. Talmai himself attempted to pursue Draaken into his underwater lair and end his rule forever, but the young hero was lost beneath the waves and never seen again.

When Finn ended his reading, the crew burst into applause.

"It would not have been that interesting if I'd read it," admitted Jariel.

"What I want to know is how you made your voice sound like it was coming from other places," said Connor.

Finn shrugged modestly. "Shanachai mischief. I can imitate noises, project them from other places." Suddenly everyone turned as the squawk of an island bird sounded from the cave doorway. But there was nothing there. Finn cracked a smile. "See?"

"A useful trick," said Kai.

Ellie, however, was lost in thought. A bold idea was taking shape in her mind. It could give the fleet a future full of hope, or it might get her expelled from the Council—maybe even from the Vestigia Roi. Was it worth it? If the orders of those in authority were wrong, could disobedience possibly be the right thing?

As the others trickled into the cave to sleep, Ellie pulled aside Alyce and Finn and whispered her idea to them. They agreed, their eyes shining.

Before Ellie curled up in her blanket for the night, she carefully tore twelve blank pages out of her sketchbook. The next few days were going to be busy.

The next morning in the Council, Katha was back to talking about the ball she wanted to host. "It would be held in this very room, and we could have bottlebrush garlands and lots of lanterns for decorations. It wouldn't be visible from the outside at all. Oh, how I miss dancing…"

Meggie's mouth was already open to object when Ellie surprised everyone by speaking up.

"I know my opinion may not count for much, but I think the ball is a wonderful idea. It's exactly what the people need to lift their spirits."

Meggie's mouth hung open. Katha squinted suspiciously. "You're…*agreeing* with me?"

Ellie nodded. Katha relaxed in her chair. "Well. Maybe you do have some taste after all." She turned to Councilman Tobin. "Godfather, the seer is on my side. Now can we please have the ball?"

Councilman Tobin looked as if he were wavering. Councilwoman Phylla broke in. "But…the expense…there simply aren't resources for such an extravagance!"

"It doesn't have to cost extra, though," said Ellie. "Why not just send people through the regular supper line? It would be the same food they'd normally eat, but with a little music and dancing to go with it. The only extra things we'd need are a few more lanterns, some simple decorations, and some musicians. Alyce has already volunteered. We could use the opportunity to host a community singing of the Song as well. I was thinking Canto Twelve would be a good choice, in honor of Oron Talmai."

Alyce studiously kept her face still.

Katha looked pleadingly at the Council. "You must agree that the community's morale is down. And low morale can lead to unrest and rebellion. We can't afford *not* to host this ball."

"The amusement does seem harmless enough," agreed Councilman Serle. "If the expense will be small, I offer my support."

"As…do I," said Councilman Tobin.

Councilwoman Phylla shrugged. "Then it appears I am overruled even if I disagree, so I will not. A ball there will be."

Katha clapped her hands. "Splendid! I will oversee the decorations."

Meggie looked from Katha to Ellie with confusion. "Whatever you two are up to, I hope it's for the best."

When the Council adjourned for the day, Ellie and Alyce headed for the library, Ellie's twelve loose pages tucked inside her sketchbook. Meggie caught up to them on the way.

"Ellie, won't you tell me what's going on? I never thought you'd side with Katha. I thought you'd think the ball was a frivolous waste."

Ellie shrugged. She might have forgiven Meggie for past wrongs, but that didn't mean she trusted her with the truth yet. "I guess I came to see her side."

"Does it have anything to do with the new Song music you talked about the other day?"

Ellie tried not to let her face betray her emotions. "Why would it?"

"Because..." Meggie looked desperate. She glanced at Alyce.

"Whatever you have to say, you can trust her as you'd trust me," said Ellie.

Meggie lowered her voice to a whisper. "I had a dream last night."

Ellie raised her eyebrows, hushing her voice to match Meggie's. "What kind of a dream?"

"I dreamed..." Meggie licked her lips. "I saw a map of Aletheia, with Rhynlyr just a burned black spot in the middle. But the islands around it were all golden, and they shot arrows of light toward the center. When the arrows touched Rhynlyr, they turned the island gold again. I think...I think maybe Ishua wants us to rally the islands and retake Rhynlyr." Her eyes were wide and frightened. "I don't know what to think. I've never had a dream like that before. Am I going crazy?"

Meggie had had a dream from Ishua. Ellie grabbed her hand. "You're not crazy. Come with me."

They arrived at the library just in time to see Vivian's students leaving their first class. There were twelve or fifteen children too young to work, but Korrina came out of the cave as well. Apparently Makundo had persuaded her to rest until her injury was healed. Vivian stood inside, beaming as the last of the students left. Only Aimee and Owen remained with her.

"I've always loved research so much that I never thought I'd enjoy teaching," she said. "But something about watching students learn…it's magical."

"Now that they've left, can I work on…a project in here?" Ellie asked. "I don't want everyone to see it all at once."

"Of course," said Vivian. "You can spread out some sailcloth to keep it dry."

Ellie spread out her twelve blank pages on a piece of sailcloth to form a large rectangle. From her pocket, she produced two slender needles and a spool of white thread. She handed Meggie a needle.

"Here. We can sew these pages together while I tell you what this is going to be."

News of the ball spread quickly. People talked excitedly about it in the supper line and the passageways. It seemed a frivolous thing, but the prospect of a single night of celebration gave the weary Vestigians something to look forward to, something to remind them of Rhynlyr. Katha was busy overseeing the decorations and being scrupulously nice to Ellie. Councilman Serle and Councilwoman Phylla were coordinating the room layout and food service, and Meggie was helping Ellie plan the entertainment. There would be music and dancing, followed by a community singing at the end of the evening.

The rest of the *Legend's* crew was busy as well. Repairs on the *Legend* and the other ships were now complete, so Connor and Jariel joined the hunters to catch extra game. The underground fever continued to spread, and Jude worked in the infirmary from morning until night, caring for patients and searching for a way to kill the spores. Vivian continued to teach children during the day, but she added extra evening lessons so the Janakim could keep learning the Common Tongue. She kept talking about Korrina's exceptional language skills and praising her progress. Korrina just grunted, but her proud eyes glinted with pleasure.

Owen's helkath bite had faded to a light purple splotch like an old bruise, but the darkness he carried within him had only deepened. He barely slept, and he kept trying to slip away from the library when Vivian wasn't looking. Vivian had left him under Laralyn's watchful eye for a while, but one afternoon Gresha was taken to the infirmary with a fever, and Laralyn could not leave her side. Now every time Ellie entered the library to work on her project, Owen was there. He caused trouble, trying to upset her paints and tear the paper she was working on. But even when he wasn't in the way, he watched her progress, his eyes hungry and wild.

The onot was Ellie's one escape. Jariel had decided she liked being a swimming teacher and went with Ellie as often as she could.

"Now, wade in all the way up to your neck. Then push off and start moving your arms and legs in big circles. Like this." Jariel pushed off into the sapphire depths of the pool and began treading water, easily keeping her head above the surface.

Ellie flailed, trying to copy her. She bobbed up for a quick moment, then sank back down, her feet reaching for solid ground. "It didn't work!"

"You didn't give it a fair chance! Don't flail. Just make big, slow circles. See how I'm doing it? Try it where you're standing first."

Standing in place, Ellie began to form circles with her arms until she found a slow, steady rhythm. Her left arm now gave her no more than an occasional twinge of discomfort.

"Okay, now in the deeper water again."

Taking a deep breath, Ellie pushed off. Her feet no longer touched the ground. But her head stayed above water. She was swimming!

Jariel grinned. "Good job, Ellie!"

"Does it...look right?" Ellie was out of breath, trying to keep both her arms and legs moving at the same time.

"Whatever keeps you above water is right."

After an hour, Ellie could both tread water and paddle her way forward. She felt both thrilled and exhausted.

"I'm going to go dry off on the beach and rest for a while," she said, squeezing water out of her hair.

"Aren't you going to come exploring with me? Look at all those caves!" Jariel pointed to the dark hollows at the waterline.

Ellie shook her head. "I've had enough swimming for one day. You go ahead. And thanks for teaching me, Jariel. I'm less afraid of the water now."

"It was easy. You're a quick learner." With a wink, Jariel flipped onto her stomach and swam off, slippery and graceful as a dolphin. As Ellie sat on the beach, wringing out her dripping clothes, she could hear the echoes of her friend's voice from the caves. The first one seemed to be a dead end, but in the next, Jariel's voice got farther and farther away.

"Wow! This one goes back really far! And the water has a...current. It's flowing out, like an underground river! Ooh, a fish! Here, fishy fishy..."

Jariel's voice got fainter and fainter. Ellie began to worry.

"Jariel! Come back! Don't go too far alone!"

Jariel didn't answer. Ellie hesitated. Was her friend all right? As the moments of silence stretched out, Ellie made up her mind. Wading into the water again, she began to paddle forward, the way Jariel had shown her. It felt wonderful to know she could cross the expanse of blue water and not be afraid of sinking. When she reached the mouth of the cave where Jariel had gone in, Ellie hesitated. Light from the onot traveled only a few feet before it disappeared into utter blackness. A few eerie reflections danced on the ceiling of the tunnel. What was in there? Was she a strong enough swimmer to make it back? But what if Jariel was stuck and needed her help? Taking a deep breath, Ellie paddled into the dark water. But she had only gone a few feet when she heard the sound of splashing.

A few moments later, Jariel reappeared. Ellie let out a sigh of relief.

"Jariel, I was worried! You shouldn't have gone so far alone. Are you okay?"

Jariel pushed wet hair from her eyes, her face alight. "Ellie, you'll never guess what's on the other side of that cave!"

"Um...what?"

"An opening! This isn't a cave—it's a tunnel!"

"A tunnel? Where does it lead?"

"The sheltered harbor where the ships are kept."

"Interesting."

"Yeah." Jariel looked thoughtful. "Interesting."

Chapter 10
Rising

At last the day of the ball arrived. There were no new clothes to wear, no special food or fancy decorations. But after bathing and washing her uniform in the onot, having Vivian braid her hair in a circlet around her head, and fastening her shiny Scholastic House pin near her collar, Ellie felt a little more equal to the important task before her tonight.

Alyce and Finn had gone ahead to prepare with the other musicians, and Jude was working a late shift, but the rest of the *Legend's* crew entered the great cavern together. Even Owen came, though they were all watching him closely. Normally the big room was dim and gloomy, but tonight it was almost festive. Katha had done her part well. Leaping torchlight warmed the walls and illuminated the vast space. Graceful garlands of red bottlebrush and fern leaves adorned the entrance and the stage area set up for the musicians. Alyce was there, talking with a few choir members, and Finn was tuning up his harp with a fiddler and a flutist. A few children hung around the musicians, watching them curiously. Ellie glanced to the side of the stage to make sure her project was safe. The large sailcloth was right where she'd left it, carefully draped over something hanging on the wall. Good.

At the far end of the room, Ellie noticed a tall woman sitting beside the cot where Councilman Tobin lay, with Meggie attending him. The woman's nautical coat was sleeveless, revealing green tattoos winding down her right arm, and it was cut out at the back to make room for her enormous, feathery, shimmering green wings. Ellie ran over to her.

"Lady Lilia!" Ellie knew it was probably bad manners to hug an Alirya, but she threw herself into Lilia's arms anyway.

"Ellie!" The Alirya's beautiful face, with its smooth olive complexion, defined cheekbones, and clear dark eyes, wore a genuine smile. "How good it is to see you alive. I did not think you had perished on your voyage here, but many things may happen in the wide world."

"How we've needed you," Ellie burst out. "So much has happened here, and…"

Lilia's expression grew serious. "I know. Councilman Tobin and Miss Radburne have been telling me the news. And I myself sense something…" she glanced around the room, her forehead puckering darkly. "Well. We will speak more at tomorrow's Council meeting. For tonight, let us enjoy the festivities."

"I hope you like the ball," Ellie said, suddenly feeling embarrassed as she thought of what was to come. "We have…lots of plans."

"I can tell." Lilia's eyes twinkled knowingly.

There weren't nearly enough tables to go around, but Ellie joined her shipmates in a circle on the floor. Deniev came and joined them, but Laralyn and Gresha were not with him. Vivian introduced the Janakim, and she beamed with pride when Korrina, her wound now healed, said the full sentence, "We are pleased to meet you." Kai raised his eyebrows.

"How is Gresha?" Vivian asked. "We miss her here tonight."

Deniev shook his head. "The healers say it's the underground fever. They told me it's just a matter of time before it burns itself out, or…doesn't. There's only room in the infirmary for one visitor at a time, though, and Laralyn won't leave her."

"Poor Gresha," said Jariel. "She's so funny and cheerful. I hate to think of her being sick."

"So do I." Deniev's fist clenched. "What we really need is to get out of here, go somewhere we can breathe fresh air again. These tunnels are killing us. We could stop hiding and fight back if we all worked together."

"Hear, hear," said Connor. "I've had enough of skulking around and letting the Enemy have his way. If we're to fall, I say we fall from the sky, not wait like rabbits for death to find us here."

Ellie stirred her soup, trying to keep her expression neutral. Connor and Deniev were going to like tonight's entertainment.

A few minutes later, Jude joined them, his sleeves rolled up, balancing a bowl of hot soup in one hand.

"You made it," said Vivian, kissing his cheek, which was rough with a day-old beard.

"Barely," Jude sighed. "I feel wrong, being here when all those sick people can't rise from their beds. But I'm so tired I can barely keep my hands steady. I'll have some food and rest, then go back later. Besides, my research is moving forward. I think I may be close to finding a cure for the underground fever."

"Really?" Deniev asked eagerly. "What is it?"

"I'd rather not say just yet. I don't want to get anyone's hopes up before I'm sure. But I did check on Gresha before I left. We're controlling her fever with cold compresses and crushed *aton* leaves. She's not out of danger, but I told Laralyn she could take a bit of sleep. She looked exhausted. I'll check in on them again later."

Deniev nodded. "Thank you for paying such careful attention to my daughter."

Jude's eyes were full of compassion. "I'd do the same if it were my child."

Vivian slipped her arm through his. "Before you go back to more important business, will you promise me one dance?"

Jude smiled, weary lines creasing beside his eyes. "Anything for you, my love."

Connor courteously cleared everyone's dishes away. Moments later, the musicians struck up the dance music, starting with a lively reel.

Jude looked at Vivian. "How about this one?"

"Let's wait for something slower," she smiled. "I'm not moving as quickly as I used to."

Jariel tapped out the rhythm with her foot. "I like fast dances."

"Then you should dance," Ellie said.

"Nah. You need a partner for this one."

"So? Find one," said Connor, rejoining the group.

"What? You volunteering?" Jariel rolled her eyes.

"Sure."

"Sure? You don't even know how to dance!"

"I do too."

"Then why haven't I ever seen you?"

"Maybe I didn't want to."

"You're bluffing."

"Am not."

"Are too."

"Then dance with me." Connor cocked an eyebrow. "I dare you. Or are you too scared?"

"I am *not* scared." Jariel stood up, dusting herself off. "Hurry up, slowpoke."

Ellie watched as Jariel and Connor joined a reel on the dance floor. They fumbled awkwardly to find each other's hands and perform the first set of spins. But then they seemed to find a rhythm. Both of them were strong and athletic, and they both had a good sense for the music. They began to clap in time and skipped down the line with energy. Their movements fell into practiced unison, as if they were working together to trim a sail or polish a deck.

"Do you…like to dance?" Kai asked Korrina.

Korrina gave a fierce laugh. "I like to fight."

Kai nodded briskly. "Yes. Fighting is better. At least you know if you're winning or losing."

Jariel and Connor finished their reel and plopped back down across the circle from each other, panting.

"*Now* will you admit that I can dance?" said Connor.

"Only if you'll admit that I can dance circles around you," retorted Jariel.

The next tune was slower, and the sentry Ravago approached their circle.

"Hullo, Ellie," he said, his voice cracking. "How's your arm?"

"Fine," Ellie said, smiling as she rolled her shoulder in a circle. "I have a scar, but I can do just about everything again."

Ravago blushed. "I'm just—I still feel so bad about that. Can I make it up to you? Do you—would you like to dance?"

"Um…" Ellie squirmed, surprised by the sudden question. "I guess that would be okay."

She hadn't danced in a long time, and Ravago wasn't very good at it. He kept accidentally stepping on her toes, then apologizing. Out of the corner of her eye, Ellie saw Jude and Vivian dancing slowly, holding each other as they rocked in rhythm.

"My turn." Connor cut in, pulling Ellie away.

Ravago grinned. Ellie guessed he was relieved not have to figure out any more dance steps. "Okay. I hope your arm is—well, that it doesn't give you—get better soon. Bye."

As soon as Ravago was out of earshot, Connor rolled his eyes. "And just what do you call *that*?"

"I call it being nice." Ellie found waltz position again. "He was trying to apologize."

"After shooting you."

"It was an accident."

"An accident that now likes to dance?"

"Oh, give it up." Ellie felt her cheeks heating up. "It's nothing like that, and you know it."

"Do I?"

Suddenly Finn appeared behind Connor and tapped him on the shoulder. He still didn't have a nautical uniform, but he was wearing his Innish tunic, woven with intricate knots. The green in the fabric made his red hair look even more brilliant.

"Can I have a turn? The fiddler's playing solo for this one."

Connor looked at him as if he'd grown another head. "You too? What's going on tonight?"

Ellie felt her face turning red again. "Relax, Connor. It's just dancing."

Grumbling, Connor tromped off to sit with the group again. Ellie caught a glimpse of Jariel smothering a grin. Ellie ignored her, turning back toward Finn.

"I'm sorry about that," she apologized.

"I hope I didn't upset him," said Finn.

"I don't think so. Connor's the best brother ever, and I wouldn't trade him for anything. But he's…not always good with changes." She lifted her hands to return to waltz position. But Finn adjusted her hold, resting both her palms on top of his.

"This is how we dance on Innish." Lifting Ellie's hands straight up, Finn twirled her around and around. Ellie laughed, caught up in the fast movements. Around her, the room blurred into a swirl of lights and colors. When she stopped spinning, she was dizzy and giggling. Finn caught her as she lurched to one side.

"That was fun," she grinned. "Thanks."

Finn smiled back, his crooked grin crinkling up one side of his face. "You're welcome. I had fun too."

The music ended, and Ellie stepped away. "I…we should go get ready. The choir's going up soon."

Ellie took her place to the side of the main stage, in front of the hanging sailcloth. Finn joined the fiddler and flutist, and Alyce and the small choir formed lines behind them. Meggie stood at the front and spoke to the crowd.

"Good evening, everyone," she said, her clear voice sailing to the back of the room. The hubbub of conversations quieted down. "We hope you are enjoying the festivities. Now we invite you to join in the Song of Ishua. Please stand and follow the choir."

Like a rising wave, the crowd got up. Finn and the other musicians tuned to a starting note, and Alyce stepped to the front of the choir. She took a deep breath and opened her mouth. People leaned forward, expecting to hear the sweet and familiar music of Canto Twelve.

But they did not hear it.

Alyce's pure voice soared into a high note, then into a melody they had never heard before. It was swift and stirring, like a blend of a hymn and a battle anthem. As Alyce sang the first wordless phrases, people began to murmur. What was this strange new music? And who would dare call it the Song?

Ellie scanned the room nervously, her changed vision showing her swirls of mixed colors. Across the room, she saw Councilman Serle, a dark gray thundercloud swirling over his head, and Councilman Tobin, his face creased into a weak smile, his fingers as clear as glass.

Then the words began.

Come awake, O sleepers...

The choir, both men and women, joined in with Alyce. There was a ripple of grumbling as some people refused to echo the line. But Ellie saw others stir as if they really were coming awake from sleep. She sang along, swelling the weak response.

...from the silence of night.

A little stronger now. More voices joined the echo.

Dawn rises...

They were drowning out the grumbling...

...new life from fire!

Ellie had once seen a vision of her shipmates wearing golden circlets emblazoned with flames of fire. Now she saw the circlets again, this time on the head of every Vestigian man, woman, and child in the great cavern. As they sang, the flames grew brighter. Tears pooled in Ellie's eyes until the flames blurred together into an orange-and-gold sunrise.

Rise up, O golden ones,
Keep time with the music.
Come follow the kingdom
to its glorious day.

The choir's voices swelled, becoming a mighty and inescapable tide. As they began to repeat the stanza, Ellie knew it was time. She gave the dropcloth a sharp tug.

There was a gasp as the illumination was unveiled. On a canvas of stitched pages, as tall as Ellie herself, was the vision Rua had been showing her over these past few weeks. In a circle in the center, a new hakara pushed up its head from the ocean. Fiery lava bubbled down its sides. From its center, golden beams of light burst through the edge of the circle like the spokes of a wheel, spreading out into the blue sky above and the sea below. At the edges of the canvas, the light became the words of the new Song, the golden letters shaped like tongues of flame: RISE UP. The rich blue, deep red, and glittering gold of the illumination glowed in the lantern light, and a bolt of energy surged through the room. The singing swelled to its highest point. From the back of the room, Ellie heard a shout.

"Retake Rhynlyr!"

"Fight back against Draaken!"

"Follow the Kingdom!"

The last strains of music were still trembling in the air as the individual shouts became knots of people talking animatedly. Fists pumped the air. Voices rose and fell with vigor. Ellie let out her breath and sagged against the wall, her gaze lifting up to the dim ceiling of the cavern.

The Song had done its work.

The Vestigia Roi had been roused.

And Ishua's Kingdom was once more on the move.

Chapter 11
A Call to Arms

When the ball was over and Ellie had helped clean up, she couldn't find any of her shipmates. Wearily, she walked all the way back to the cave and found them huddled around the mouth of the cave.

"What's wrong?" Ellie asked Vivian.

"It's Owen," said Vivian, worry in her voice. "He...started acting strange about the time the singing started. By the end, he was on the floor writhing. Kai had to carry him back here. Jariel's gone to get Jude, but I don't know what else to do."

A hideous scream issued from the cave, like the cry of a dying animal. Ellie edged forward to see Kai inside, firmly pinning Owen's arms and legs to the ground while the boy's head thrashed back and forth. His glasses had been flung off and his eyes were bloodshot and wild.

"Let me *go!*" he shrieked, his voice sounding unnaturally loud and deep. "I'll kill you! I'll kill you all!"

As Ellie stood frozen in horror, something soft and feathery brushed against her face. Lady Lilia gently but firmly stepped through the knot of onlookers and knelt beside Owen and Kai in the cave. For a moment, Owen stopped thrashing and his eyes focused on her.

"Ishua, Rua, and Adona Roi," Lilia breathed. "I cannot believe it. A *dshinn,* here in our very midst."

She nodded to Kai and he stepped aside. Lilia put her hands on either side of Owen's face and looked into his eyes.

"Owen. Owen Mardel. Clever mind and lover of animals. Can you hear me?"

For a moment Owen looked up at her with the open expression of the curious ten-year-old he had been. Then his expression crumpled and became a leer. The irises of his eyes turned yellow, his pupils became vertical slits. Ellie covered her mouth.

"We hear all. We see all." The voice coming out of Owen's mouth was rough and throaty.

"What is your name, dshinn?"

Owen bared his teeth. "Why should we tell you our name?"

Lilia gripped Owen's face more firmly. "I am a servant of The Three Who Ever Live. This is their Kingdom, and you have no power here."

Owen choked and hissed. "We are called Mordaz. One day your master will serve ours…one day soon."

Lilia appeared to ignore the comment. "What have you seen, Mordaz?"

Owen's face contorted into a hideous smile that was not his own. "We have seen all. Our master, Lord Draaken, whose wisdom is greater than the sea, knows of the hole where the Ulfurssh worms dwell. He knows the seer is here." Owen's eyes moved to rest on Ellie, standing in the doorway. "He is coming for you."

"Coming here? When? How large is his force?"

"He will not rest until the Ulfurssh worms are exterminated. Then Khum Lagor will come. He will be here in ten days."

Lilia pulled in a deep breath. Her great wings extended, arching like a canopy over Owen.

"Mordaz, I command you to release this boy and leave this place forever."

Owen let out a scream that chilled Ellie's blood. "No! You cannot banish me! You do not have the power!"

"In the name of Ishua, Rua, and Adona Roi, I do have the power. You are banished."

Then Lady Lilia began to sing. From her lips came the new Song music. Owen immediately began to thrash. Ellie's mouth felt as dry as sandpaper, but she hoarsely tried to sing too. It felt like the only thing she could do to help.

As her vision changed, Ellie caught a hideous glimpse of Owen reduced to nothing but bones and eyes. His skeleton writhed convulsively on the floor. Flecks of white spittle bubbled to his mouth, and his eyes rolled back in his skull.

"I command you to leave him," Lilia said again. "Owen, you are free."

Ellie saw the skeleton exhale a puff of what looked like black smoke. The smoke lingered a moment in the air, then dissipated suddenly, as if blown away by a clean wind. Owen's body twitched once and went limp.

The singing stopped and the vision slid away from Ellie. There was Owen, his eyes closed, lying pale and still on the cave floor. Running footsteps sounded in the passageway, and Jude and Jariel burst inside.

"I came as fast as I could," said Jude breathlessly, dropping to his knees beside Owen.

"Is he...dead?" Jariel asked, her voice sounding small.

"No." Lilia slowly stood up, her wings drooping a little. "Owen will be all right now. All he needs is rest. He will need much of that, after the ordeal he has passed through."

The crowd at the doorway parted respectfully to let Lilia through. The Alirya met Ellie's eyes. "We have much work ahead of us tonight. Come, little one. Bring the singer as well."

Ellie met Alyce's eyes. They left the others huddling around Owen and followed Lilia through the passageway.

"What...what *was* that?" Ellie said when she could find breath to speak.

"It was a dshinn," said Lilia, her voice husky and tired. "It is one of Draaken's most powerful servants, and all the more dangerous because it cannot be seen. It inhabits a human's mind, controls their thoughts, sees through their eyes, and communicates all it learns to its master. How long has Owen been like this?"

Ellie could hardly think. Panic swirled inside her as she digested this new information.

"Owen's been sick almost four weeks, Lady Lilia," Alyce filled in. "He changed about the time we arrived here. But he was bitten by a helkath a week before that. Jude thought he was having really strange complications from the bite."

Lilia nodded. "That makes more sense. It is likely that the helkath bite weakened his defenses. When Owen was in the grip of hopelessness and despair, too weary to resist, the dshinn crept in and took control of his mind. I am only sorry I was not here to identify it sooner. It is beyond the skill of any human healer to remove."

"But...he'll be all right now, won't he?" Ellie asked.

"Yes. Owen is a healthy young boy, full of life, and he will make a full recovery, though it will take time. His mind and body have been pushed to their limit, and he will not be ready for active service for some weeks. And we do not have that long."

"What do you mean?" said Alyce.

"The dshinn was communicating with Draaken the whole time it was inhabiting Owen's mind. You heard its report: the Lagorites know where we are, and they will be here in ten days, if not sooner. The Council must determine a plan of action tonight."

Lady Lilia dispatched sentries to gather the rest of the Council to the great cavern. Serle and Phylla were yawning as they came. Meggie appeared with the news that Councilman Tobin had taken to his bed after the ball. He was too ill to be moved, and Katha was staying with him, but he had sent Meggie as his representative. Lilia ordered another sentry to send Jude to the old man's bedside.

The great cavern, still hung with drooping garlands of flowers, was dim again, though Ellie's illumination still glinted dimly on the far wall. Alyce collected the remaining lanterns into a bastion at the Council's table. Lilia rolled out a map of Aletheia and quickly explained what had happened.

"We have seen our Enemy's plan," she said. "His forces will be here in ten days. He means to wipe us out...and with us, all hope of reuniting the islands and restoring the One Kingdom. I am only an adviser to this Council and cannot make decisions directly, but if the

Vestigia Roi is to survive, let alone take back Rhynlyr, we must move now."

"So it's...true," said Councilman Serle. The lantern light illuminated his face and glittered on unshed tears in his eyes. "The One Kingdom...it's not just a figure of speech."

"It cannot be. I might have believed that once, but not after seeing all those people singing," said Councilwoman Phylla.

Councilman Serle looked up at the ceiling. "I have served Ishua all my life and sought to understand him as best I could. But last night...in that music...I heard him *moving*. Yes, the One Kingdom is a joy to be gained after death, and it will be fully realized one day. But last night I understood that it is *also* coming here, now. It is future, and it is present. It is *both*."

Ellie shivered. Had she really worked this drastic change in the councilmembers? She knew she'd coordinated some music and painted a picture, and that was something. But it did not add up to this transformation she was seeing. Suddenly she felt small in the presence of a power both mighty and uncontrollable.

"I am sorry, but we must keep moving," Lilia urged. "The Enemy now knows we plan to attack Rhynlyr. If we are to have any chance of success, we will need an army of unprecedented size and a safe base from which to attack."

"To build that kind of an army, we will need every Vestigian and every sympathizer from every island," said Councilman Serle. "Our first task is to gather them from the islands and unite them under one banner."

"But how?" said Councilwoman Phylla. "The attack on Rhynlyr scattered the Vestigia Roi in all directions."

"We could send out another eyret message, for one," said Meggie. "The birds home to our tattoos. That would reach the Vestigian sailors, at least."

"But what about the sympathizers without tattoos?" said Alyce. "All the people we left on Innish now follow Ishua, but none of them have tattoos."

"For them, we may have to send word in person," said Councilman Serle. "The same for the island of Nakuru, our last aid mission before Rhynlyr was taken. On the advice of Consul Radburne, most of our fleet sailed there with supplies after the island was devastated by a tidal wave. Some of our forces may still be there, if they received our first message and did not attempt to return to Rhynlyr, but we have no way of knowing."

"But these sympathetic forces may already be besieged by the Enemy," objected Councilwoman Phylla. "We may have to free them before they can fight for us, and we have only thirty ships, most of which were built for cargo transport, not war."

"We'll have to choose our islands carefully," said Councilman Serle. "Identify three or four islands with the largest populations of sympathizers. Group the ships into convoys and send them there. Rely on the eyrets to do the rest."

Meggie placed a stone counter over the island of Nakuru on the map, and more stones joined it as the Council identified other islands with strong populations of sympathizers. Ellie placed one on the Orkent island of Innish. The islands were scattered all over Aletheia. To reach them, Vestigians would be spreading out all over the world, like the beams of light in her illumination.

"That still leaves us with the problem of where to regroup—a base from which to stage our attack on Rhynlyr," said Serle. He traced the seven Havens marked on the map. "A Haven would be ideal, as Rhynlyr is also a flying island. But we know that Sylt is taken. Ilorin holds Vestigian prisoners and…traitors undergoing rehabilitation. But from the other five Havens we've had no word."

"Jura has fallen to the Enemy," said Lady Lilia. "That much my earlier mission confirmed."

"Then I propose sending out eyret messages to the four Havens that may yet stand," said Serle. "Either Dhar or Ajmer would make a good staging ground for an attack on Rhynlyr."

"We must also have somewhere safe to send those who cannot sail or fight now," said Councilwoman Phylla. "Many of the people here are too young, too old, or too sick to undertake a mission."

"A safe island." Meggie rubbed her forehead. "I wonder if such a place even exists anymore."

"We also have to think about how to get all these people safely off Mharra," said Ellie. "The Enemy's forces are only ten days away, and we're going to need a head start."

"What if we set up a decoy, a rearguard, to make them think the island is still inhabited?" said Meggie.

"Wouldn't it be terribly dangerous for those who stayed behind?" said Ellie. "What if the Enemy catches them here?"

"Yet a live presence would make the Lagorites more likely to actually make a landing and investigate, slowing them down and giving the rest of the Vestigia Roi a greater chance of escape," said Serle.

"It seems every course is fraught with danger," said Phylla with a sigh.

"And yet the Kingdom comes," said Meggie. "I propose we call a muster of our sailors tomorrow, first thing in the morning. Then we can start making plans and deploying ships—maybe as soon as the day after that, under cover of darkness."

"But I don't think we can *order* anyone to stay behind as the rearguard," said Ellie. "I mean, I know the Council has the power to command, but I just don't think it would be right. If sailors are going to risk their lives like that, I think it's only fair to ask for volunteers."

"Then we muster at dawn," said Serle.

"Wonderful," said Lilia, her smile weary but proud. "You are fully equipped for the task ahead of you. Which is why I do not worry, even though I must leave you for a while. I am undertaking a mission of my own."

"What? You can't leave us! We need you!" said Meggie.

"Lilia, what are you thinking of?" added Phylla.

"If I am successful, I will bring help for the war against Draaken," Lilia answered, her face grave. "I will also take responsibility for scouting the remaining Havens. In the meanwhile, I know the Vestigia Roi is well cared for."

"We'll miss you, Lilia," said Ellie, suddenly feeling smaller than ever. "Come back to us safely and soon."

Lilia nodded. "I will do my best."

It was very late by the time Ellie and Alyce stumbled back into their cave. Jude hadn't returned yet. Ellie knew the sentries had orders to summon the Vestigians at dawn, and she needed rest desperately. But still, as her mind turned over tomorrow's plans, it was a long time before she fell asleep.

Chapter 12
Hard Choices

Early the next morning, Ellie sleepily entered the great cavern. Lady Lilia, Councilman Serle, and Councilwoman Phylla were already there, as were Katha, Meggie, and Jude. Everyone looked somber. Katha and Meggie's eyes were red, as if they had been crying.

Ellie looked around worriedly. "What's wrong?"

Katha blew her nose into a handkerchief. Jude put a hand on Ellie's shoulder.

"Councilman Tobin—he didn't make it through the night, Ellie," Jude said, his voice husky. He looked as if he hadn't slept. "He was very sick and weak, and he died peacefully in his sleep."

Ellie felt tears spring to her eyes. She hadn't been especially close to Councilman Tobin. He wasn't her godfather. But nevertheless, she felt a hole open up in her heart at the news.

"Before he went, he left instructions," Jude continued. "I witnessed them, as did Lady Lilia."

"He nominated Ellie, Meggie, and Katha as acting councilmembers," said Lady Lilia. "The position is a temporary one, only until official elections can be held, but with the upheaval at hand, who knows when that will be."

Ellie's knees felt suddenly weak and she sat down in a chair. "What? Me? Why?"

Lilia shook her head. "Tobin was too weak to speak at length, but he clearly had confidence in you—all three of you. And I support his confidence. Each of you brings your own gift to Vestigian leadership."

"But...I'm only thirteen," Ellie said faintly. "What do I know about leading the Vestigia Roi?"

"What do any of us know about leading the Vestigia Roi in this hour of darkness? What do we know about defeating Draaken—about saving this world from his control?" asked Lilia. "You may be young, Ellie, but your gift of Sight makes you as qualified as anyone—maybe more. And you are not alone. You are connected to Ishua, Rua, and Adona Roi. And to these people." Lilia swept her arm around the room, gesturing to the other councilmembers.

"Please say yes, Ellie," Meggie said, her voice thick. "We need your help."

Ellie let out a long breath, gazing into the lantern on the table. The little yellow flame inside bobbed and flickered. It reminded Ellie of something her teacher Zarifah had said: *Rua's power gives Vestigians the courage to dream in the direction of the One Kingdom.* Ellie glanced up, catching sight of her illumination on the far wall—the volcano, the beams of light spreading out in every direction.

"Okay," she said haltingly. "I still don't know why Councilman Tobin picked me, but I'll do my best." She stood up slowly and hugged first Meggie, then Katha. "I'm sorry about your godfather."

There was very little time to grieve. The sentries' summons had already gone out, and the Vestigians began to assemble in the great cavern. They were a bedraggled lot, but after last night, Ellie saw new vigor and resolution in their eyes. She spotted the crew of the *Legend* standing together with the Janakim. Owen was with them, though he was sitting on the floor, leaning against Kai.

Councilman Serle got up to speak. He announced the sad news of Tobin's death and introduced the three new acting councilmembers. Then he explained the plan: four missions to rally Vestigians from all parts of Aletheia. The target islands would be Nakuru in the Numed Archipelago, Sukka in Arjun Mador, Twyrild in Newdonia, and Innish in the Orkent Isles. When the missions were complete, all the ships would regroup at a Haven for the attack on Rhynlyr. Which Haven it would be depended on Lilia's scouting mission.

The able-bodied sailors were divided up for the four missions. The *Legend* and the *Venture* were assigned the Nakuru mission, since they had experience working together and Janaki and Nakuran were similar dialects of Numbani, the language of the Numed Archipelago. There would be a hasty Ceremony of Vows that evening to officially induct the new sailors. Finn was asked if he wanted to join the mission to Innish, but he shook his head.

"Chieftain Ahearn and draoi on Innish are already loyal to Ishua. They speak Common, and they'll recognize a Vestigian ship when they see one. My place is with my crew now."

Three ships would carry those too old, young, weak, or sick to fight to an island of safety. The Council would also accompany them. Councilwoman Phylla announced that they were seeking nominations for such an island, but no one stepped forward.

Last and most difficult, Councilman Serle explained the rearguard mission. He called for a few volunteers who would be willing to give their lives to offer their brothers and sisters a better chance of escape. There would, of course, be an escape plan for the rearguard, but no one knew if it would be successful. Five people volunteered: a young husband and wife, Ravago, a middle-aged widow, and Deniev. He was standing near Ellie at the front, and she tried to change his mind.

"Deniev, you don't have to do this," she urged quietly. "You can let someone else stay. Think about Laralyn and Gresha."

"I am thinking about them," he said grimly. He looked at Ellie and his eyes softened. "Gresha is still very sick. If she and Laralyn can get away, go somewhere they will be safe and healthy…and if I can give them a chance to get there…"

"But don't you…don't you want to see Gresha grow up?" Ellie asked, her throat tight.

"Of course I want to see her grow up." Deniev smiled sadly and chucked Ellie under the chin. "Of course I do. But more than that, I want to know that she *will* grow up." He slipped away to join the other rearguard volunteers.

Ellie stayed with the Council all day, using her Sight to project the best routes for the mission ships and dividing up tasks and supplies. The fleet had enough eyret birds for each ship to take one. In the evening, the cavern filled with people again as all new sailors prepared to take their Vows of Dedication and receive their tattoos. Ellie remembered her own ceremony clearly: the knocking on the doors of Main Hall, the new Academy pins, the robed choir. Now there were no robes, no pins, no hall, and she was standing with the Council, presiding over the ceremony. And yet the new Vestigians made the same solemn vow:

> ...that I shall serve Adona Roi and his son Ishua
> as a loyal citizen of the One Kingdom.
> All Vestigians will be my brothers and sisters.
> I commit myself to the Kingdom's principles
> and will faithfully uphold and respect its laws.
> I will support all things that advance the Kingdom
> and oppose any that harm it.
> I will defend the Kingdom in its hour of need.
> To Adona Roi, to Ishua, to Rua, and to the Vestigia Roi,
> I dedicate myself in eternal devotion.

One by one, Lady Lilia tattooed the VR insignia in the crook of the novices' left arms, forever bonding them to the fleet. Ellie watched as Finn received his tattoo. She had been terribly afraid during hers, but Finn's expression stayed calm even as the freezing brand marked his skin.

Ellie was exhausted by the time she stumbled back to the cave that night. Jude wasn't back yet. Aimee and Sunny were snoring, curled up together in a corner. Owen was also sleeping, his face calm and peaceful. Everyone else was awake, mending trousers or sharpening blades as they talked in soft voices. Makundo, Korrina, and Deniev were there with them, though Laralyn and Gresha were still at the infirmary.

"So when are we leaving?" said Jariel.

"Not for another week," said Connor.

"But some of the other missions are leaving sooner," said Finn, twisting his left arm to watch his silvery tattoo catch the lantern light. "The ships bound for Innish leave the day after tomorrow, since they have the longest way to go."

"It'll be a busy week," said Kai. "We need to hunt enough game to dry for our voyage. There's no guarantee we'll find anywhere to stop for supplies along the way."

"That's a lot of game," said Connor. "According to the map, I estimate it'll take us two weeks to get to Nakuru."

"If no storms," put in Korrina.

Just then, Jude arrived. He sat down next to Vivian, rubbing the bridge of his nose as if to relieve a headache.

"You need sleep," said Vivian, rubbing his back.

"I can't," he said tensely. "Another woman died of the underground fever today." He looked at Deniev, meeting the other man's worried gaze.

"Deniev, Gresha's not doing well. Her fever is rising again. I think I may have found a medicine that will kill the spores and cure the fever permanently, and I'd like your permission to try it on Gresha."

Deniev's forehead was lined with worry. "Is it safe?"

Jude sighed. "The remedy is new and I can't be sure. But I'm more worried about what will happen to Gresha if we don't try it."

Deniev frowned. "What does Laralyn say?"

"She was against it at first, but when Gresha's fever spiked again this afternoon, she changed her mind. But I need your consent as well."

Deniev nodded slowly, though he was still frowning. "I trust you, Jude. If you say this remedy will give Gresha a better chance, I'll agree to anything. But I want to be there."

"Of course. I'd like to administer it as soon as possible. Are you ready to go now?"

Deniev nodded, and the two men went out.

When Ellie woke the next morning, Kai, Finn, Connor, and Jariel were already out hunting. Jude was also gone. But Owen had his eyes open. Ellie crawled over to him.

"You're awake," she whispered.

Owen's eyes wandered to her face and squinted, his glasses still in his pocket. Ellie looked at his eyes nervously, but relaxed as she saw the hazel-green irises and round pupils. Owen, the real Owen, was back.

"I sure hope I never have a dream like that again," Owen muttered sleepily. "I can't remember if it was last night or the night before. But it was awful."

"Yes." Ellie reached down, lifted a lock of brown hair out of his eyes. "You were...sick. Really sick. But you're better now."

"I *feel* better," said Owen with a yawn. "I feel...light, like I set down something really heavy. But I'm so tired, too. I feel like I could sleep for days."

"Then do. You've earned it."

Owen didn't argue. His eyes drifted shut again.

Ellie headed to the Council as soon as Alyce was awake. They spent a busy morning writing eyret messages, planning a funeral for Tobin, and meeting with the captains of the Innish mission, who were leaving the next morning. About noon, a sentry approached, with Jude, Laralyn, and Deniev following him. Laralyn carried a bundle in her arms.

"An urgent message from the infirmary, your honors."

Jude's face looked haggard, but he was smiling.

"I believe I have found a cure for the underground fever."

Councilwoman Phylla stood up. "What?"

"I have been doing research for the past few weeks, but after Councilman Tobin's death, I knew we could wait no longer. I asked Deniev and Laralyn's permission to test the new treatment on their daughter."

Laralyn stepped forward, smiling through her tears. She opened the front flap of the bundle, and Gresha peeked out, her little face pinched, but her eyes clear and bright.

"He did it," said Deniev, his voice thick with emotion. "Gresha's going to be all right."

Ellie smiled, tears welling up in her own eyes. Some good news at last.

"What is the cure?" Councilman Serle asked, leaning forward.

"*Caris* powder, of all things," said Jude. "I knew the leaf of the *stellaria* tree healed coral, but I did not know of its healing power for human beings. I was a bit worried about its potency, but I dissolved it in hot water and administered it to Gresha as a tea last night. By this morning, the fever was completely gone."

Meggie let out a slow sigh. "That's...wonderful news."

"If only it had come in time to save our godfather," said Katha with a sniffle.

Councilman Serle frowned. "But how practical is this remedy? The great stellaria tree on Rhynlyr was destroyed, and for all we know, the Enemy controls all the offshoots on the Havens. Our supply of caris powder is limited."

"And we must send what we have with the ships as they go out on their missions," said Councilwoman Phylla.

"How much caris do we have?" said Meggie. "Maybe we could send some with the ships, and use some to heal the sickest patients."

Sentries were dispatched to inventory the fleet's supply of caris. They returned a few hours later with a discouraging report. The ships that had made it to Mharra had been poorly stocked with caris, and some had used theirs up at islands along the way. There were only fifteen pouches left: enough for each mission to take one, including the convoy taking the sick and weak to a safe island, with ten doses left over. Jude looked grave when he heard the news. "I wish we had enough to treat every patient, rule out any possibility that the fever could return later. But this will save the sickest ones."

That night, Gresha was well enough to come home from the infirmary, and Deniev and Laralyn brought her into the *Legend*'s cave to say hello. Ellie had attended Councilman Tobin's simple funeral and didn't feel much like talking, but Jariel and Aimee made faces to draw sleepy smiles from the little girl. Jude knelt down next to her when he came in, a smile smoothing the tired lines in his face.

"Her progress is amazing," he said. "The fever weakened her body, and she'll need rest and good care, but I see no reason she shouldn't make a full recovery."

Laralyn beamed. "I'll see that she rests up on the island they send us to, wherever it is." She looked at Deniev. "You sure you can't change your mind and come with us?"

Deniev shook his head, squeezing her shoulder. "I've made my decision. And I stand by it even more now that we know Gresha is going to get well. The most important thing to me is that you and she get away safely."

"Do you have an escape plan for getting off the island?" Vivian asked softly, making room for Jude to sit down in the circle.

"Yes, but not a very good one," Deniev admitted, clasping and unclasping his fingers. "We're going to create a lot of noise and ruckus, light some fires aboveground, make our position obvious. Then we'll make a run for the last boat and try to slip off unnoticed. What has me the most worried, though, is that stretch of open beach between us and the harbor where the ship will be. If the enemies are close enough to see our fires, they'll surely be close enough to shoot down a few fools running across a beach. I just wish there were a more protected way to reach the ship."

The scrape of Jariel's sword against her whetstone went silent. "Maybe there is." She looked at Ellie. "Remember? That day in the onot?" Quickly she told Deniev about the underground river she had discovered, the one that opened onto the harbor. Deniev listened gravely.

"I'll investigate it in the morning. It's certainly worth a try."

"You'll give yourselves a better chance if you have some traps." Everyone turned. The voice was Owen's. He was lying on his back, staring at the ceiling. "Set up some mirrors to reflect torchlight in lots of different directions. Create some tubes to amplify noise. Lure the enemies here, into the passageways, then set some snares to keep them busy."

"That's...brilliant," said Jariel.

"Knew we could count on you for a good idea," said Connor, smiling and shaking Owen's shoulder.

Owen shrugged. "Not much else I can do right now. I can help design them if you like."

"We'll be happy for any help," said Deniev. He looked at Vivian. "Will you keep an eye on Laralyn and Gresha? Make sure they settle in on the safe island where you're going?"

Vivian smiled apologetically. "Normally I'd be happy to. But I won't be going with them."

"You won't?" said Deniev.

"What?" said Jude.

"No," said Vivian. She took Jude's hand. "My husband and my crew are going to Nakuru. And I'm going with them."

"No, you're not," said Jude.

Vivian raised her eyebrows.

"Vivian…" he sighed, trying to control the expression on his haggard face. "Can I talk to you? Alone?"

The two of them got up. Deniev and Laralyn also rose to go.

"We'd better get back. Gresha needs her rest."

The crew of the *Legend* got ready for bed, and Ellie walked down the hall to the lavatory. As she was coming back, she heard voices coming up the tunnel. She hesitated in a dim alcove.

"Vivian, you're not coming with us. How can you be so thoughtless of your own safety? This plan of yours—it's senseless and selfish!"

"*My* plan is selfish? Because I stand by my principles? Because I choose to be loyal to my kingdom and my husband?"

"No! Because you're a mother now. Can't you see? It's not just your life at stake anymore. I can't let you go on this mission."

"*Let* me?" Vivian's voice became dangerously quiet. Ellie shifted nervously, wanting to leave, but now she was stuck in the alcove with Jude and Vivian just around the corner.

Jude heaved a sigh. "That's not what I meant."

"And what *did* you mean?"

"I'm just…terrified that something will happen to you, or to the baby." Jude's voice grew thick and tight. "I've seen so much death and suffering these past few weeks. I…I couldn't bear for anything to happen to you. I could bear anything else, but not that."

Vivian's voice softened. "And nothing *will* happen to us, darling. You and I have weathered dangers before. Can't we trust that we'll weather this one too? I hate to think of being shipped off like a piece of baggage. I want to help."

"You will be helping. But this time, you have a mission no one else can do: taking care of the life inside you. You are responsible for its future."

"And what about you? How can I send you off to battle and danger alone?"

"I hope that there will not be a battle," came Jude's voice softly. "But if there is, the best peace, the best help you can give me is to know that you and the baby are safe."

Now Vivian's voice was choked with tears. "I wish it were anything but wartime. I wish we were back in our sunny flat on Rhynlyr, with my books and your garden, where we could dream of our child's future in peace."

"So do I," said Jude fervently. "I wish that every day—that all we had to think about was knitting booties and building a cradle, though I doubt such a quiet life would keep you happy for very long." Vivian chuckled, but her voice cracked. Jude's voice resumed, more serious now. "I wish from the bottom of my heart that we did not have to wonder, now of all times, if we'd ever see each other again. But it is now that the future is being decided—what kind of a world our child will grow up in, or if it will have a chance to grow up at all. I would give my life to make sure that future has hope for you and for the baby."

There was a break in the conversation, and Ellie heard the muffled sound of weeping—whose, she couldn't tell. She felt embarrassed for having overheard so much, but she couldn't move now without crossing in front of them. Vivian's voice spoke up again.

"If you can be brave to protect our baby's future, then so can I. My old home island, Vahye, is as safe an island as any. I will nominate it as a destination, and I will go with the convoy of those unable to fight. But you had better come back alive and in one piece. This baby is going to need raising, and I'm counting on your help."

Jude chuckled softly. "If I am spared, I will change any number of diapers without complaining."

"Good. But truly, be safe. Please be careful."

"I will."

"If you don't, I'm going to give the baby a Knerusse name nobody can pronounce."

"Then I'll be twice as careful. I promise."

"Jude?"

"Mmm?"

"I love you."

"Oh, my darling." A pause. "Our baby has the best and bravest woman in the Vestigia Roi for a mother."

Their voices dropped too low for Ellie to hear. When their footsteps walked on down the passage, Ellie slipped back to the cave. Though she was embarrassed to have heard so much, she wondered if her parents had ever had a conversation like this one. They'd taken risks as Vestigian agents on Freith, and it had ultimately cost them their lives. But both their children had survived and found their way into the Vestigia Roi. Now Ellie was an acting councilmember and Connor was captaining a ship. There was a lot Ellie didn't know about her parents, but now she understood that they'd been brave, like Vivian and Jude. Life in this fleet was full of difficult choices. But Ellie felt lucky to have had parents who loved her so much.

As Ellie was working with the Council the next morning, a sentry brought Vivian in. She looked tired and solemn.

"Yesterday you asked about a safe island that could serve as a refuge for those unable to fight," she said, looking at the floor. "I think I can suggest one. I grew up on Vahye in Arjun Mador, and my father was a senator there. When I returned for his funeral nearly five years ago, it was still a peaceful island. At that time, an…acquaintance of mine was the son of the First Minister, the highest official in the land. If he is still in power, I believe I could negotiate asylum for us there, at least until we find a more permanent base."

"Vahye," Meggie murmured, unrolling a map.

"Northwest Arjun Mador. Good location. And it looks like a large island, too," said Councilman Serle. "The only other person who came forward suggested a tiny, mountainous island in eastern Newdonia. Even if we could avoid the risk of sailing so close to Rhynlyr, a voyage of that length would be a threat in itself. Not to mention the inhospitable climate once we reached the island."

"Vahye is tropical, with a warm and temperate climate," said Vivian, her face softening as she remembered her home. "It is well cultivated, and every kind of necessity is available."

"How do we know that it is not under the control of...the Enemy?" said Phylla nervously.

"I cannot guarantee it," said Vivian. "But in all the time I was growing up there, I never saw any outright presence of the Enemy. That was still true five years ago."

"There is much we don't know, but our options are limited," mused Councilman Serle. "And we can't afford to wait much longer. We have only a few days left."

"I do not know if the islanders know about the Vestigia Roi, or what the current attitude is toward outsiders," said Vivian. "To avoid suspicion, we could sail in by water, as if fleeing from an island struck by a natural disaster. It would also make it easier to show we are not a military threat."

"I say we go to Vahye," said Katha. "At least someone here has seen it, and Vivian has influence there. Besides, I like the sound of a tropical climate."

Meggie rolled her eyes. "Except for that last comment, I have to say I agree with Katha. For once."

"All in favor?" All the Council raised their hands.

"Thank you, Vivian," said Councilwoman Phylla. "It seems Vahye is our safe island."

Chapter 13
Nakuru

Four days later, Connor stood on the black sand beach of Mharra's harbor to say his goodbyes. The *Legend* and the *Venture* were departing for Nakuru, and three ships were leaving for Vahye. The tunnels and caves were now empty, except for the five people in the rearguard and the variety of traps Owen had devised. If Deniev and his team survived, they would join the group on Vahye later.

The sun had already set behind the volcanoes, and the sky was aflame with orange clouds. While Connor waited for his sister, who was getting smothered by one of Jariel's hugs, he glanced around. Gresha held on to Deniev's neck. Jude held Vivian close, kissing her as if he'd never get another chance. Ugh. Connor wished they could just get the goodbyes part over with and go back to sailing.

"Will you hurry up and give me a turn?" he huffed at Jariel.

"No. I'm not letting go."

"She's *my* sister!"

"She's my sister too." Jariel finally let Ellie go. "We might not have the same parents, but that's not the only thing that makes sisters." She glanced at Alyce and Aimee. "Maybe we all are, in a way."

Ellie tried to smile, but her eyes swam with tears. "It seems like we're stars in an enormous sky, and the darkness will swallow us up if we get too far apart."

"No amount of darkness can put out even *one* star," said Jariel. "No matter how far apart we get." She squeezed Ellie again.

"Okay, okay. My turn." Connor nudged Jariel over and hugged Ellie his own way, pinning her arms to her sides and lifting her off the ground. She squeaked as her feet flailed in the air.

"When you're sitting on a warm, sandy beach, eating delicious tropical fruit, think of your poor brother, okay?"

Ellie gave a watery smile. "I'll try." Then her blue eyes filled up again. "I'll miss you, Connor. Be careful—please."

He nudged her shoulder playfully. "You too. Don't make yourself sick on those tropical fruits."

"Connor! I'm being serious."

"Okay, I'll be careful. Take care of yourself too, and of Owen and Vivian and the baby. Jude's going to be a soppy mess the whole time."

Owen, who was wrapped in a blanket as he stood beside Ellie, offered a weak smile. He had a long road of recovery ahead of him. His pet snake Moby was wrapped around his wrist and Sunny's tail thumped against his leg. "We'll look after each other."

Ellie glanced over her shoulder. Her ship, the *Spark,* and the other two convoy ships were almost finished boarding passengers.

"I'd better go." Ellie hugged Connor one more time.

"Ellie—wait." Finn came up, cradling his harp in his arms. The polished wood of the instrument was carved with vines and flying falcons.

"Will you take care of Tangwystl for me, Ellie?" he asked.

Ellie frowned. "Why don't you take it with you? It's your most precious possession."

"Well…we're going into danger and maybe battle, and I don't want to risk her. Besides, I hear it's a desert climate on Nakuru. The dry air could crack her frame. I trust you to take care of her."

Ellie carefully cushioned the weight of the harp as Finn passed it to her. "Well…okay. But you'll have to come back and get it—her—when you're done. I don't know anything about harps."

Finn cracked a smile, then hesitated for a moment. "'Bye, Ellie," he said at last, dropping an arm awkwardly around her shoulders. Then he hurried off to the *Legend*. Connor looked from the Innish boy to Ellie, who slowly ran her fingers over the harp's frame. Connor frowned.

"You'd better hurry up. You'll miss the boat."

Ellie picked up her knapsack, its top flap stretched tight over her sketchbook. "Ready, Owen, Vivian?"

Vivian wiped her eyes with her sleeve. "Ready as I'll ever be." She gave Jude's hand a last squeeze, then the three of them turned and boarded the *Spark*. Connor stood with his arms crossed, watching until Ellie gave a last wave and disappeared through the hatch.

"They'd better take care of our girl," said Jariel with a sniff, turning to head for the *Legend*.

"Yeah," Connor agreed.

It was good to be back aboard his ship. Sailors scurried about the deck, and there was no more time to think about goodbyes. There was only the beautiful, familiar helm and deck, rudder and sails, lines and propellers of the *Legend*. Connor and the crew, which again included

Korrina and a few Janakim, had been working on the ship all week, getting her ready to sail again. He couldn't wait to get airborne. He'd be willing to brave a lot of storms before he lived in any more dark, stuffy tunnels. He took his place at the helm, compass in hand.

"Lines ready?" he shouted.

"Lines ready, Captain," called Jariel, testing a cleated knot.

"Are the Janakim ready to sail?"

"Aye." Kai pointed at the blue flag the Janaki navigator was waving. Connor nodded to Jariel, who returned the flag signal.

"Then weigh anchor. Hoist sails."

The crew scrambled to heave on the lines, and Connor shifted the brass lever to warm up the lumena. The mechanisms growled as the *Legend* sailed out of the harbor, the *Venture* close behind. By the time they reached the middle of the lagoon, the lumena was humming happily.

"Ready?" he shouted.

"Ready, Captain!"

"And—up ship!" Connor pushed the brass lever forward to full power. The propellers began to whirl. Connor's stomach dropped and he bent his knees as the *Legend* rose out of the water, the deck pressing into the soles of his boots. The crew let the sails flap loosely as the ship gained altitude, then trimmed them to full power as they leveled out, high above the volcano range. As the lava-streaked volcanoes faded behind them, Connor checked their bearings. Their course was clear, and the ship's lantern twinkled like a star in the darkening sky. A clean gust of wind whipped through Connor's hair, and he grinned, the cold air chilling his teeth. They were off!

After two weeks, though, Connor had to admit he was ready for a sight of land. They'd hit a gale near Halliu, and almost everyone had had airsickness. Alyce's had lasted for days, and she still scowled at Connor as if the gale had been his fault. Most of the Janaki sailors were very hardworking, but two of them were lazy and had to be watched constantly. They either didn't understand Connor or pretended not to, and it usually took a tongue-lashing from Korrina to get them back in line. Connor wondered if the whole crew was secretly mocking him behind his back. And then there was Finn. The gangly storyteller took orders well and seemed to stay cheerful, but sometimes Connor felt an urge to punch the smug smile straight off the other boy's face.

At least Aimee was helpful. The little girl had been developing her skill of communicating with animals. Zira the falcon had run several missions. Today she'd flown ahead to scout as they approached Nakuru. She returned about noon, and Aimee took the bird's report.

"She says the island is about one hour away, and there's a sun on it," Aimee said, looking into the bird's golden eyes. "The light was so hot and bright she couldn't go any closer."

"A *sun?*" Connor frowned, looking at Kai. "What do you make of that?"

Kai shook his head. "Could be a watchtower or a lighthouse. Let's keep an eye out."

Connor called Jude, Kai, and Jariel into his cabin to plan their descent strategy. The map showed Nakuru to be a large island that was mostly desert, except for a rocky system of plateaus and canyons to the northeast.

"We're looking first for the Vestigian fleet, and then for any sympathetic Nakurans we can recruit to our cause," said Connor. "We'd probably have the most luck starting with a city or big town. I see a few marked here."

"We should circle the island by air before deciding where to land," said Kai. "We don't know how much the tidal wave changed the island's landscape."

"I hope the main cities are still in the desert area," said Connor. "I don't want to try a landing in those canyons unless we really have to."

"We should send an eyret message ahead of us," said Jude. "If any Vestigian ships are still on the island, they'll send a return message and save us a search."

"Good idea," said Connor. "You can write the message and send it right away. In the meanwhile, Jariel, we'll need a sharp lookout. We want signs of life, ideally the ships of the Vestigian fleet."

"Aye, Captain."

"Then let's go. Signal the Janakim."

In about ten minutes, a smudge appeared on the horizon; in about twenty minutes more, it had resolved into an island. As they approached from the northeast, Connor could see that the map was still mostly accurate. On the side of the island closest to them, vast gorges cut between rocky plateaus. Beyond the canyons, a few clouds cast a dappled pattern of shadows over a barren desert that stretched for miles.

As the *Legend* sailed over the island, the crew looked down, looking for any sign of flying ships, people, civilization. But there was nothing. The rocky landscape was as lifeless as a skeleton picked clean by vultures. Connor began to worry. What if the tidal wave had swept the island's population completely away? What if the Vestigian fleet was no longer here?

There was a sudden ripple as one of the clifftops moved. A covering was jerked away, and a beam of blinding light flashed forth.

"Agh!" Jariel cried, dropping her spyglass and covering her eyes. "Right in my eyes! It's like someone's playing with a mirror!"

Connor shielded his eyes against the brightness. "That would be one gigantic mirror. It *is* like another sun." He squinted at the starboard wing sail, itself bright in the noonday sun. Was it...?

"Fire!" he shouted. The beam of light was setting their wing sail on fire!

Kai grabbed the pail of drinking water sitting on deck and soaked the scorching fabric. But the beam of light moved, now focusing on the mainsail. The oil in the cloth made it dangerously flammable. Kai dashed belowdecks to the Oratory for more water, followed by Finn and Korrina.

"We're under attack!" shouted Connor. He yanked back on the altitude lever, and his stomach lurched as the ship dropped sharply. "We have to get below that mirror! Jariel, signal the Janakim!"

Connor piloted the ship straight forward and down. If he could only put that mirror between them and the sun, they'd be out of danger. But the ship moved with painful slowness, and the focused light beam kept moving, setting fires faster than the crew could put them out. There must be more than one mirror, because the *Venture* was also smoking. Both ships' sails were riddled with holes. They were losing altitude quickly.

Suddenly everything went mercifully dim. A cloud glided across the sun, lessening the mirror's power for a moment. Seizing the chance, Connor made a quick scan of the landscape below. The canyons all bottomed out in rocky gullies or sandy flats. Perfect places to crash a ship and blow up its lumena on impact. They'd all die in a fiery inferno.

"Jariel, help me find some water to land on!" Connor shouted. Nervously he worked the altitude lever, trying to slow their fall, but the tattered sails weren't helping. The red cliffs rushed up to meet them. The *Legend* was almost level with the tallest plateaus now. The sun reappeared from behind the cloud, and a new section of the mainsail caught fire.

"There are *urken* wielding those mirrors!" Jariel shouted. "It's an enemy outpost!"

"That's nice! But I need water *now!*"

"I see it!" Jariel cried. "A lake! It's at the end of this canyon."

"Big enough to land on?"

"Aye."

"Then that's where we're landing." Connor adjusted the helm, steering them toward the canyon.

"What are you doing?" shouted Jude. "The ship won't fit in there!"

Connor didn't move. Everything he'd learned about navigation at the Academy rushed through his mind. He stared straight ahead, measuring the width of the canyon with his eyes, feeling the wingspan of the ship as if it were his own body.

At last they dropped below the level of the mirror, and the burning beam blinked out. At least now he could see. Connor set his jaw and piloted the *Legend* into the canyon.

The red walls rushed past them on either side, clearing the *Legend's* wingtips by mere feet. Connor breathed slowly, focusing on keeping his hands steady. They were coming up on a turn. Connor twisted the wheel sharply—a little too sharply. There was a *crunch* as a jutting rock crushed some of the wooden supports in the port wing sail. The ship listed to port.

"You're *sure* there's water here, Jariel?" he shouted.

"Sure! Just ahead, Captain!"

After two more agonizing turns, Connor spotted it: a reservoir of clear blue water, backing up into a wall of rock. Gratefully, Connor lowered the *Legend* down and glided her onto the lake. When he took his hands from the helm, he realized they were shaking.

"Well *done*," said Jariel, climbing down from the rigging. "That's the fanciest bit of shipcraft I've seen in a while."

"It was also the most foolish," said Kai, glowering. "Very foolish—but well done."

The *Venture* splashed down a moment later. It was intact, but striped with burn marks and badly gashed from collisions with the canyon walls. Connor felt a private surge of pride as he noticed how little damage the *Legend* had sustained.

The misshapen heads of two urken peered over the lip of the canyon far above them, shouting in their grating language. Suddenly one fell screaming into the reservoir, sinking like a stone in its heavy armor. Kai aimed his crossbow for a second shot. But the urken fell first, its neck pierced by a javelin.

Kai looked at Korrina. "Good shot."

She looked into the water with a grimace. "Waste of good javelin."

"We need cover," said Connor. "More will come."

It looked like there was a rock overhang at the back of the reservoir. If they could shelter under that, at least they'd be hidden from above. But as they reached the overhang, Connor realized that what had appeared to be a rear wall, hidden in shadow, was actually a cave.

"Light the ship's lantern, Alyce," he instructed quietly.

As the lantern flickered to life, Connor looked around the huge cavern in amazement. Moored in the water were ships. Dozens of ships. Ships with propellers and wing sails.

Connor shut off the *Legend's* rear propeller and the ship bobbed silently for a moment. What were these seemingly deserted ships doing here? Were they under Vestigian or Lagorite control? And what had happened to their crews? The makeshift harbor had the eerie feel of a graveyard.

"What do we do now?" Jariel said.

"Well…" Connor thought for a moment. "We can't get off the island while those mirrors are up there. And our ships need repairs. I say we moor here and send a party to scout the area. I volunteer."

Jude, Jariel, Korrina, and a few other Janakim also volunteered. They had let down the lifeboat and were making for a rock ledge at the back of the cave when a group of figures stepped out from the shadow of a moored ship. There were four men and a woman, all of them tall and dark-skinned, their clothing woven in subtle colors that blended with the rocks. In the light of the torches they carried, their dark eyes glittered as fiercely as the arrowheads on their drawn bows.

Chapter 14
Grounded

"Kucha!" the woman commanded. Her hair was silvering, but she looked wiry and strong. She barked out a few more words in a harsh foreign tongue.

"We are Vestigians who come in peace…" Jude began, but the bowstrings only pulled tighter. Korrina cut him off.

"Marafi!" she yelled. "Marafi!"

The bowstrings relaxed, though the shining arrowheads remained pointed at the Vestigians' eyes. The Nakuran woman's voice, while still wary, sounded calmer.

"Ay Numbani?"

Korrina answered. Though Nakuran sounded slightly different from Janaki, both were dialects of Numbani, and Korrina communicated easily. She translated for the others. "They say we must wait on shore, or they will shoot."

Connor let out his breath. "Nice people."

The four sailors slowly got out of the boat and sat down on the rock ledge, their hands folded on their heads. The woman trained her arrow on Jude and stepped closer, barking something in her language. Jude took a deep breath, his eyes fixed on the arrowhead, but Korrina responded quickly, pointing at Connor. The Nakuran woman just shook her head.

"She think Jude captain," Korrina said. Connor scowled. What did he have to do to convince people that he was a captain?

Just then, more torchlight and the sounds of movement entered the cave. A large, powerful man led a group of sailors in Vestigian uniforms. Connor had never been more relieved to see anything.

"Let 'em go, Hasheya," the big man boomed. "They're with us."

The Nakuran woman looked up. "More of yours, Trull? Do these ones need food and shelter too? Do they also follow your thoughtless orders?"

The bulldog-like man crossed his thick arms. "One failed mission doesn't make a failed war. Now put down those bows. We've had word these ones were coming." He turned and solemnly saluted Connor's group. "To the One Kingdom."

Connor returned the salute. "May it be found."

Seeing their recognition, Hasheya pursed her lips and lowered her bow.

"Jude? Jude Sterlen?" A wiry, freckled man with a mop of brown curls stepped out from beside Trull.

"Markos?" said Jude hesitantly. Connor raised his eyebrows. Markos? The former lookout and navigator of the *Legend*?

"It *is* you!" Markos shook Jude's hand warmly and helped him to his feet. "When Vice-Admiral Trull showed me the eyret message, I thought I recognized your handwriting. Practically unreadable, as always."

"Enough small talk," said Trull. "These Nakurans will as soon shoot you as talk to you. Come with us."

Hasheya narrowed her eyes and said something to Korrina in the Nakuran language.

"With thanks, no," Korrina answered in Common. "We stay with crew."

Hasheya's nostrils flared. "Very well. Take them all, Mister Trull. With my son sick, we have our own problems." She said something else to Korrina in Nakuran, then signaled the guards and left.

"What did she say?" Connor whispered.

"She say we Numbani, so we always have home with them," said Korrina. "She tell me where to go. But we not leave you."

Under Vice-Admiral Trull's supervision, the crews of the *Legend* and *Venture* disembarked. He instructed them to bring whatever food, blankets, and shelters they had with them. When they were finished unloading, they followed Trull down a canyon. The sandy ground ate the sound of the group's footfalls. Connor looked up at the rock formations towering over them. Some were as delicate as peaks of frosting on a cake; others towered like the walls of a fortress; still others looked so rickety and unstable that a good gust of wind would knock them over. All of them were striped in a brilliant variety of reds, oranges, browns, and sandy yellows. They were actually interesting when they weren't threatening to wreck your ship.

At last they turned into a broad valley that looked like it had been carved by a wide river. The gravelly floor sloped gently upwards. Tents crowded the dry riverbed like a city, punctuated by a few scrubby trees and bushes. Sailors, at least a thousand of them, stood in formations, practicing drills. Now, in the late afternoon, the walls of the canyon shaded the camp, but Connor realized that at midday it would be an inferno out here.

Their guides directed them to an empty patch of ground and told them to pitch their shelters there, then report to Vice-Admiral Trull's tent. It was only slightly larger than any other tent in the valley, and no better furnished. The cot, the small table, and even the water in the washbasin were coated in a fine layer of red dust. The vice admiral, sitting in a camp chair, motioned for them to take seats on the ground. A young boy in uniform offered them a cool drink he said was called *temkal* juice. Connor accepted gratefully. His dry tongue felt twice its normal size. He took a big gulp, then fought hard not to spit the juice back into the cup. The drink's tangy bitterness went straight up his nose, and it had a thick, slimy texture like raw eggs.

"Which one of you is the commanding officer here?" said Trull, looking from Kai to Jude. Connor felt his ears getting hot.

"Connor Reid is the captain of the *Legend*," said Jude, placing a hand on Connor's shoulder.

The vice admiral raised his eyebrows. "You? Wouldn't have thought you'd been through the Academy yet."

"Connor successfully piloted the *Legend* through a canyon to a safe landing, and he has all of our loyalty." Connor's chest swelled at Jude's praise.

"Well. Let's hope you're up to the task. We received the eyret message that you were coming, but it didn't say much else. What brings you to Nakuru?"

Connor crossed his arms, hoping he looked authoritative. "Council business. The Vestigia Roi has decided to retake Rhynlyr from Draaken's forces, and we're here to rally reinforcements. I take it you heard about the attack on the island?"

Vice-Admiral Trull gave a curt nod. "Heard of it, and received the Council's message not to return there. We got another message with a funny riddle in it, too, but by then we were grounded here by the mirrors. You were lucky with the cloud cover today—bought you a little time—but there were no clouds for us. The mirrors blasted us out of the sky—ships going up in flames, crashing into the rocks, lumenai exploding. Of the two hundred ships dispatched here, fifty-one landed safely, but I'd estimate as many more were destroyed."

"And the rest?" asked Kai.

Trull shrugged. "Escaped, we hope. Though whether they were scattered to the four archipelagos or reunited somewhere, we don't know. In either case, it doesn't help us. The mirrors have us trapped on this blasted island until further notice. They've also got a lumena rigged up there, so it's no good trying to escape at night either."

"Has anyone tried to disarm the mirrors?" said Connor.

The vice admiral barked a laugh. "Of course we tried! Tried, and failed, and paid dearly. The mirrors are on a high plateau called the Red Horn, controlled by Lagorite forces, and the only way up is a narrow cliff path. I led the attack with a strong force of Vestigians, and the Nakurans gave us troops as well. But our attack force was destroyed. The Lagorites had the advantage of height, and the path was so narrow that we couldn't advance more than two or three at a time. They mowed us down. There were urken, but also some higher-ranking officers who fought like black lightning."

Connor suddenly remembered Nikira, the web-fingered agent of the Enemy who had twice tried to capture Ellie. He wondered if others like her were part of the plateau garrison.

Trull continued. "We lost three hundred good soldiers that day, and it's on that count the Nakurans have no love left for us. When we first came here with supplies, they cared for us, took us into their cliff houses. But after the battle, that stiff-necked woman Hasheya—she shook us off like dust from her shoes, left us to fend for ourselves in this confounded hot camp. The sailors get sick from the heat, and they're idle. I run 'em through drills to keep 'em fit, but their morale's low. They'd love to lift off, go fight for Rhynlyr. So would I, I don't mind saying. But there's not much we can do about it now. Best make yourselves comfortable here. Looks like you'll be staying a while."

When the conference was over, the crew of the *Legend* headed back to their tents. Jude wrote another eyret message, notifying the Council that they had arrived at Nakuru but were detained by enemy resistance. Connor kicked at a loose stone, thinking about what the vice admiral had said. Had they come all this way only to be grounded along with these demoralized sailors? Were they just supposed to sit here, helpless, while the rest of the Vestigia Roi raced to defeat Draaken?

When the sun set, the desert air grew cold, and brilliant stars came out in an ink-dark sky. The *Legend*'s crew sat around a small cookfire, eating Alyce's attempt at stew. Some other sailors had brought them a dead rattlesnake as a gift. Alyce had been disgusted, but Jude had removed the skin and poison glands and added it to the stew. Connor chewed a bite slowly, spitting out the bones, and swallowed. The meat was tough, but it tasted like chicken. Mostly.

Markos entered their circle of firelight. "May I join you?"

Jude cleared a seat for him, and Alyce offered him a bowl of stew.

"So how's the *Legend* these days? Now I'm third mate on Vice-Admiral Trull's ship, the *Intrepid,* but sometimes I still miss the old girl."

"Well, Connor here's the captain now. Daevin, rest his soul, has been gone nine months. And this is our crew—part of it, at least. Three of them are on a safer island now, including my wife, Vivian."

"Your wife? Jude, I didn't know you'd got married! Have any kids?"

Jude smiled into the fire. "One on the way."

Markos chuckled. "Never expected you'd get married. When we sailed together, you couldn't even talk to a girl without getting all tongue-tied."

"He didn't exactly win Vivian over by talking," Jariel put in slyly.

Jude's face flushed in the firelight. "That's another story. But tell me what's going on here. Are the Nakurans really set against helping us?"

Markos sighed. "Afraid so. They were plenty hospitable when we first arrived—fed us, put us up in their cave dwellings. The caves are only emergency housing, where the Nakurans retreated after the tidal wave, but they're amazing places. I'd have liked to stay there. But after so many Nakurans were killed in Trull's charge..." he lowered his voice. "Between you and me, I think the massacre was unnecessary. The vice admiral is a good commander and a brave man, but he didn't take time to survey the land properly or ask for advice. He saw that cliff path as the way in, and he set out to take it by storm. But the Nakurans know this land like their own skin. If Trull had asked them to help with the strategy, maybe we could have both captured the Red Horn and saved lives."

"So...do you think there might be another way up the plateau?" said Connor.

Markos shrugged. "Maybe. If anyone knows, the Nakurans would."

Connor glanced over at Makundo and Korrina. An idea began to form in his mind.

"Maybe it would help us to get to know the land ourselves," said Jariel. "Do you know your way around, Markos?"

"I do," said Markos. He sized her up. "What do you do aboard the *Legend*?"

"I'm the lookout."

"So you're my replacement, eh? A bit on the small side."

Jariel bristled. "I'm tough, though."

"Can you rock climb?"

"I can learn."

"Then I'll tell you what. I have tomorrow afternoon off. I'll teach you to climb. There's no learning the land around here without some climbing skills. *Then* we'll see if you're tougher than you look."

"Done." Jariel's eyes flashed.

"Can I come too?" said Connor, grinning at Jariel. "This is going to be funny."

"Anyone can come, as long as you can keep quiet and follow orders. I'll find you all some ponchos. Gifts from the Nakurans, before things went sour. We use them for camouflage on the cliffs."

"You can count me out," said Alyce grumpily. "If it's as hot tomorrow as it was today, I'm finding a patch of shade and staying in it."

"Are you sure? It sounds like such an adventure!" said Finn.

"Oh, I'm sure. Besides, someone has to stay with Aimee."

When Markos had left, agreeing to take Jariel, Connor, Finn, and Kai on the climbing expedition, Connor turned to Makundo and Korrina.

"I have an idea," he whispered. "To get off this island, we're going to need the Nakurans' help. If you'll help me, I think we can get the two groups talking again."

Chapter 15
Vahye

Ellie leaned over the railing of the *Spark*, feeling the ocean's salty spray on her face as she strained for her first glimpse of the island of Vahye. Ocean sailing wasn't quite the same as flying among the clouds, surrounded by cygnera birds and cloud trout, but Ellie was fascinated by the ever-shifting blues and greens of the sea.

There! A dark blob on the horizon began to take shape. Ellie squinted against the bright ocean. A little at a time, she began to make out details: stone walls, lush palm trees, a slim tower that tapered to a pointed tip. From the tower, the haunting, eerie wail of a horn traveled across the water.

"Well, now they've seen us. No turning back now." Meggie leaned her elbows on the railing beside Ellie. After two and a half weeks at sea, Meggie's face was tanned and her arms were developing wiry muscles from ship work. "Let's hope Vivian was right about this island."

Ellie nodded, returning her gaze to Vahye. "Vivian knows what she's doing."

She turned back as she heard a groan. Katha was holding on to the foremast, gazing longingly at the land in the distance. Her face had a sickly greenish pallor. "If we reach that island, I swear I'll never leave land again."

Meggie laughed. "Some Vestigian that'd make you. But cheer up, Katha. Captain Urian said we'll reach land within an hour."

As the three ships approached Vahye's docks, Ellie stood on deck between Owen and Vivian, cradling Finn's harp in her arms. After two and a half weeks of sea air and sunshine, Owen looked stronger and healthier, but Vivian looked as green as Katha had. The baby, apparently, did not enjoy sea voyages. Still, she stood up straight, fingering a letter in her hands.

"How do I look?" she asked Ellie with a nervous smile.

Ellie examined Vivian. She had helped her carefully wash and press her only dress, which gracefully made room for her very round belly. Her hair was carefully curled and piled atop her head.

"You look perfect," Ellie answered.

"Good." Vivian sighed. "He has to recognize me if this is going to work."

A large party of burly guards awaited them on the docks, standing at attention even in the hot island sun. The brown-skinned men wore white uniform jackets, loose white pants, and round red caps with black tassels. In their hands were long pikes, and not one of them was smiling.

Captain Urian, a sturdy man in late middle age, called out to the guards. Vivian had told them that the Common Tongue was spoken here alongside the native dialect of Ayva, so they would be able to communicate freely.

"Permission to dock?" shouted the captain.

"What is your business?"

"We have business with a Vahyan official—"

"Ahlmet Mukkech," said Vivian, stepping forward. She held up the letter in her hand.

The uniformed guard raised his thick black eyebrows. "The First Minister?"

Vivian hesitated. "Yes. Please deliver this to him right away. We will wait here for his response."

The guard reached up for the letter and passed it to a young boy, who took off at a run. Vivian nodded her thanks.

"I didn't realize he was the First Minister now," she murmured to Ellie. "Mukkech's father was First Minister when I lived here, but the office is elected, not passed from father to son. It's lucky for us that he's in such a powerful position." She pressed her lips together. "I think."

"Wait—" Ellie paused. "Is this the same son of the First Minister you had to dance with that one time? The one you said had eyes like a fish and breath like a goat?"

Vivian reddened. "Is that what I said about him? For heaven's sake, don't mention that here. But yes, it is the same person. He wanted to marry me once. My father urged me to accept."

"I'm glad you didn't," said Ellie. "Then I might never have met you."

"Jude's prob'ly glad too," observed Owen, scratching Sunny's head.

Vivian smiled. "I'm glad too. Still, we don't want to remind the First Minister of that if we don't have to."

About half an hour later, a procession approached the docks. More white-clad guards surrounded a golden litter, which was carried by eight men and canopied in rich red and purple cloths. At the dock, the litter bearers set down their burden and a man stepped out. He was dressed like the guards, but more grandly. His white coat was so long it brushed the ground, his red hat stood up off his head like a crown, and he had a thick gold chain around his neck and gold rings on his fingers. He was a head shorter than any of the guards, but all bowed to him as he passed. He strode down the pier briskly, his short, sharp beard sticking out stiffly from his chin. When he caught sight of Vivian, his thick black eyebrows rose. He whirled angrily and barked something to the guards standing there. Bowing apologetically, they called Captain Urian to lay down the gangplank at his pleasure. Vivian left the ship first, followed by the members of the Council. On the pier, she began to curtsy, but the First Minister raised her up. He took a long, slow look over her.

"Vivian Edrei," he said at last, his voice smooth and deep. "I never expected to see you again. Yet here you are, and looking very well indeed."

Vivian smiled, blushing a little. "As are you, Ahlmet. It seems life has been good to you since our last meeting. But I am Vivian Edrei no longer. My husband's last name is Sterlen."

The First Minister coughed and quickly looked up, scanning the ships' decks. "And your…husband. Is he here?"

Vivian shook her head. "He is away on…business. The people you see here are refugees. Our island was destroyed in a disaster. We simply need a safe place to shelter for a short time. We do not need much—a few huts, or even just a place to dock our ships—and we are willing to work."

"And you the daughter of the great Senator Edrei? And in your condition? Nonsense!" He beckoned one of the guards with a motion of two fingers. "Send word to the palace to prepare room for Lady Vivian and all her guests. See that they have every necessity and comfort."

Vivian nodded. "Thank you for your generosity."

Mukkech studied her face closely. "As you may observe, I have become wealthy and powerful since you left. At a wave of my hand, men jump to obey me. But I can see that there is more to your story that you are not telling me. Come! Refresh yourselves, you and all your people. You shall be my guests at supper. Then we shall speak more of this matter." His dark eyes glittered as he bent and kissed Vivian's hand. Then he returned to his litter and disappeared.

When he was gone, Ellie raised her eyebrows. "I'd say that went pretty well."

"Please, please, please let there be bathtubs in the palace," muttered Katha.

But Vivian did not speak. She had an absent expression on her face, and a pucker between her eyebrows.

Guards stood ready to escort the group of about sixty refugees to the palace, and pony carts were provided for those who could not walk easily. Vivian insisted she could walk, but Ellie casually pointed out how hot it was, and that Vivian would need all her energy for later. In the end, Ellie had to climb into a cart herself to convince her stubborn friend to ride. Besides, even though they were off the ship, Ellie could still feel the ground rolling beneath her. The sleek black pony, driven by a young man who kept smiling at Katha, pulled them down a smooth dirt road through a bustling port city. Vivian smiled almost the whole way.

"Look, Ellie! That's the market." She pointed out a sprawling maze of brightly colored tents, loud with the voices of hawkers. "You can buy almost anything there, from jewelry to spices to preserved monkey brains for telling the future." She laughed at Ellie's disgusted expression. "Don't worry, only the old women from the villages use them. Oh! Do you see that little boy drinking out of what looks like a big nut? That's a *sidra* fruit. People hammer holes in the hard shell and drink the juice straight out. I used to do that when I was a little girl. We'll have to come down here so you can try it."

"Does it taste like monkey brains?" Ellie asked, wrinkling her nose.

"Only a little." Vivian winked.

Ellie tried not to blink as they drove up the gently sloping main road. She didn't want to miss a moment of the colorful sights: the old men drinking tea and playing board games in the shade; the ropes of dried red chilies hanging from covered booths; the whitewashed houses, their balconies patterned with painted tiles and spilling over with bright flowers. Ellie could almost imagine Vivian growing up here as a mischievous, sunburned little girl who drank sidra juice from the shell.

At last the road led them to a fortress with thick stone walls patrolled by pairs of white-clad guards. As the cart passed through a great gate shaped like an enormous keyhole, Ellie sucked in her breath. Before her sprawled an enormous garden. Neatly trimmed hedges lined either side of the road, punctuated by avenues of the most dazzling roses and other tropical flowers Ellie couldn't name. Some of the flowers had delicate, fluttery petals as big as her head; some grew in bright pink sheets that clung gracefully to whitewashed walls and red tile roofs; still others showered down the weeping branches of evenly spaced trees. The carefully sculpted plants framed views of bubbling fountains, shady benches, and reflecting pools dotted with white water lilies.

"Your mouth is open," Vivian teased gently.

Ellie shut it with a click, not wanting to tear her eyes away from the gardens. "I just…can't *believe* all this. Jude would love it here."

"Yes, he would," Vivian agreed. "I wish he could see it."

At last the cart stopped in front of a pair of grand wooden doors engraved with intricate, curling designs that might be letters in another language. A middle-aged woman, her round brown face furrowed with wrinkles and her graying hair rolled into a bun, bowed with her palms pressed together as the travelers approached. She wore a flowing brown garment, and her posture communicated both respect and dignity.

"Welcome to the First Minister's summer palace. I am Anaya, the head housekeeper, and my staff and I will attend to your needs. Talia here will show you to your apartments."

As the Vestigian refugees followed the young maid inside, Anaya's eyes focused on Vivian. She squinted and frowned.

"Forgive me, but…have you visited here before?"

Vivian smiled. "I was born and raised on Vahye. My father was Senator Edrei."

"Senator Edrei! Then that would make you…you're not young Vivian Edrei?"

Vivian's smile broadened. "Vivian Sterlen now, but yes."

"Well, I'll be! I remember you as a girl, back when I served here under the old First Minister, my master's father. You used to dance like air and clouds in the gardens. I don't expect you remember me, though."

"Of course I do! You were the one I'd come to for a snack after everyone else was asleep," Vivian laughed. "It's good to see you well."

"And the same to you. How lovely you are now! I remember thinking what a fine thing it'd be if you and my master were to marry. If he thought about having a family a tenth as much as he thought about building projects, then maybe I'd have some little ones to cuddle by now." She touched Vivian's belly tenderly. "A shame, it is." As if coming to herself, she quickly cleared her throat. "I apologize. I forget my place. Let me show you to your rooms. I will personally see that you are made comfortable."

Ellie followed Anaya through cool, marble-floored halls and under domed ceilings patterned with tile mosaics or intricate stonework. Ellie's senses felt saturated with so much beauty. After weeks of cramped quarters on a ship and weeks before that of living in dark, stuffy tunnels underground, this felt like waking up after a bad dream.

Finally Anaya led them into a courtyard where swallows swooped and dipped over a pool that reflected a slender tower overhead. The refugees were housed two to a room, and Ellie was with Vivian. Anaya showed them into a room grander than any Ellie had ever slept in. There was an enormous bed, surrounded by gauzy red curtains and spread with a rich, embroidered coverlet. One wall was hung with an embroidered tapestry showing a man and woman walking in an orange grove. Another wall was completely covered with colorful tiles. The room was supplied with everything they could wish for: a pair of cushioned wicker chairs, a small writing desk with stationery under a real coral paperweight, and even a balcony overlooking the gardens.

"This door leads to the washroom," Anaya instructed. "Hot baths have already been prepared for you and your friends. My master will provide you with clothing for tonight's banquet, and your other clothes will be washed."

Vivian bowed her head. "Your kindness and your master's generosity are beyond goodness. *Mirin te.*"

Anaya's round face dimpled, and her eyes shrank to smiling slits. "Mirin te." She nodded and went out.

"What did you say to her?" Ellie asked.

"It's a greeting in Ayva, the native dialect of the island. The merchants, politicians, and leaders here all speak Common, but most of the servants and farmers use Ayva. 'Mirin te' is a friendly phrase that can mean hello, goodbye, thank you, or a number of other things. My childhood nurse spoke Ayva and taught me a few phrases."

"So you were already learning languages when you were little."

Vivian smiled. "I guess so." She sank down on the bed. "Ah! How wonderful it is to be back! I hadn't even realized how much I missed this place. I only came to the summer palace for political suppers and parties, but it reminds me of old times. The villa where I grew up wasn't nearly as grand as this, but it was still beautiful. I wonder if Senator Koren still owns it."

"I'd like to see it, if we can," said Ellie.

"Really? I'd be delighted to show you. Not all my memories from there are happy, but one always cherishes the memories of one's childhood home."

Ellie said nothing. She had no memories of a childhood home. Everywhere she'd lived had been only temporary, a place to stay until someone returned her to the next orphanage. Even her quarters at the Academy hadn't been permanent.

"How thoughtless of me," said Vivian, realizing what she'd said. "I'm sorry, Ellie. I'll see if we can arrange a visit to the villa. But at the moment, I think I'd be happy to spend the next two weeks in the bath." Vivian pulled the pins from her long hair and shook it loose.

"Why don't you have the first bath, then?" said Ellie. "I want to have a look around."

Vivian agreed, and Ellie went out to the balcony and looked over the gardens. They had yet a different orderly and symmetrical loveliness when seen from above. The rich perfume of full-blown flowers wafted up to her. Beyond the green maze of hedges was the stone wall of the palace, and beyond that, she caught a glimpse of the sparkling sea. For some reason, the sight of the ocean made her feel a pang of loneliness for Connor, Jariel, Finn, and her other shipmates who were out there recruiting troops to retake Rhynlyr. Ellie felt guilty that she was enjoying Vahye's comforts while they were probably sleeping in tents and eating ship's rations. With a sigh, she turned away from the view.

While Vivian bathed, Ellie walked around the courtyard. It was open to the sky, but the sun had now dipped below the wall, leaving the courtyard in cool shadow. Laralyn watched from her doorway as Gresha twirled in dizzy circles outside, giggling every time she fell over. Ellie smiled. It was good to see the little girl so healthy and energetic again. She hoped Deniev was safe and already on his way to join them.

Owen was sharing a room with Councilman Serle. The door was open and the councilman was out conferring with Phylla, so Ellie stepped inside. Owen was lying on one of two small beds with Sunny curled up at his feet. He lay still, staring up at the ceiling.

"How are you feeling?" Ellie asked.

"Okay. A little tired after all the traveling." His voice trailed off, and Ellie sensed there was something else he wanted to say. She was too tired to probe for it now, though.

"Do you like it here so far?" she asked instead.

"Oh yes. I'll bet there are lots of bugs to find in those gardens. Councilman Serle doesn't like Sunny yet, but he'll see. Sunny's quiet and clean, and he's nicer than a lot of people."

"Councilman Serle does take a while to get used to things," Ellie agreed. "But for now, get some rest. Maybe I can help you look for bugs in the garden tomorrow?"

"Okay."

Ellie left and went to check on Katha and Meggie, who were sharing a room. Katha sat in a chair by the window, combing through her golden hair, while Meggie paced the room, fuming.

"I couldn't help taking a long bath," sniffed Katha. "I needed it. There were positively pounds of salt in my hair after that sea voyage, and you can't rush a good cleaning."

"Of course you can't, especially not when your sister's waiting!" huffed Meggie, snatching up a towel. "You're always thinking of yourself first!" She stomped into the washroom and shut the door.

Ellie sat down on the large, green-covered bed. "Er...how are you both settling in?"

"*I'm* just fine, though Meggie's worked herself into a state," said Katha, stretching luxuriously. "This place suits me very well. I was born to live like this."

Ellie tried not to smile. "Remember we're only here until we find a safe base for the Rhynlyr attack." She looked up at the room's ceiling, painted with a lush pattern of flowers. "Something about this place...I don't know. It's beautiful, but it makes me a little uneasy."

"Don't insult the First Minister's hospitality when he's been so kind to us!" retorted Katha.

"I'm not insulting him. I just don't know if I trust him. Not yet, anyway."

Katha harrumphed and went back to combing her hair, and Ellie returned to her own room. Vivian had finished her bath and was taking a nap. In the washroom was a huge stone tub filled with warm, scented water. Ellie slipped into it with a sigh of happiness. She knew there would be things to do tomorrow, but for now it was delicious to be all by herself, enveloped in a cloud of flower-scented steam.

Chapter 16
Mukkech

Ellie was drying her hair when there was a knock on the door. The young maid, Talia, entered, carrying a packet wrapped in tissue paper. Inside were two gowns made in the island style. Ellie sighed in amazement as the rich, slippery fabric unfolded. She slipped into hers while Talia helped Vivian.

"How long have you worked in the palace, Talia?" Vivian asked as the girl fastened the clasps at the back of the dress.

"About four months, your ladyship. My father's only a farmer out in the hills near Tixra, so it's an honor for me to work here."

"And is the First Minister a kind master?" Vivian asked, sitting down to brush her hair.

Talia hesitated. "I don't know if…well, yes, your ladyship."

"Go ahead. What were you going to say?"

"Well…I don't know if *kind* is the word I'd use, exactly. It's hard work, and the rules are strict. But the master—he always pays us fair and makes sure we get enough to eat."

"How does he punish disobedience?" Vivian asked casually, teasing out a tangle in her hair.

"We…don't have that, your ladyship. The staff, we either obey, or we're turned out by morning." Talia blushed as she began to twist

Vivian's hair up. "Now my tongue's flapping again. Please don't say that I said anything, your ladyship. He really is a good master, and I'm grateful for this job."

"I'm sure you are. And don't worry. Your secrets are safe with me." Vivian smiled at Talia in the mirror, but her eyes looked thoughtful.

Talia finished helping them get ready and gave them directions to the banquet hall, then left. Vivian stood up and smiled at Ellie.

"Don't you look beautiful."

Ellie swished her skirt shyly. Her dress was deep blue, with long, wide sleeves, a high waist, and a square neckline edged in gold. The gauzy skirt had a long, trailing piece of fabric, which Talia had expertly looped around Ellie's body and pinned to her shoulder with a gold clasp. Vivian's gown was the same style, but her bodice was deep red, with a loose skirt of gauzy ivory. The fabric was patterned with a subtle design of roses. It reminded Ellie of the vision she'd seen on Mharra. A pearl-and-gold necklace and tiara had been sent especially for Vivian to wear.

"You look like a queen," Ellie said.

"That's what I'm afraid of," said Vivian, carefully removing the tiara and setting it on the desk. "Did you hear what Talia was saying? Our host is a powerful man who is used to getting what he wants. Tonight it is not very hard to guess what that is."

"I wish Jude were here," said Ellie.

"So do I. But tonight we are on our own. We must use the wits we have to keep ourselves and those in our care out of trouble."

"Still, I'd give a lot to see Jude's face if he could see you now," Ellie smirked. "I know exactly what he'd look like." She opened her mouth and used her hands to make her expression as long and shocked as possible. She and Vivian both dissolved into giggles.

"Come on! We can't be late to the banquet," Vivian managed at last, pulling Ellie out the door.

The entire group of refugees found their way to the banquet hall together. Pairs of guards stood at each entrance, and serving women wearing flowing brown garments were posted around the room. The First Minister was seated at a raised table at the head of the room. He wore a loose white robe, and his hair was slicked back and shiny. He bowed deeply to Vivian and again kissed her hand, then looked at her appreciatively.

"You have surpassed your former beauty as the full-blown rose surpasses the bud." He frowned. "But you are not wearing the crown I sent you."

Vivian smiled. "I did not wish to be presumptuous."

"That would be impossible. I intend for you to feel like royalty here." He offered her his arm and led her to the head of the table. Ellie quietly took the seat to Vivian's other side.

In all her life, Ellie had never seen anything like this banquet. Seemingly endless courses were served on platters of silver and gold: olives and cucumbers with a dizzying number of dipping sauces, yogurts and cheeses, savory roasted meats, plump tomatoes and peppers stuffed with flavored rice. The guests were not given utensils, but instead were served large rounds of soft bread that were perfect for scooping and for dipping up sauces. Throughout the meal, they were entertained by musicians playing wooden flutes and tiny stringed instruments, men and women who danced in glittering costumes that flowed with their movements, and even a giant wild beast, sinuous as a cat but striped with orange and ten times as big, that could stand on its hind legs and dance with a man.

Though the entertainments were fascinating, Ellie kept an eye on Mukkech and listened as he questioned Vivian about their real reason for being here.

"I told you the truth at the pier—we are refugees without a home," said Vivian, tearing her bread into neat strips.

"And how did that come to be? Last I heard, you were pursuing the life of a Scholar on Mundarva."

Vivian cleared her throat. "Yes, well…much has happened since then. There isn't time for the whole story tonight."

"Then what do you say to an outing tomorrow? I imagine you'd like to see some of the old sights while you're here."

"Oh yes! That would be delightful. I was telling Ellie here about all the strange and wonderful things to be found in the marketplace. Would you like to see it, Ellie?"

Ellie nodded eagerly.

"Then tomorrow it is. I will order carriages for us, and we will leave after breakfast."

The next morning, two of the First Minister's sleek, canopied carriages took Mukkech, Vivian, Ellie, Owen, Meggie, and Katha down to the marketplace. Councilman Serle and Councilwoman Phylla had been invited, but the island's damp heat, already noticeable in the early morning, did not agree with them, so they stayed indoors.

The streets of the marketplace were so narrow that they had to explore on foot. Four of Mukkech's guards surrounded them, making room for their party to pass through. Ellie carried her sketchbook, but there was so much to see that she could only scribble down the barest ideas and hope to remember them later. People jostled shoulder to shoulder, haggling loudly over the prices of bright cloth, carved wooden daggers, colored glass lamps, and painted tiles. Hawkers shouted their wares, trying to catch the attention of everyone who passed by. Racks of gold bracelets glinted in the sun, and unfamiliar scents tickled Ellie's nose as they passed heaps of orange, yellow, and red spices. They stopped at the stall of a sidra fruit seller, and Mukkech bought fruit for everyone. The merchant, who wore a bright red cap and had a gold tooth, hammered holes into the tops of the hard fruits and poked thin reeds inside. Ellie sucked up the juice, which was thin and watery, but sweet.

Owen wrinkled up his nose. "I don't like it. Tastes like plain water with sugar in it."

"I think it tastes like flowers," Ellie said.

"It's what my childhood tasted like," Vivian smiled as she sipped hers. "My father always told me it wasn't proper to drink it out of the shell like this, but I did it anyway. It doesn't taste the same from a glass."

"I couldn't agree more," said Mukkech. "I'll order a shipment of them for supper tonight."

The merchant's face lit up, and Vivian smiled. "That's very kind of you."

In an open square, a young man was swallowing fire, then breathing it back out like a living volcano. They watched an old woman telling a wealthy merchant's fortune, picking apart a dried monkey brain with a stick to see how his years would unfold. Katha looked away quickly.

"I think I'm going to be sick," she groaned.

Mukkech seemed to be nothing but kind and attentive, especially to Vivian, but something about him still made Ellie uneasy. From the slight tension in Vivian's body language, she could tell her friend wasn't completely comfortable either. Ellie dropped back slightly from the group and began to hum softly. When her vision changed, she was disturbed by how dim everything grew. Lights and colors encircled her companions: Owen was surrounded by a nimbus of bright green, Meggie by warm, rich brown, and Katha by a blend of light gray and lavender. Up ahead, Ellie saw light around Vivian too, and that strange golden coral branch she'd seen once before. But Mukkech—he wore a robe as black as the night sky, with tiny stars winking at the edges. Ellie cocked her head. What was that supposed to mean? She wished once again that her old teacher, Zarifah, were alive and here to help her understand.

On the way out of the market, Owen suddenly crouched down beside something in the dirt. Ellie thought it was a pebble, until it moved. Then she saw that it was a tiny tortoise about half the size of her palm, its legs no longer than a fingernail.

"It's so cute!" Meggie exclaimed.

"I think it's hurt. One of its legs isn't working right," Owen muttered, frowning. He carefully opened one palm and scooted the tortoise onto it. "I'm going to take it home and take care of it."

"In other words, you have a new pet," Ellie smiled.

"Yeah." Owen climbed into the carriage, not taking his eyes off the tortoise. "I guess so."

Ellie watched him gently brushing dirt off the tortoise's shell. It was good to have the real Owen back.

That night at supper, Mukkech again seated Vivian beside him. Around the tables, the Vestigian refugees drank sidra juice. Some of them grimaced at the taste; others gulped down big swallows. Vivian smiled, watching them.

"Thank you for giving them this opportunity, Ahlmet. I am glad they are able to get a taste of life on Vahye while we are here."

"It is my pleasure," said Mukkech. "But I still see that you have not told me everything about why you are here. Did something happen on Mundarva? Is that the island you fled?"

"Well..." Vivian paused, choosing her words carefully. "Yes, something did happen on Mundarva. But that is not the island this group escaped from. What do you say to another outing?"

Mukkech smiled. "Of course. Where to this time?"

"I thought we could go see my old home. I promised Ellie a look at it. I'd also like a glimpse of the island core."

Mukkech's smile slipped. "Why not leave the children behind this time? We could take a carriage and make a day of it, just the two of us."

Vivian's smile also tensed. "Ahlmet, I'm surprised at you. You know it would be improper for us to go alone, without chaperones."

"I am the First Minister, and nothing that I do is improper. But if it would make you more comfortable, I will order a second carriage for the children."

"Thank you. But I do not think we will need the carriages. I have...another form of transportation in mind."

Mukkech raised an eyebrow. "Very well. I am curious. Tomorrow, then?"

"Perhaps the day after. I'm feeling a bit tired after the market visit today."

"Of course." Mukkech took a sip of wine from a sparkling crystal goblet. "In the meanwhile, tell me about this husband of yours. What sort of man is he? It's difficult to imagine someone good enough for you."

Vivian smiled. "It wouldn't be if you'd met Jude. He's a wonderful person. He's a doctor, but he's also brilliant with gardening and carpentry. He's brave and kind, and the children love him. He's humble and absolutely truthful—" Observing the storm clouds rolling over Mukkech's face, Vivian cleared her throat. "I couldn't have asked for a better man."

"No," Mukkech grumbled into his wine glass. "Apparently you couldn't."

Ellie met with the Council the next day to take stock of their situation.

"It seems we've landed on our feet here," said Councilwoman Phylla, looking refreshed after spending yesterday in the cool palace. "There's plenty of space for everyone, and we have a powerful benefactor looking after our welfare. I couldn't have picked a better safe island."

"I agree," said Katha, sipping a glass of freshly squeezed orange juice. "I like it here, and the First Minister is an absolutely lovely person."

Meggie rolled her eyes. "You just like living in a palace."

"So what if I do?"

Ellie looked down. "I'm not so sure we should trust him."

"Why not?" Katha objected. "He's perfect: rich, powerful, handsome..."

Meggie snorted. "You'd say a *baboon* was perfect if it were rich and handsome."

"Well, baboons *aren't* handsome, Miss Know-It-All."

"I saw a vision of the First Minister yesterday," Ellie continued. "I'm not exactly sure what it meant, but it was...troubling."

"We mustn't be ungrateful when he's done so much for us," warned Phylla.

"And yet Ellie's visions are trustworthy," put in Meggie.

"*If* I know what they mean," Ellie said. "I don't want to be ungrateful. I just think we should be...cautious. At least until we know more."

Councilman Serle cleared his throat. "Very well. Ellie, since you are the closest to Vivian, and the First Minister spends the most time with her, you can keep an eye on him. That being settled, we do have other business today. We've received eyret messages that the missions to Sukka and Nakuru have arrived safely." Ellie's heart leaped. Her friends aboard the *Legend* were safe.

"However," Serle continued, putting on a pair of spectacles to read the tiny rolls of paper, "while rallying troops on Sukka appears to be going well, the Nakuru detachment has hit several difficulties. The message is short, but it seems the mission crews have run into enemy forces, which they will have to overcome before they can leave the island."

Ellie frowned. She wondered what that meant.

"In addition, the rearguard has sent us a message. It seems, against all hope, that four out of the five members survived the mission and are on their way here."

"Does it say which four?" Ellie asked, instantly worried about Deniev.

"No—the message is extremely brief. We'll find out in person in a few days."

"What about the missions to Twyrild and Innish?" Meggie asked. "And have we had any word from Lady Lilia?"

Serle shook his head. "Twyrild and Innish are farther away, so it will take us longer to hear from them. And there's nothing from Lilia yet, either. When she reports back, we can tell the other missions where to regroup."

In the afternoon, Ellie found Owen in the gardens. He was offering his new tortoise a selection of leaves to see what it liked.

"I named her Pinta," Owen said without looking up. "I cleaned her leg, and it's working better already." He watched as the tiny creature began to scrape a hole in the damp sand by a fountain.

"What does Councilman Serle say about your new pet?" Ellie asked, smiling.

"He doesn't know about her. I figured he doesn't need any more surprises. He already got a surprise this morning when Moby tried to crawl up his bedpost and fell on his face instead."

"I'll say," Ellie chuckled, imagining the stern councilmember waking up with a snake on his face. But as Owen crouched on the ground, Ellie could see the faint purple scar of the helkath bite on his neck.

"How are you feeling these days, Owen? I mean...really."

Owen pushed one of the leaves closer to Pinta. "I'm feeling okay, I guess," he shrugged, not looking up. "I can walk and talk and do everything normal again."

Ellie crouched down beside him. "But there's something else going on, isn't there?"

Owen kept his eyes fixed on the tortoise. "Yeah," he said, his voice barely a whisper. "The...thing, the dshinn...it's gone, I know it. I don't feel it anymore. What I do feel is..." Owen's finger idly drew circles in the sand. "I feel so guilty. Like I betrayed you all. I don't feel like I deserve to be in the Vestigia Roi anymore." Suddenly he looked up, his hazel eyes worried. "I didn't do it on purpose, you know. After the helkath bit me, I felt like...nothing. I didn't want to keep sailing, or stay part of the Vestigia Roi, or...or anything. There was no hope. Nothing mattered. And when they put me in that dark room on the *Legend*, I felt so empty inside. That's when it—the dshinn—came to me. It was like a voice inside my head. It told me that you all—that the Vestigia Roi only wanted me for the things I could do, and now that I couldn't help with anything, you were just going to leave me behind somewhere. But the dshinn told me *it* appreciated me just for me. I'd been feeling so cold, and it made me feel warm again, at least for a moment. So...I let it in. Inside me." Owen's lip trembled. "Once it was inside, it wouldn't leave. It wouldn't let me sleep. It told me what things to look at, and it filled up my head with such hateful thoughts—for the Vestigia Roi, for Ishua, for all of you." Owen crossed his arms on his knees and leaned his forehead on them. "I don't feel like I belong here anymore. I put the whole Vestigia Roi, especially you, in danger. I should go somewhere else, alone, where I can't hurt anybody else."

Ellie sat down and put her arm around Owen's shoulders. He didn't make a sound, but she could feel his shoulders shaking. She didn't say anything for a long time, until the shaking calmed.

"Owen," she said at last. The boy lifted his head. His eyes and nose were red. "Owen. That...thing wasn't you. That was the Enemy. He attacked you when you were weak from the helkath poison. The bad things the dshinn did—that's its fault, not yours. You were no more a traitor than someone who caught the underground fever. Okay?"

Owen leaned his forehead on his arms again. "I just feel like...how could Ishua ever want me again when I was so weak? When I gave in to the Enemy?"

Ellie squeezed Owen's shoulder. "He does want you. When you were...sick, I saw a vision of you. You were wearing a big black cloak, but underneath you were your normal self. I think that's how Ishua sees you. The Enemy had you all wrapped up, but inside, Ishua knew you were just the same. Now the cloak is gone, and it doesn't matter anymore."

Owen sniffled, not looking up. "You really think so?"

"I do. I should know. He took me back, gave me back my Sight, even after I got so proud and told lies about it. You remember that. In fact, you were one of the first ones who forgave me."

"And...do you forgive me? Even though you were the one in the most danger?"

Ellie smiled. "There's nothing to forgive."

Chapter 17
Climbing

C onnor told the other crewmembers about his plan to get the Vestigians and Nakurans talking again. By morning, Kai was ready to play his part. Around the camp, sailors were lighting breakfast fires and holding quiet conversations in the still morning air. Connor watched from his tent as Kai swaggered up to the Janakim's fire.

"This area belongs to our crew! Move along, you lot!"

Korrina stood up, lifting her chin. "Our crew bigger! *You* move out!"

Curious heads were turning toward the raised voices. Kai talked even louder.

"I don't care how big your crews are! There's not room in this camp for you Janaki scum!"

Makundo leapt to his feet and shouted something in his language. Sailors started to crowd toward the fight. A moment later, Korrina punched Kai and sent him sprawling. Hubbub erupted, and Connor rushed in.

"…a threat!" someone was shouting.

"Disturbing the peace!"

"How Vestigian *are* they really?"

Korrina shouted, "Finished! We finished here! We go to Nakurans!"

The Janakim immediately began to break down their tents. Some of the sailors jeered until the entire group of about forty people was headed out of the camp. Vice-Admiral Trull stepped out of his tent as the procession marched by.

"What is the meaning of this?" he demanded.

"The Janakim—they're leaving!" shouted Connor. "Had a fight, and now they're going to join the Nakurans!"

"Hm," said the vice admiral. "Well, let 'em go where they belong. Too much like those stubborn Nakurans, if you ask me."

Connor followed the procession, grimacing. He hadn't realized just how easy this scheme would be. How could Vestigian sailors mistrust their own sworn and tattooed brothers and sisters so easily?

A curious band of sailors followed the Janakim back toward the lake, stopping at the base of a cliff.

"Mudra Hasheya! Ay kujunga e minifu!" Korrina called up.

A sentry's face appeared over a ledge in the cliff. He barked down what sounded like a question.

"Ay! Kujunga!" Korrina answered.

Behind the sentry, Hasheya herself appeared. She called out in the Common Tongue. "These Numbani stay with us. The rest of you, go! We want nothing to do with you!"

The Nakuran leader's voice carried authority. A few sailors jeered, but most turned and trickled quietly back the way they had come. Connor followed them, but cast a glance over his shoulder. The Janakim were beginning their ascent to the cliff dwellings on a slender rope ladder the Nakurans had let down. And Makundo had his falcon. Good.

"I think it's working," Connor said to Kai in a low voice. "How's your face? That fight looked convincing."

Kai's one eye was swollen and already bruising. "She hits hard," he muttered.

A passing sailor slapped Kai on the back. "That eye looks painful. I'll bring you some *zelfmyr* leaf for it later. Those Numbani—can't trust 'em."

Connor watched the man walk away. "Why did the other sailors do that—push out the Janakim so easily? I mean, today it's what we wanted. But they were so ready to hate them, when the Janakim follow Ishua, same as us. They have their tattoos, and they're just as willing to fight for the One Kingdom."

"Same reason the Council rejected the new Song music at first, I'll wager," said Kai grimly. "People are afraid of things that are different. They hate what they don't understand. Trouble is, hate never got anything new off the ground. Only faith can do that."

"So letting yourself get punched in the face this morning was faith?" said Connor with a sly grin.

"I just hope that sailor's leaf works," Kai growled. "I don't want to give Korrina the satisfaction of seeing me with a black eye."

That afternoon, Markos stood at the base of a cliff with Jariel, Connor, Finn, and Kai. All of them wore belted brown ponchos that blended with the rocks.

"Right. Everyone remember the instructions?" Markos said.

"You're going up first to place the climbing wedges and secure the anchor at the top of the cliff. Then we'll belay each other up," said Jariel with a bored expression. "We know, we know."

"Then let's see if you can do it," Markos challenged. "See you at the top."

The cliff was only about twenty feet high, but it was sheer after the first few feet. Markos scrambled up the boulders piled at the base. When he could no longer find a handhold, he took a metal wedge from a pouch at his belt and pushed it into a crack in the rock. The wedge gave him a handhold, and he pulled himself up to the next level.

Connor watched as Markos slowly made his way to the top, leaving a trail of metal wedges behind him. When he reached the top, he uncoiled a long rope slung across his chest, looped the rope around a huge boulder, and dropped both ends down. One end went around Jariel's waist with the knot Markos had shown them. Connor held the other end taut as Jariel began to climb. At first her hands groped wildly, trying to find holds in the crumbly rock. But soon Connor was watching in admiration as she worked her way up the wall, her long arms splayed out like a spider's for maximum balance. She looked as comfortable climbing a cliff as she did in a ship's rigging.

Finn belayed for Connor, though Connor didn't like the idea of trusting his whole weight to that skinny storyteller. He was surprised at how tired his arms got, and once he slipped as he reached for a hold and missed. But Finn held the safety rope taut and caught him. Connor was relieved when he reached the top. Finn came next. Kai brought up the rear, with Markos belaying him from above.

At the top, Markos led them into a narrow, twisting canyon. They had to walk single file, and the rocks crowded overhead, blocking any glimpse of the sky. But it wasn't dark inside. Light, coming from somewhere Connor couldn't see, ricocheted off the sandy walls, warming their natural orange-brown color to a deep, intense red. The rocks took on acrobatic shapes, now jutting out in sharp spikes over their heads, now sucking into fantastic caves and recesses. Sometimes they looked like clouds in an orange-and-gold sunset, sometimes like mountain ranges set against a twilight sky. Connor craned his neck, fascinated. He had thought they were simply going to learn the lay of the land, as they had done in the blank tunnels of Mharra, but these light tricks were magical. He was sorry when the canyon ended and he stood blinking in the direct sunlight.

"I'll take you to a plateau where we can get a decent view of the enemy base," Markos said. "Raise your hoods, and be silent as we travel. This landscape carries sound in extraordinary, if not always accurate, ways."

"Not always accurate?" said Finn. "What do you mean?"

"Well..." Markos walked back about twenty feet into the canyon. "The smooth surfaces of the rocks reflect sound the way they do light. It travels far without effort." The whispered words sounded as if they were spoken inches from Connor's ear. Markos put his lips to a hole in the rock, and his next words sounded as if they were coming from overhead. "And yet the shapes of the rocks can also distort noise, making some things sound closer than they are, or as if they're coming from a different direction."

Finn's gray eyes were darting over the walls of the fissure. He stepped into an alcove. "So in a curve like this, sounds are amplified?" His voice boomed like thunder.

"Yes."

Finn leaned his shoulder against a sheer wall and looked up. "And against a smooth wall, sound travels straight up."

"Good."

"Hm. Interesting."

"So that's why we have to be silent," said Markos. "Come on."

After the enclosed canyon, the top of the plateau felt empty and exposed. The group stayed under cover as much as possible, flitting silently from clumps of scrubby bushes to tumbles of boulders. The moments of shade were a welcome relief from the relentless beating of the sun.

Finally they approached the sheer edge of the plateau. Markos gestured for them to drop to the ground, and they wriggled to the edge. Connor looked down. Hundreds of feet below, the sandy floor of the canyon looked like a smooth golden snake, and the few bushes looked like grasshoppers. Connor imagined the tidal wave surging through that canyon, its fury polishing the striped red walls smooth. But straight ahead was a bright light that hurt Connor's eyes. *The mirrors.* He pulled out his spyglass, being careful not to aim it directly at the light. The huge mirrors made the air above them shimmer with heat. Connor suddenly remembered the sections of mirror Kai had found in the hold of the ship *Defiance.* Maybe that ship had been headed here when they captured it.

In the center of the plateau was what looked like a slender wooden tower with a bright lamp on top—that must be the lumena. On the east side was a large stone gate, blocking the narrow cliff path where Trull had made his attack. No wonder it had been a massacre. But on all other sides, the Red Horn plateau fell off into sheer cliffs, except for a mountain backing it from the north. Tiny, dark figures of urken patrolled on all sides. Could there really be another way into such a fortress?

The next morning, Connor's body ached everywhere from the rock climbing. He got the cookfire going, shook some biting red ants out of his boot, and looked up to admire the clear blue of the morning sky. Then he spotted a black dot circling overhead. He frowned. Was it a vulture? An eyret bird with a message from the Council? As it got closer, Connor realized it was neither. The falcon Zira landed on a big rock and ruffled her feathers, eyeing Connor imperiously. Careful not to make any sudden moves, Connor glided quietly over to the girls' tent and slapped the canvas.

"Psst! Aimee! Are you awake?"

Jariel's head poked out, her red hair rumpled into a bush. "What?"

"Is Aimee awake?"

"Why?"

Connor pointed at the rock where the bird sat preening. "Makundo's falcon just arrived. It might have a message."

Jariel ducked back inside. A few minutes later, all three girls emerged, sleepy-eyed but dressed and curious. Aimee held out her arm, and Zira gently perched on it. The girl and the bird stared into the each other's eyes, the falcon bobbing its head back and forth. After a few moments of this silent conversation, Aimee looked up.

"Did she say anything?" Connor asked anxiously.

"Zira says her humans have lots of new friends in the caves. But one of their new friends is very sick. He is an important person, like a prince. The prince's mother wishes for a doctor who could make him better."

"Then it's our move," said Connor. "Will Zira carry back a written message from us?"

Aimee looked deep into the falcon's eyes again, cocking her head. "She says yes, as long as you don't tie it to her leg too tightly."

Connor was just fishing in his pocket for a pencil and paper when Jude emerged from his tent.

"Jude, the plan worked," Connor said. "You have an invitation to treat the Nakuran prince."

Jude nodded solemnly. "I'll do my best."

Connor wrote a note and carefully wound it around the bird's leg, covered in a strip of cloth. Aimee lifted her arm and the falcon took to the sky.

Jude's eyes watched the bird go. "If only we could send messages to and from Vahye that easily. I know we have to save our eyrets for official business, but I wish we could keep up on how things are with Vivian, Owen, and Ellie."

"They're probably having a good time while we're working ourselves to the bone out here," Connor joked, bumping Jude's arm. "Come on. Time to bring the vice admiral in on our plan. Won't be long before some Nakurans arrive to ask for you."

Trull paced his tent, arms crossed. "And it never occurred to you to ask my permission before launching your plan?"

Connor stood with his hands behind his back, trying to look meek. "We weren't sure if it would work, sir. And the other sailors couldn't know about it. We needed it to look like they were pushing the Janakim out. Otherwise the Nakurans might not have accepted them."

Trull's lips were pressed into a tight line. "Still. This is insubordination. I should have you all horsewhipped."

"But would you have listened to us earlier, sir?"

Trull's jaw muscles flexed before he continued pacing. "At any rate, it's too late to look back now. The idea may be foolish, but it just might work. Second Mate Sterlen, you have permission to go to the Nakuran prince. But if you want to avoid an outright war with the Nakurans, I hope you're half as good a doctor as Captain Reid says."

"I will do my best, sir," said Jude.

Before the sun reached its zenith, a Nakuran embassy had arrived with the expected message. Jude agreed to their request and returned with them to the Nakuran caves. When he was gone, Connor sat outside his tent, poking a trail of ants with a stick. Now the only thing to do was wait.

The next morning, Connor and Kai stood at the base of the Nakuran cliff dwelling to collect Jude's message. Korrina descended the rope ladder to meet them. Kai bent his head, turning his black eye away. The zelfmyr leaf hadn't worked. When Korrina landed, she squinted at Kai.

"What wrong? You hiding?"

"I'm not hiding," growled Kai. Slowly he lifted his chin.

When Korrina saw his face, she looked shocked. "Your eye purple. I hit you hard."

Kai scowled. "Yes, you did. It was supposed to be a sham fight."

She smiled. "I need to...how you say? Convince."

"And a lighter punch couldn't have been convincing?" said Kai. Korrina laughed, her dark eyes sparkling.

"What does Jude say, Korrina?" Connor asked. "How is Hasheya's son?"

Korrina's face grew serious. "He bad, very bad. Jude still with him. Omondi is very good—good cliff climber, good man. We hope he not die."

Connor nodded. "So do we."

As Korrina climbed back up the rope ladder, Kai watched her, his gaze traveling up to the dark cave mouth dozens of feet overhead. "I wonder if the rest of us will ever be allowed in there."

Connor shrugged. "Let's just hope Jude can heal Omondi."

The report was the same the next day. Omondi's condition held steady, and they could not tell yet if he would pull through. Connor, Jariel, Finn, and Kai spent their spare time cliff climbing with Markos, now that he had decided they weren't useless weaklings. Connor still felt sore each morning, but he felt his muscles gaining strength and flexibility. Besides, there was a certain focus, a rhythm he liked about climbing. All you had to think about was your next handhold. There wasn't room for anything else.

Connor was awakened by a smack on the side of his tent.

"Connor! Get dressed!" Kai hissed.

Connor tumbled outside, hastily tucking in his shirt. "What is it?"

Kai only jerked his head in the direction of Vice-Admiral Trull's tent.

Outside the tent, a Nakuran embassy stood talking with Vice-Admiral Trull. The messengers carried wooden platters heaped with food: quail and owls with the feathers still on, plump prickly pears, jugs of what Connor guessed was that nasty temkal juice. Korrina was there, translating for the party. Connor and Kai drew close enough to hear.

"...happy for recovery of Prince Omondi," she was saying. "Mother Hasheya, she send these gifts to you, friends of good healer Jude. She also wish to meet with leaders at sunset. Meet at caves."

"Inviting us to the caves?" Trull puffed out his chest, sticking his thumbs into his belt. "Well, that's a change in Hasheya's tune. Very well. We accept your offer. Our leaders will be at the caves this evening."

As the Nakuran spokesman replied, Korrina spotted Connor and Kai. She winked.

That evening, Connor and Kai accompanied Vice-Admiral Trull and a handful of other fleet officers to the base of the Nakuran cliff dwellings. Overhead, the sky blazed with streaks of pink, orange, and gold, and the cliff walls glowed in the reflected light.

"Hasheya!" called Vice Admiral Trull. Two Numbani heads appeared in the cliff above them, and the rope ladder tumbled down.

Connor ascended after Kai, the motion reminding him of the climb up the ladder to a rescue ship. A group of Numbani was waiting at the top, richly dressed and carrying clay lamps. The light flickered over their striking and mysterious faces. Korrina and Makundo were with them, both wearing decorative Nakuran ponchos woven in bright colors and belted at the waist. Korrina also wore a necklace studded with polished turquoise stones, and her shiny, waist-length black hair shimmered in the lamplight. Connor moved to follow them and almost tripped over Kai, who stood still as a statue.

"You coming? Or you just going to stand there all night?" Connor said, annoyed.

Kai coughed and muttered something unintelligible, hurrying to catch up.

The Nakuran guides led them through a maze of passageways. Connor had expected these caves to be damp and dark like the lava tunnels on Mharra, but he was surprised. Lamps in wall sconces illuminated spacious, sandy-floored passageways, and fresh air flowed in through unseen cracks in the rock. Most importantly, the caves were cool and sheltered, unlike the exposed Vestigian camp.

At last they entered a large room filled with soft, warm light. The rock walls and ceiling were etched with geometrical shapes of humans and animals. Long, low tables were set up in a three-sided prong shape, and some Nakurans were already seated on cushions on the floor. Connor spotted Jude sitting beside a young Nakuran man. All rose as the newcomers entered.

"Welcome," said Hasheya, who looked dignified in a flowing white poncho with silver bangles on her arms. She crossed her arms over her chest and bowed slightly to the newcomers. "We welcome our Vestigian guests."

Connor imitated her respectful bow, but out of the corner of his eye he saw Trull give only a stiff nod of acknowledgment. Ignoring him, Hasheya continued.

"Tonight we give thanks for the life of my son Omondi and the skill of the Vestigian healer Jude. Please enjoy our hospitality. We welcome you."

Jude reddened and was the first to sit down. Connor moved quickly and got a seat across from the doctor. Kai was not so quick. He ended up at one end of the prong of tables, sandwiched between Makundo and Korrina.

Connor's mouth watered as he saw platters of roasted, crispy desert fowl, crunchy salads of roots and succulents, and hot flatbreads drizzled with honey. Rations at camp had been short and boring. Actually, he couldn't remember the last time he'd had a really satisfying meal. When someone came around with a pitcher of temkal juice, though, he quickly covered his cup with his hand. He would rather eat a raw frog than drink that juice again.

"Good to see you," he said to Jude as other conversations started up in the room. "I was beginning to get worried."

Jude's face was calm, though Connor saw telltale shadows under his eyes. "It was touch and go for a while." He clapped a hand to the shoulder of the tall Nakuran man beside him. "But Omondi here has the spirit of a warrior. He wouldn't give up without a fight."

Omondi's face was drawn, in evidence of his illness, but he still smiled, his teeth gleaming white in his dark face. "Jude is warrior. He not sleep for two days."

"I'm just glad you're all right," said Jude. "Hopefully you'll be back to climbing in a few days. I feel lucky to have met you and your mother, and to have seen your magnificent caves."

"They are amazing," Connor agreed. "What kind of climbing do you do, Omondi?"

"All climbing," Omondi grinned. "Anything that goes..." he held one long hand at a vertical angle, like a steep cliff.

"Omondi won't admit it, but people here say he's the finest cliff climber among them," said Jude. "He holds the record for the fastest scaling of a cliff they call Tower Rock."

Connor leaned forward. "Have you ever climbed the Red Horn?"

Omondi shook his head. "No. *Al-akalea*, Red Horn, very steep. Hard climb."

"But could it be done? Is there another way up besides the path?"

The lamplight flickered in Omondi's eyes. "If there is rock, there is way. Always way. Omondi could find it."

Connor sat back on his cushion, his eyes meeting Jude's for a moment. "How interesting."

After supper, some of the Nakurans drifted away from the table, and the remaining Vestigians and their hosts drew closer together. Trull sat down on a cushion across from Hasheya.

"Thanks for your hospitality," he said bluntly, taking a swig of temkal juice. "Glad to know we're on speaking terms again."

Hasheya nodded with dignity, the silver streaks in her hair glinting in the low light. "I am grateful for you sending Jude."

Trull rubbed the back of his neck. "So, any chance of you helping us make another attempt on the Red Horn? I know that the last attack didn't go so well, but…"

Hasheya's eyes flashed dangerously. "Speak not of it. We are at peace. Your sailors may even return to the caves. But do not speak of another attack."

"What do you think we're here for?" Trull banged his fist on the table. "To be your guests forever? A little holiday? There's a *war* going on, and we need to get to it!"

"That is not our trouble," said Hasheya coldly.

"Not your—" Trull stood up, his face getting red. "And when will it be your trouble? When Draaken sends another tidal wave to your island? When he takes over the world? You think you can hide out here in your caves, but you can't! You're just—"

"And *you* think you are king because you have many ships and many men!" Hasheya also stood up. Though she was fully a foot shorter than Trull, her stance commanded authority. "You think because you are strong, you are right. Not here! Leave now, and take your—"

"Mother Hasheya," said Jude, crossing his arms over his chest and bowing deeply. "May I say something?"

Hasheya looked across Omondi to Jude, and her expression softened. "Speak."

Jude cleared his throat. "While Vice-Admiral Trull does not use gentle words—" the commanding officer sputtered angrily—"his message is true. There is a great Enemy, the one who sent the tidal wave to destroy Nakuru, and he means to command all Aletheia. He wants to make every island his territory and all people his slaves. If we are going to stop him, all enemies of the one Enemy must work together. Our ships must find a way to leave Nakuru so we can fight him.

"But even if you do not wish to help us for this reason, even if the Enemy means nothing to you…" he paused, considering his words. "Then because I have reunited you with your son, I ask a favor. I too have a family, a wife and child, somewhere in the wide ocean, and I long to see them again. If you will not help us for the sake of our cause, then I ask your help for my own sake. Please, I beg you, help us to destroy the Enemy's mirrors so I, too, can be reunited with my family."

Hasheya sat down, visibly calmed. She opened her mouth to speak, but Omondi interrupted. "I help you, Jude. You save my life, and you are my friend. I find way up Red Horn for you. Omondi can do it."

Hasheya pursed her lips. She still looked displeased, but no longer angry. "If any Nakurans wish to fight with you, they have my permission. But I will not command more of my people to be killed, not while this vulture leads." She jerked her head at Trull. "But you, Jude, have helped us, and so we will help you. We will scout Red Horn, find ways to approach it, and prepare the rock for climbing. We know the rock better than those evil creatures at the top do. But then you are on your own. You are a good man and I hope you find your family again."

Jude bowed his head gratefully. "Thank you."

Chapter 18
Traitors

A re you sure this is a good idea?" Ellie whispered to Vivian as they stepped aboard the *Spark*. Katha, Owen, Meggie, Captain Urian, and a few deckhands moved about the ship, preparing to set sail. "I mean—the First Minister doesn't seem to know about the Vestigia Roi. Are you sure we should tell him…everything?"

"I'm trying to see what he's ready for," said Vivian. She wore a light cloak, though the weather was warm. "But after all, the other four missions are out recruiting support for the war against Draaken. We may not be fighting, but that doesn't mean we can't work for the One Kingdom."

"I just hope you know what you're doing," Ellie sighed.

Mukkech, several of his advisers, and a group of guards boarded the *Spark*. Mukkech looked amused as he offered Vivian his arm.

"This is a charming vessel, though I don't know how you plan to visit your old villa in it. The holding is at least half a mile inland."

Vivian smiled. "Wait and see."

When everyone was aboard, the captain gave orders to the crew.

"Weigh anchor! Hoist sails!"

Ellie, Owen, and Meggie pitched in to help. The white sails billowed down from the yards and filled with wind. The lumena began to hum. When the *Spark* was safely away from the docks, the captain pushed the altitude lever all the way forward. Ellie saw Mukkech frown as the propellers began to whirr. Then all the Vahyans stumbled as the ship rose out of the water. One of the advisers lost his balance and sprawled on the deck.

"What in the name of…Vivian, what is going on?" Mukkech demanded loudly.

"Another form of transportation," said Vivian, calmly holding on to the railing.

As the ship leveled out, Mukkech regained his composure and moved to stand beside Vivian at the railing. Their voices were low, but Ellie could hear their conversation.

"Would you care to explain why you are in possession of a flying ship?" Mukkech asked, his tone cool. "Or why you chose not to tell me about this at the beginning of your visit?"

"I did not want to overwhelm you with too much information at once," Vivian smiled disarmingly before becoming more serious. "The other night, you asked me if something had happened to Mundarva, and the answer is yes. Have you…ever heard tell of the Vestigia Roi? Or perhaps you've heard them called Basileans?"

Mukkech frowned, stroking his pointed beard thoughtfully. "I have heard of them. Word has it they're a troublesome group of rebels in parts of Newdonia, though news does not often come to us from that part of the world. Anyway, I've never had to deal with them on Vahye. Why do you ask?"

Vivian carefully kept her expression neutral. "Because Mundarva was destroyed. The island broke loose from its coral tree and was lost over the Edge of the world. I alone was saved by the crew of Basileans sailing a flying ship. They called themselves the Vestigia Roi, sailors who serve a king called Adona Roi and his son Ishua."

The First Minister raised one eyebrow, smiling incredulously. "I don't know what part of that story sounds the most absurd: your rescue by dangerous rebels, or the notion of an island breaking loose from its coral and falling off the edge of the world, when the world is well known to be round. If I didn't know better, I'd say all that schooling had turned your head."

Vivian pursed her lips. "And yet my story is true. I know we were taught that the world is round—that is also what I learned at the Mundarva Library. But I have seen the Edge with my own eyes, and seen an island fall over it. It is no laughing matter."

"Well." Mukkech patted her hand. "I do not wish to upset you. Let us leave the matter alone. Look! We are nearing the villa."

Ellie looked over the railing as the *Spark* flew low over a sprawling two-story house surrounded by what had once been a garden. Now it was more like a jungle. Thickets of weeds swallowed up the cultivated plants, and untrained vines ran up the walls of the house. Many of the windows were boarded up, and the once-white walls were smeared with dark patches of dirt and mold.

"Unfortunately, Senator Koren lost most of his fortune in a foolish bet," Mukkech explained. "The man always did have a weakness for gambling. Now he cannot afford to keep up the whole villa. He is living in a few of the rooms and letting the rest deteriorate."

"How sad," Vivian said, looking mournfully at the run-down house and garden. "I used to climb that tall tree to look over the wall. It was such a beautiful place then."

"Most things change over time," Mukkech observed, looking intently at Vivian. "Only a few stay the same." Vivian's hand lay on the railing, and he covered it with his. "You may remember me as a boy, Vivian, but now I am the most powerful man on Vahye. However, I find you as beautiful now as I did when we were young. If you marry me, I could make you comfortable. I would even make provision for your child."

Vivian pulled her hand away. "You seem to forget that I already have a husband, whom I happen to love very much."

Mukkech's expression hardened. "Ah yes, absent on mysterious business. What makes you think he is coming back?"

"What makes you think he isn't?"

Mukkech shrugged. "The ocean is wide, and men are fickle, my dear. Many misfortunes may befall a man on the high seas. Even if your husband is still alive, why should he return? What's to stop him from settling down on a warm island with a pretty local girl?"

Vivian's eyes flashed. "Because Jude is *loyal* to me, that's why! He loves me!"

Mukkech looked out over the island landscape. "Suit yourself. But consider my offer. You may think differently as time goes by."

Vivian withdrew into silence, her mouth tight.

About half an hour later, the *Spark* sailed over the island core, which was a simple, stone-circled well. The noonday sun shone straight down, illuminating the shapes of gray, brittle coral branches below. Ellie stood beside Vivian.

"That does not look like healthy coral," Ellie muttered.

Vivian shook her head. Her face looked pale and tired. "The island will not last long without caris powder. We have our pouch inside the safe on board; we just need someone to go down there."

Mukkech was standing a few feet away, looking over the side of the ship. "I don't know what we came out here to see," he commented. "It's just a well."

Taking a deep breath, Vivian stood up straight and faced him. "It's not just a well. That is the coral branch that holds Vahye to its place in the ocean. Healthy coral is supposed to be pink. Ahlmet, do you remember the story I told you about Mundarva?"

He sneered. "The one about islands falling over the world's edge?"

Vivian held him with a steely gaze. "Yes. The same thing will happen to Vahye if you don't do something quickly. Fortunately, I have the remedy on board this ship: a powder called caris that can heal the coral."

"And what proof do you have for this nonsensical story?"

Vivian hesitated a moment. "Because I wasn't simply rescued by the Vestigia Roi, Ahlmet. I'm one of them." She pulled back her left sleeve, revealing the silver VR tattoo in the crook of her arm. "We are not rebels, but servants of the Good King and his One Kingdom. We fight for the reunion and restoration of all the islands. Please let one of us go down and save your island."

Mukkech took a wary step backward. His guards and advisers watched him carefully.

"And you...are you all...*Basileans?*" Mukkech said, the word escaping through clenched teeth.

Vivian looked at the others, unwilling to give them away. But Ellie pulled back her own sleeve, as did the others. Their tattoos glinted like stars.

Mukkech looked from one of them to the other, his face turning a deep red. "You...traitors! You came here to bring rebellion and overthrow me! And you..." his eyes locked onto Vivian. "You brought them here...told me lies, let me bring them into my very palace...how dare you? Guards!"

Eight well-armed guards instantly stepped forward.

"Surround them. We will return to my palace immediately."

The blood drained from Vivian's face. "Ahlmet, don't do this! Think of the island—your people!"

"I am thinking of them," he grunted, turning away to stand by the ship's bow.

Prodded by the sharp tip of a guard's pike, Captain Urian turned the *Spark* back toward the harbor. Vivian sat down on the steps to the quarterdeck. Ellie sat down beside her.

"It's okay, Vivian. It's not your fault," she whispered.

Vivian leaned her head against the railing. "I'm afraid it is, Ellie. I misjudged his willingness to listen."

Ellie laid her hand on Vivian's and was about to speak when she noticed the warmth of her friend's skin.

"Vivian, are you...all right? You're so...warm."

"I know. I haven't felt very well all day. I'll lie down when we get back."

When the *Spark* docked back at the pier, the guards immediately escorted the Vestigians back to the palace. The great gates in the palace wall were shut and bolted behind them. So were the doors to the wing where the Vestigians were housed. They were locked in.

"What are you going to do with us?" Vivian demanded as Mukkech turned to leave.

"I will think on it. In the meanwhile, you are under house arrest—you and all the traitors you brought here with you." He turned on his heel, and the doors shut and locked behind him.

Vivian returned to her room to lie down. Ellie went with Meggie and Katha to report the bad news to the Council. On the way, they passed Laralyn and Gresha, and again Ellie wondered if Deniev had survived the rearguard mission—or if he would be able to reach them now that they were Mukkech's prisoners.

When he heard the news, Councilman Serle rubbed his forehead. "So the government here is hostile to Vestigians. I wish Vivian had been more careful."

"She thought she was doing the right thing," Ellie argued. "The First Minister seemed calm up until the very last moment."

"There was no way to know," Meggie agreed. "And we needed his help if we were going to administer the caris. It was a necessary risk. And at least we found out that the coral here is truly sick."

"And now we can do nothing about it," fretted Councilwoman Phylla. "Why didn't you at least retrieve the caris from its safe aboard the *Spark*?"

"We didn't have a chance," said Katha. "The guards had us at the end of their pikes the whole way back. I thought it was quite rude, after all the hospitality we've been shown here."

"We'll find a way to get it back," said Meggie.

"Hopefully before Vahye falls over the Edge," said Serle gloomily.

At suppertime, servants opened the gates a crack and slid in baskets of food for the prisoners. They did not speak, and their expressions were grim.

While the other Councilmembers worked to distribute the food, Ellie went to wake Vivian. She was still lying in bed, but she was mumbling and shaking her head back and forth.

"Vivian?" Ellie said. Vivian did not respond. Her cheeks had an unnatural pink flush. "Vivian?" Ellie tried again, louder, shaking Vivian's arm. Her skin was hot to the touch.

"Oh no," Ellie breathed. "Vivian, wake up!"

When Vivian still did not respond, Ellie ran for Laralyn. Laralyn felt her forehead, then bit her lip.

"Oh Ishua, please don't let it be a relapse of the underground fever. Get wet towels, Ellie. We have to cool her down right away."

Ellie's stomach knotted as she soaked every towel she could find in cold water. She remembered Jude saying that the disease could return anytime as long as the spores lived. Where was Jude now?

"Hurry!" said Laralyn.

Together, Ellie and Laralyn managed to bring down Vivian's temperature. About midnight, Laralyn left to collect Gresha from a neighbor and get some sleep. Ellie leaned back in one of the wicker chairs and closed her eyes.

It seemed she'd barely gone to sleep when she was awakened by a fit of coughing. Early-morning light was coming through the window, and Vivian was coughing as if she couldn't breathe. Frantically, Ellie patted her back and helped her sit up, but the coughing continued until the fit passed. When it was over, Vivian sank back on her pillow, exhausted.

Ellie squeezed her hand tightly. "You're going to be all right. We're going to get you well."

Vivian looked back at her with hollow, weary eyes. The next coughing fit began a few minutes later.

When the servants brought breakfast in baskets, Ellie sent a note to Mukkech, asking him for a doctor. The doctor came, but Vivian's illness baffled him. He'd never seen anything like the underground fever before, and he knew of no remedy for it. He merely repeated Laralyn's advice to keep the fever down and hope for the best. In the early afternoon, Mukkech himself paid a visit. Ellie was glad Vivian was asleep when he came. She looked exhausted and weak, her skin damp with perspiration and little curls of hair sticking to her forehead and neck. Mukkech watched her with his hands clasped behind his back, an unreadable expression on his face. Ellie wondered if he was regretting his harsh words of yesterday. He left without speaking to Ellie, but he did tell the doctor to return later.

That afternoon, as Ellie replaced a dry towel with a wet one, Vivian opened her eyes. She had slept a bit, and her gaze was almost uncannily bright.

"Ellie," she whispered.

"Shhh, Vivian. I'm right here."

"Remember—what you promised me."

Ellie's stomach sank as she remembered their conversation in the tunnels, when Vivian had first contracted the underground fever. It seemed so long ago. "Yes, I remember. But it doesn't matter. You're going to be fine," she said, hoping she sounded more confident than she felt.

"Look after—my baby. If I die." Vivian slowly moved her hand to rest on top of Ellie's. "Promise."

Ellie nodded, her eyes filling with tears. "I promise."

As Vivian relaxed, Ellie's mind flitted to Jude's cure for the underground fever. Caris powder had completely healed Gresha. But the only caris powder on Vahye was locked up aboard the *Spark*, where no one could get to it. And even if they could, how could they ever justify…no. It was impossible.

Laralyn came by later, bringing fresh towels. She took a long look at Vivian, lying pale and still in the bed.

"I think you ought to send a message to Jude," she said softly.

Ellie looked up in alarm. "Why? Do you think she's that bad?"

Laralyn's forehead puckered. "I'm no doctor. But when my Gresha was sick…well, the disease moves fast, and it's hard to predict. If I were Jude, I'd want to know."

Ellie chewed on her lip. "If she's not better in the morning, I'll send the message."

Chapter 19
Caris

In the morning, Vivian was worse. Her coughing fits were closer together, and her fever wouldn't come down. Two more eyrets had come in, confirming the safety of the Twyrild and Innish missions, and Ellie asked the Council for permission to send one of the birds with a message to Nakuru. It cost her much effort to write the short note. *Jude: Vivian ill. Please come quickly. Ellie.*

Later on, Katha and Meggie came by to see Vivian, but they could only watch with compassion as she struggled to breathe. When the coughing subsided for a moment, they pulled Ellie out to the balcony.

"Katha and I were talking last night," said Meggie, "and we have a plan to get the caris powder from the *Spark.*"

"Really?" said Ellie.

"When the maids bring supper this evening, we're going to convince them to come inside the compound for something—we can ask them to check on Vivian—and then get their clothes soaking wet. We'll offer for them to wait here and wear our clothes while theirs dry. Meanwhile, we'll put on the maids' wet clothes and slip out to the ships. Captain Urian has already given us the key to the safe where the caris is kept. No one will stop a couple of servants. We'll get the caris and be back here before the maids suspect anything."

"Before they suspect anything? It's a long way to the docks," said Ellie.

"Not if you have wheels," Meggie smirked. "Katha made friends with our cart driver, Yesef, the first day we arrived. He'll be waiting for us at the gate."

"And the guards at the docks?"

"Oh," said Katha breezily. "I think I know how to take care of *them*."

Ellie raised her eyebrows. "It sounds risky."

"We have to get the caris *somehow*," said Meggie. "It's only a matter of time before Vahye breaks loose and sends us all toward the Edge."

"Even if you succeed, how are you going to get the caris to the island core?"

"We'll figure that out later. One thing at a time."

Ellie sighed. "Please be careful. I don't like to think what the First Minister would do if he catches you."

"That's why he won't catch us," said Meggie.

That evening, Katha and Meggie carried out their plan. It wasn't hard to "accidentally" soak the two maids as they brought water for Vivian's towels, and it wasn't hard for Ellie to distract them while Katha and Meggie snuck out in their disguises. In fact, Ellie was glad for their help. There was scarcely a break between Vivian's coughing fits now. Once Vivian coughed so hard she vomited. Her body was reaching the limits of its strength.

When the coughing finally paused, Ellie sat down beside Vivian and sang a passage from the Song, hoping to soothe both Vivian and herself. The two maids listened with a mixture of nervousness and curiosity.

Ellie saw the same vision she had seen all those weeks ago in the tunnels—Vivian wearing a gown patterned with roses, with a golden emblem of coral over the growing baby. The only differences were that now the roses were in full bloom and the golden coral had grown into a tree. It lifted into the air, branching out in all directions. One bright arm reached toward the gray coral paperweight that lay on the desk. As the light touched it, the coral also began to glow.

Coral. Something to do with coral…and the baby. Ellie racked her brains. This vision was important. She just wished she knew what it meant.

It seemed like ages before Katha and Meggie solemnly entered the room, carrying the maids' folded clothing.

"They're dry," said Meggie. "Sorry it took so long."

When the maids had changed and left, Katha and Meggie burst into squeals.

"We did it!" Meggie exclaimed, producing the leather pouch of caris. "And you should have seen Katha! The guard on the pier tried to stop us, but she just turned so charming and stopped him in his tracks…"

"And then Meggie climbed a rope over the side of the ship like a monkey," giggled Katha. "You were up in less than a minute, I'm sure. I didn't know you could do that. It's a good thing, though, because that guard's breath smelled like a whole field of onions."

"I didn't know I could do it either," admitted Meggie. "I just knew that I had to, so I did. Anyway, we succeeded. Now we just have to find a way to get to the island core."

Katha yawned. "But first, sleep. I'm exhausted. We can talk it over with the Council tomorrow."

The next morning, Owen came to visit Ellie and Vivian. He brought Sunny, who nosed Vivian's hand affectionately, but she was too weak even to smile.

When Vivian fell asleep for a few minutes, Owen looked at Ellie.

"Do you remember the cure Jude found for the underground fever?"

Ellie nodded. "Caris powder. I've thought about it, but until last night it was out of our reach."

"Well, now the caris is here. We could use it to save Vivian."

Ellie shook her head. "We can't. We need it to save the island's coral."

Owen fell silent, but the idea stayed in Ellie's mind even after Owen had left. She kept thinking about yesterday's vision—the roses, the growing coral. There was something important about this baby. And if...if anything happened to Vivian, she wasn't sure they could save the baby either. But using the caris on Vivian would mean sentencing an entire island of people to death. How could that possibly be right?

Later that afternoon, Laralyn stayed with Vivian while Ellie met with the Council to discuss what to do with the caris powder. The leather pouch lay on a table between them.

"We could borrow a horse," suggested Meggie. "A single rider could get to the core fairly quickly."

"But where would we get a horse, even assuming someone could slip out again?" objected Councilman Serle.

"Getting out shouldn't be a problem," said Katha airily. "And I don't see why Yesef wouldn't take me. He's awfully nice."

"But what would you tell him the mission was about? And why would he disobey the First Minister's orders?" said Serle.

The arguments went back and forth as the Council tried to figure out a way to get the caris to the island core. Ellie was only half listening. Finally she blurted out the thought that had been growing in her mind.

"I think we should give the caris to Vivian."

Silence fell over the Council.

"Ellie…" Meggie sighed. "I know you want to save Vivian. We all want to see her come through this. But we only have one pouch of caris, and we need the whole dose to save the island's coral."

Ellie shook her head. "No, you don't understand. I saw a vision. Vivian's baby has something to do with the coral. I don't know exactly what it is, but it's important. The baby has to live."

"You can't seriously be thinking of giving the caris to one person when it means everyone on this island—the islanders, us, even Vivian—will die," said Councilman Serle.

"I am thinking of it," said Ellie. "In fact, I think that's what Ishua means for us to do. The trails of light in the visions…they usually show where the One Kingdom is moving."

"No!" said Katha, grabbing the pouch of caris and clutching it close to her. "I won't let you! I don't want to die here!"

"We do have our three ships," ventured Phylla timidly. "We, at least, could escape the island."

"Not while we're under house arrest," countered Serle. "And that would still leave all the Vahyans here to die. We're a rescue fleet. We can't do that. The only solution is to administer the caris to the coral and save the island."

"But have Ellie's visions ever been wrong?" Meggie said. "We know her gift comes from Ishua. What would happen if this vision were true, if it were Ishua's will to save Vivian, and we ignored it?"

"Well…Vivian might die," reasoned Katha nervously. Ellie's stomach clenched at the very words. "And…the baby might too. Especially if it's already infected with the spore sickness."

"So, what if Ishua does have important plans for the baby?" Meggie reasoned. "What if saving its life is worth the sacrifices we'd have to make?"

"But what about us? And…and all the people on this island?" said Katha, her voice shrill and desperate.

"There *is* that message Ellie sent to Nakuru," said Phylla. "Perhaps those ships will come to rescue us."

"They are besieged by enemies," said Serle. "By the time they get here, it might be too late—even if they could rescue us from house arrest."

"If Ishua sent Ellie this vision, he must have thought through the consequences," Meggie argued.

"Let's take some time to think about it," said Phylla. "I say we adjourn until after supper."

"But then we have to decide," said Ellie. "Vivian can't wait much longer."

"Nor can the island," said Councilman Serle.

After supper, the Council met again. Serious faces encircled the table.

"Have we reached a decision?" Meggie asked. "*I* think we ought to listen to Ellie and give Vivian the caris powder."

Katha crossed her arms. "I still think it's foolish to give it to one person when everyone else could die."

Serle bowed his head. "Rationally, it makes no sense. But... I have been thinking." He looked up at the ceiling. "In the caves on Mharra, we saw what Ishua, Rua, and Adona Roi can do. They sent us new Song music that gave hope to our hopeless fleet. They gave some of our sailors new gifts to empower us against the Enemy. Lilia even arrived at just such a time to drive out the dshinn and learn its knowledge before the Enemy reached us. And Ellie's visions have always been true signs of the One Kingdom." He glanced at the pouch of caris on the table and sighed. "So while it makes no sense to me, I think we should heed Ellie's vision and use the caris powder to save Vivian. We are, after all, Ishua's fleet. I trust that he will either provide rescue for us, or that this is the sacrifice he intends for us to make."

Phylla pressed her lips together. "I cannot say I am not afraid of the consequences of this choice. But after what we saw on Mharra, I agree with Serle."

"So we have a majority vote," said Meggie.

Ellie looked at Katha. "I don't want to do this without your agreement."

Katha looked away.

"Think carefully, Katha," Meggie urged. "This isn't just about you. The One Kingdom is bigger than all of us. Think of Godfather

Tobin. He worked until the very last day of his life to help that Kingdom come. What would he do if he were here?"

Katha looked up with a sniff. Her nose was red. "All right. I agree, but on one condition. I want to pour the powder into the tea for Vivian."

Ellie smiled. "I'll go boil some water."

A few minutes later, the entire Council stood in Vivian's room. Owen was there too. Ellie held a steaming bowl as Katha opened the leather pouch of caris and slowly emptied its faintly shimmering contents into the water. Her hands were shaking. "I hope Ishua knows what he's doing," she muttered under her breath.

A freshness like a spring breeze filled the room as the powdered caris dissolved into the bowl. Vivian was barely conscious, but Laralyn helped her sit up, and Ellie put the bowl to Vivian's lips. At the first touch of water, Vivian spluttered and began to cough again, spilling precious drops of caris onto the bedspread. But when she paused for breath, Ellie tipped a little of the tea into her mouth. Vivian swallowed. After a few more sips, the coughing began to ease, and Vivian drank the rest of the tea.

"There," said Ellie, as Vivian relaxed back onto the pillow.

"I really hope this works," said Meggie.

Vivian slept through the night, and in the morning she was well enough to sit up and eat something. Ellie had also slept, though her dreams had been dark and frightening. Even in the daylight, she could see the image of Connor being squeezed by a constricting black snake, and she shuddered. *Ishua, let Connor be all right, wherever he is.*

Ellie slid pillows behind Vivian's back, propping her up. "How are you feeling?"

"Much, much better," said Vivian. Her eyes were clear, though her face looked thin and shadowed. "How long have I been ill?"

Ellie handed her a bowl of thin porridge. "A little over three days. We think you had a relapse of the underground fever."

Vivian paused, the spoon halfway to her mouth. "The underground fever? But didn't Jude say relapses of that could be…"

Ellie nodded slowly. "We were really afraid for you. I even sent a message to Jude. Do you remember asking me to look after the baby?"

Vivian shook her head slowly. "I don't remember anything— only dreams filled with dark, reaching…nightmares." She frowned. "How did I recover, then?"

Ellie looked down, tracing the pattern of the bedspread. "You know how there was one packet of caris aboard the *Spark*?"

Vivian's face paled and she set the porridge down. "No, Ellie. Please don't tell me…"

Ellie nodded. "We gave it to you last night, and you recovered. But it wasn't a quick decision. I had a vision…" She told Vivian about the roses and the golden coral tree. Ellie's eyes came to rest on the coral paperweight on the desk. "I think that Ishua meant for you and the baby to be saved. That's why the Council voted to give you the caris. We all agreed."

Many emotions chased each other across Vivian's face: relief, regret, happiness, guilt. She sighed and looked up at the bed's canopy. "Of course I'm grateful. I'm terribly, wonderfully grateful to be alive, that the baby and I are going to be all right. But at the same time…the island..." she looked out the window, her face haunted. "How can I live with myself if I am the cause of my home island's destruction?"

"I don't know what we're supposed to do next," Ellie admitted. "After all, we're still under house arrest as traitors, and the First Minister hasn't said what he's going to do with us. But I really am grateful you're better. Why don't you eat your porridge for now, and then we'll think about what to do?"

By the next day, Vivian was well enough to get out of bed and make the short walk to the balcony with Ellie's help. She was standing there, a light shawl draped around her shoulders, when there was a knock at the door. Ellie opened it to see Mukkech standing there.

"May I come in?"

Ellie looked at Vivian, and she nodded. Mukkech approached the balcony slowly.

"You are...better?" he asked awkwardly.

Vivian wrapped the shawl more tightly around her and nodded, her expression hard.

"And the...child? It has suffered no ill effects?"

"Not that I know of."

"I am glad...truly. While you were ill, I had time to think. I was indeed surprised to find out that you were a Basilean—"

"—Vestigian," Vivian corrected.

"Very well. Vestigian. I acted hastily and in anger. But I have considered the situation more carefully now. I meant what I said that day—I do wish to marry you. And I know that you are a woman of honor. So I have decided to let your people go free—on two conditions."

"What are the conditions?"

"One—that you give me your word that these Vestigians do not intend to overthrow my rule."

"I could have told you that at the beginning," said Vivian. "And the other condition?"

"That you stay here and marry me."

Vivian snorted and looked out at the garden. "I've already told you, that's impossible."

"Why is it impossible? I love you, Vivian."

Vivian turned toward him again, her eyes flashing. "Love? How can you speak of love when you are using my people's freedom as bait to get what you want? That's not love. Real love gives up its own way to help other people. That's what my husband is out there doing right now. That's why I chose him and not you."

Now Mukkech's face was tight with anger too. "And it matters not to you that it was *my* doctor who brought you through your sickness when your husband left you alone? What kind of love abandons those it cares about?"

Vivian looked away, her lips pressed tightly together. "Jude didn't abandon me. He trusted me enough to let me do my duty while he did his, and he *is* coming back. And while I'm grateful for your doctor's assistance, I can assure you it wasn't him who healed me." She looked back at Mukkech coolly. "I will agree to your first condition, but never the second. I ask that you accept that and release these people immediately."

"And let you go? You must think me a fool if you…"

Suddenly the ground lurched violently beneath them. Ellie lost her balance and fell. Mukkech reached for Vivian, but she steadied

237

herself against a doorpost. A jar in the washroom fell to the floor and shattered. The curtains around the bed swayed as if in the wind. When the shaking passed, the three of them looked at each other.

"Another earthquake," muttered Mukkech. "I'd never felt even one for as long as I'd lived here, then there have been three in the last month."

"Do you think…it's the coral?" Ellie asked Vivian, slowly picking herself back up.

Vivian let go of the doorpost. "I'm afraid it might be. Ahlmet—please listen to me. Let us return to our ships. Your island is in danger, and we can help your people get away safely."

Mukkech sneered. "I've already told you the conditions of your freedom. Until both of those are met, you stay where you are." He turned on his heel and stalked out of the room.

After helping Vivian back to bed, Ellie hurried to check in with the Council. For the most part, the refugees were frightened but unhurt by the earthquake. The Council had already matched minor injuries with healers and assigned people to clean up whatever had broken during the shaking. Ellie met Meggie's eyes.

"I'm afraid this can only mean one thing," Meggie said. "The island has broken loose."

"We don't know for sure yet," Ellie said.

"We will soon," said Meggie. "I just hope you were right about the caris."

Ellie's stomach twisted in knots. She hoped so too.

Chapter 20
Sabotage

Thanks to Connor's diplomatic mission, the Vestigian fleet returned to the Nakuran caves. Safe in the vast, sheltered network of cliff dwellings, the sailors began to recover from the afflictions of the desert: sunburn, scorpion stings, snakebites, and dehydration.

Four nights after the feast, Omondi and two other skilled climbers went out on a night scouting mission. They reported that there was indeed another way to the top of the plateau—a cliff climb up the Red Horn. All sides of the plateau were steep, but one side was more textured than the others, offering better grips and more cover on the way up. Omondi said he would gather the necessary supplies and make the preparatory climb the next night. Then the night after that, the Vestigians could make their attack.

"Be careful," said Jude.

"Omondi always careful."

The next night, Omondi and his party went out, supplied with climbing wedges to prepare the way for the Vestigian climbers. Meanwhile, Vice-Admiral Trull met with the Vestigian leaders, including

Connor, Makundo, and their crews, to plan the attack. Hasheya came too. She sat down outside their circle, glowering.

The vice admiral was serious and focused. It seemed his last mistake had sobered him. He drew a circle in the sandy floor of the cave, representing the top of the Red Horn.

"We know the top of the plateau is covered with mirrors, plus a lumena. We have to take out both to free our ships and get off this island."

"How large are the enemy forces?" asked one Vestigian captain.

"We don't know," said Trull. "Though we haven't seen many coming and going in the daytime."

"That means nothing," said Hasheya, speaking up. "There is a fortress in the cliff wall behind Al-akalea. Our people built it as a second refuge, after these caves. But the urken came before the tidal wave, when the fortress was not well guarded, and they took it by force. They could hide hundreds of soldiers in there."

"Hundreds of urken? We could never get enough of our own people up the cliff wall to fight that many!" objected another captain.

"We don't have to," said Kai. "We just need a small sabotage mission to take out the lumena at night so our ships can approach from the air. Then the fleet will have until dawn to destroy the mirrors and the rest of the urken."

"It could work," said Markos. "The lumena is on a platform out in the open."

"We only get one chance," said Kai. "If we fail, they'll never let us climb the plateau again."

They agreed on the sabotage mission, and Trull called for volunteers with both climbing and battle experience. Markos, Kai,

Connor, Jariel, and Finn volunteered, as did Korrina, who had learned to climb on Janaki. Trull appointed the experienced Kai as the mission leader. He was reluctant to let the children go, but he had to admit that their smaller size and lighter weight made them ideal for the climb and the stealth mission at the top of the Red Horn. The rest of the Vestigian fleet would be waiting at the bottom of the canyon near the plateau. If the lumena exploded, they would know it was safe to approach. If it didn't, there was nothing they could do.

When the meeting was over, the troops dispersed to the caves to get some sleep. But Connor lay awake in the cave he shared with Finn, his mind full of the mission. He was eager to see some action, make some progress toward escaping this island and getting back to Rhynlyr. But at the same time, there was so much they didn't know, so many ways this mission could go wrong. Not for the first time, he wished he had Ellie's gift of Sight. Maybe then he'd be able to tell the safest way to approach the plateau, the best strategy to take out the mirrors. He knew Ellie had said he had a gift of leadership, but that just seemed a little useless compared to the ability to see what was going to happen. Why had Ishua favored his sister with such an amazing gift, and not him?

Still uncertain, Connor rolled over in his blanket. He eventually drifted into a troubled sleep.

The next day, Aimee sent Zira to scout the Red Horn. Jude was upset because another bird had arrived—an eyret bird from Vahye. Connor read the short message. *Jude: Vivian ill. Please come quickly. Ellie.*

"There's nothing we can do about it right now," Connor observed.

Jude ran a hand over his hair. "Still. If the crew agrees, I want to leave for Vahye as soon as the mirrors are destroyed, even if we go without the rest of the fleet."

"I'm sure Trull can lead them to the rendezvous island, once we get word where that is," said Connor. "In the meanwhile, try to stay calm, Jude. I know it's hard. But the first thing you can do for Vivian is to help take out these mirrors."

Jude nodded, crossing his arms. "I know. And believe me, I will."

Zira returned late in the afternoon. Aimee stroked the bird's black feathers.

"She says not very many people are up there walking around. They look sleepy, not ready to fight."

"Then we'll bring them a surprise," said Kai grimly.

The Nakurans outfitted each soldier with a pair of flexible leather moccasins for climbing, a camouflage poncho, a short wood-and-bone bow, flammable arrows wrapped in oilcloth, small grappling hooks and climbing ropes, and a tiny glowing glimmerstone attached to a headstrap. As darkness gathered and the mission prepared to leave, three more Nakurans joined them. Omondi was one of them.

"We help you with climb. Hold ropes from ground."

Kai crossed his arms and bowed in the Nakuran gesture of thanks.

As the sabotage mission began their trek toward Red Horn, the ponchos really did help them blend in—Connor's eyes skipped right over his comrades unless he was deliberately focusing on them. Omondi and his two companions led with the confidence of those who knew their way.

They approached the Red Horn from the south. About a hundred feet of tumbled boulders led up to a sheer climb of another two hundred feet. At the base of the boulders, they took a short rest and ate some dried meat and cactus fruit. No one spoke. Connor met Jariel's eyes, her gaze serious but calm. She didn't seem jittery at all. That reassured him.

When they had finished, they scrambled up the tumbled section of boulders. It was active work, but not difficult. Then they approached the cliff. Omondi and his companions had anchored three long, strong ropes at the top of the cliff, and the loose ends dangled down. Connor belted his poncho around his waist and gave his glimmerstone a sharp rap on a nearby rock. The smooth black pebble slowly began to glow from somewhere deep within. Its pale light was just bright enough for Connor to see his feet. He bound the stone to his forehead under a visor that would hide the light from above. Kai, Korrina, and Markos were climbing first. Connor shook Kai's hand as the mission leader knotted the rope around his waist.

"To the One Kingdom," Connor whispered.

Kai nodded. "May it be found."

Omondi and the other Nakurans belayed Kai, Korrina, and Markos as they climbed, keeping their ropes taut for safety. A few times a hand or foot slipped, and a few pebbles bounced down with a noise that seemed deafening in the still night. Connor winced. Was there really any chance of taking the urken by surprise?

After about twenty minutes, all three climbers were up. They each gave three sharp tugs on their ropes and let go of the loose ends.

The belayers reset the ropes and Connor, Jariel, and Finn knotted themselves in. Connor shot Jariel a glance.

"Here goes nothing," he whispered under his breath.

"If climbing Red Horn is nothing, I'd like to see what you do all day," she whispered back.

Even with the dim light of the glimmerstone, it was hard for Connor to see holds in the mottled pattern of rock. But surprisingly, he didn't need his eyes as much as he expected. His fingers became his eyes, searching out bumps and crevices in the rock surface. Where no natural hold was to be found, Omondi and his climbers had inserted metal wedges. There was no sound but Connor's own breathing and the soft scrape of stone under his moccasins. The climb became a slow, steady rhythm. He was so focused on the monotonous rock surface that he was actually surprised when his head cleared the edge of the plateau. Kai gave him a hand up. Connor unknotted the rope around his waist, tugged three times, and let it go, slipping the glimmerstone and visor back into his pack. He felt nervous as the slender rope fell away. Now he was on top of the Red Horn, and there was no way down until they accomplished their mission.

Connor took in his surroundings. The six climbers crouched on the edge of the plateau. At the center was the lumena on a raised wooden platform. Although the lumena was protected by a glass chimney and focused on nothing in particular, it lit up the whole plateau well enough to see. The only exception was one dark strip, the shadow cast by a large covered mirror on the tower. Cleverly, the Nakuran climbers had placed the climbing anchors right in the path of the shadow, giving the sabotage mission a moment of cover.

About a half-dozen urken lounged on the platform, grunting in their hideous language. Two more urken stood guard at the base of the ladder to the platform, and two other pairs patrolled the edge of the plateau, circling the huge mirrors spread out on its surface. The mirrors glimmered like a sea of glass, throwing back the lumena's light in unpredictable patterns.

One of the pairs of urken guards was headed this way.

"Jariel, Markos, take the patrol to the left," Kai breathed, his voice so soft Connor had to strain to hear. "Connor, Finn, to the right. Korrina and I will take the platform."

Finn. Why do I have to work with Finn? Connor grumbled mentally. But the two boys faced the approaching patrol. Connor readied his tiger claws and his short dagger. He had a bow, but he was less confident in his aim than in his punch.

Suddenly Connor heard the whisper of a rattlesnake's tail. It sounded very close. He looked around, but there was no sign of a snake. The urken guards also stopped, searching the ground anxiously. The rattle sounded again, this time much closer to the guards. Quickly they turned and patrolled in the other direction. Still Connor saw no sign of the snake. He turned to see Finn smirking as he crouched low to the ground, releasing a long breath of air through his teeth.

Behind them, Jariel and Markos were getting ready to dash from the shadows toward the other pair of urken. Finn grabbed Markos's shoulder. Now the sound of falling pebbles came from the mouth of a cave in the mountain fortress. The urken guards hurried off to investigate.

"Show-off," Connor whispered.

Jariel smacked his arm. "He means, 'Thank you, Finn.'"

Meanwhile, Kai and Korrina were more than halfway to the platform. They kept to the strip of shadow, and their camouflaging ponchos were so good that Connor had trouble tracking their position except when their bows caught a glint of light. They followed small dirt paths left between the mirrors, so they wouldn't risk slipping on or cracking the glass surfaces. Soundlessly, they jumped the two urken guards at the base of the ladder, the bodies dropping silently. So far, so good.

Then Kai and Korrina stepped outside the base of the platform, aiming their bows at the glass chimney encasing the lumena. With luck, the oilcloth-wrapped arrows would break the glass and catch fire in the heat of the lumena, causing it to explode.

Both bows fired.

Connor heard a loud clatter as the arrows bounced back from the glass. It must be reinforced.

The urken heard it too.

Instantly the urken sentries at the top of the platform were on the alert. They leaned over the edge. Kai and Korrina began to fire on the urken, and the creatures started shouting. They hauled up the wooden ladder, and one lifted a short horn to its mouth and blew a noisy blast. The sentries patrolling the plateau ran back to investigate. *Great*, Connor thought. *There goes our cover.*

"Come on!" Markos hissed, jerking his head toward the platform. Kai and Korrina managed to hit two of the urken on the top platform, but the creatures returned fire. Connor ducked as an arrow whistled over his head. The ground sentries raced up to meet them.

"Cover me!" Markos yelled. Whirling his grappling hook around his head, he launched it at the platform. Metal bit into wood, and

Markos began to climb. Kai, Korrina and Finn shot at the sentries, trying to hold them off.

"Connor, Jariel, take the ground patrol!" shouted Kai.

Connor braced himself as a stocky, leering beast twice his size barreled toward him. *Finally, something interesting to do.*

As the urken launched itself at him, Connor ducked and sidestepped. Carried by its own weight and momentum, the beast stumbled forward. Connor punched it in the back of the neck with his tiger claws. The urken dropped and did not get up.

Beside him, another urken bore down on Jariel, taking a swipe at her with its hooked sword. Jariel parried with her own short sword, but was pushed back by the urken's greater weight and force. As the beast lifted its sword for a second strike, Jariel took advantage of her greater speed, ducked underneath the blow, and stabbed the urken through the chest.

"Look out!" Connor spun and slashed at an urken coming up behind Jariel. His tiger claws missed, but he threw the dagger at his belt, taking the urken through the throat.

"Thanks." Jariel pulled her sword free in time to counter the blow of the fourth sentry. When another heavy stroke landed the sword in the ground, Jariel cut off the urken's head.

With a moment to breathe, Connor looked up. Kai, Korrina, and Finn had stopped shooting, unable to risk hitting Markos. The Vestigian sailor was on top of the platform, fighting the last two urken who stood between him and the lumena. At such short range, his bow was useless, and he was armed only with a short dagger. He ducked a swing and lunged at one of the urken, catching it off balance. It fell shrieking from the platform, and Finn made sure it was dead. But the other urken seized its chance. With a mighty swing, the beast's sword smashed into Markos's side and crumpled him to the floor of the platform. With a shout, Kai let fly an arrow, shooting the urken in the throat. He readied his own grappling hook to climb, but Korrina held him back. On the platform, Markos weakly pushed himself upright. He picked up his metal grappling hook and swung it around his head. The metal revolved slowly at first, but picked up speed. Finally it crashed at full force into the glass. The chimney shattered, and Connor covered his head as glass rained down. Markos collapsed to the platform.

By now, the alarm signal had drawn reinforcements. Urken were flooding out of the cave mouth toward the platform. Connor tried to guess their numbers, but gave up. He licked his lips. They had only seconds to destroy the lumena and summon the fleet before they were overwhelmed by the huge force.

"Markos, can you jump?" shouted Kai, holding out his arms.

Markos lay limp on the platform. He opened his eyes weakly. "Go."

"No, we'll get you—"

"Go!" shouted Korrina, pointing. With a trembling hand, Markos was pushing an oilcloth-wrapped arrow toward the glowing, fernlike lumena. The five sailors scrambled back toward the edge of the plateau. Suddenly there was a deafening *boom*. Connor's ears popped and he felt a rush of heat singe the back of his neck as he threw himself to the ground.

When he looked up, the surface of the plateau was dark and the platform was gone. All that was left was a blackened patch of dirt and scattered chunks of flaming wood. Connor scrubbed a sleeve across his burning eyes.

"To the One Kingdom," Kai murmured softly.

But there was no time to grieve. The urken swarming from the caves hesitated only a moment after the explosion. Kai knelt down, stripping the oilcloth off all his remaining arrows.

"Keep them at range as long as possible," he instructed. "Fire until your arrows are gone. Hopefully that will buy our ships the time they need."

Connor followed Kai's example, kneeling down and nocking an arrow to his bow.

"Don't shoot me by accident, okay?" he muttered to Jariel, who knelt next to him.

"My aim isn't *that* bad. And yours isn't much better," she grumbled in response.

Then the urken were on them. There were so many of them, so close together, that Connor didn't even have to be a good shot. His quiver was quickly emptying. He darted a quick glance into the empty night sky. Where were the ships?

He pulled back his bowstring, and his last arrow found a mark in an oncoming urken's yellow eye. Dropping his bow, he pulled out his dagger. The others also readied their hand weapons.

"Stay together," Kai ordered. "Don't let them get behind us."

Connor raised his dagger. Then there was another explosion, and he was thrown backward. Sliding to a stop on a mirror's surface, he looked up.

Ships.

The sky was full of them.

Connor let out a long breath of relief. *Thank you.*

Chapter 21
Battle on the Red Horn

The urken ran wild with terror. Vestigian cannons blasted their ranks apart and shattered the mirrors like water. The five Vestigian sailors drew back from the melee to avoid being hit. Connor identified the *Legend* near the back of the flotilla. He was too far away to identify faces, but he was sure Jude, Alyce, and Aimee were doing their best to help whatever Vestigian captain was helping pilot the ship.

When the urken ranks had been fractured down to small and scattered groups, the ships dropped their ladders and sailors began to descend. Connor saw Trull at the head of his troops, leading the ground attack. Nakuran soldiers fought alongside them. Connor and his team joined the fray, charging toward the cave entrances that continued to spit out streams of urken. Most of the Vestigian soldiers clashed with the urken outside the caves, but Connor's smaller size allowed him to slip past most of them unnoticed. He made it right to the mouth of the cave fortress before an urken swung its hooked sword at him. Connor caught the blow with his dagger. Steel rang as the dagger flew out of his hand. Connor ducked under the next swing and punched the urken in the face with his tiger claws.

Retrieving his dagger, Connor entered the fortress. It was a network of large, dry passages, like the Nakuran cave dwellings, except that these ones reeked of urken filth. Torches flickered on the walls, but the fortress was surprisingly empty inside—it seemed most of the urken had already charged out to fight. Connor ran around a bend, attacking a straggler that surprised him in a side passage. As the beast crumpled to the ground, Connor came face to face with someone he'd hoped never to see again. She was tall and slender, wearing black body armor that glinted like scales, and a black cloak flowed behind her. Two blades were sheathed behind her shoulders, but her webbed fingers didn't even reach for them. *Nikira.* Connor felt the hair rise on the back of his neck.

"*You,*" he growled, gripping the hilt of his dagger. "If you're looking for Ellie, you're in the wrong place this time."

"I'm not looking for Ellie." Nikira's lips curled into a slow smile. "I'm looking for you."

"Me?" Connor frowned. "What do you want with me? I'm the ordinary one."

"Ordinary?" Nikira's soft laughter was like oil and honey. "Only the Vestigia Roi would be so foolish as to think that."

"It's not foolish. It's a fact. Ellie's the gifted one. I'm normal."

"And yet you, a boy of thirteen years, have broken into my unassailable fortress," she said with a graceful gesture at the near-deserted cave. "You sailed a ship through a canyon to get here. You reunited two warring factions to fight against me. You overcame every obstacle I set up to test you. Ordinary? I think not."

"This…all this was a *test?*" Connor glanced back toward the cave mouth, though he couldn't see it from here. He knew that out there, Nakuran soldiers were fighting alongside Vestigian ones. It was true—it *was* his idea that had made that happen.

Nikira cocked her head, her eyes mesmerizing, sympathetic. "Do you never tire of living in your sister's shadow? Eating scraps from under the Vestigians' table while the feast is served to her? Why is she now part of the Council, in a position of trust and power, while you are a ship captain constantly mocked because of your youth?"

Connor clenched his teeth as he thought of all the people who'd laughed at him, even disbelieved that he *was* captain of the *Legend*—Makundo, Hasheya, Trull. No matter what he accomplished, it never seemed to win him the respect he wanted.

"Why settle for this? You have exceptional talent, talent enough to be captain of a warship, or someday even the admiral of a fleet. All you need is someone to recognize it. Someone who would help you make the most of your gift." Nikira tossed her silky black hair over her shoulder, smiling encouragingly.

Connor's dagger slipped from his hand, silently hitting the sandy floor of the passageway. He barely noticed.

"Lord Draaken offers you all this," Nikira crooned. "Opportunity. Promotion. Recognition. These Vestigians want to use you without offering you the advancement you deserve. But why waste your time waiting when you could start advancing now? Join my master, and he will help you develop your full potential. Why not show the world that you are just as gifted as your sister?"

Nikira was so close that Connor could catch her scent. It was a deep, heady fragrance of night-blooming flowers. But there was something else in it, too, something vaguely unpleasant. He wrinkled his nose, trying to figure out what it was.

Suddenly there was a *clang*, and Nikira hissed. Jariel stood in the passageway. Her thrown sword had glanced off Nikira's body armor.

Connor shook his head as if awakening from a dream. He knew what the undertone in Nikira's perfume was. It was the reek of rotting flesh.

Repulsed, Connor picked up his dagger. As Nikira turned toward him, Jariel tackled the creature from behind. Nikira lost her balance and stumbled as Jariel held onto her by the throat. Both of them fumbled for the blades strapped to Nikira's back.

Suddenly Nikira flipped Jariel forward, throwing her to the sand. Connor caught a glimpse of Nikira's webbed fingers as she flicked out her blades: twin swordbreakers as long as her forearms. Each blade had one notched edge to trap and break enemies' weapons. The other edge was razor sharp, ending in a deadly point. Nikira raised the swordbreakers over Jariel.

Jariel rolled out of the way as Connor charged. Steel clashed as his dagger caught in the swordbreakers. With an easy flick of her wrist, Nikira snapped the dagger a few inches below the hilt. Connor tossed the useless weapon away, taking a step backward.

From the other end of the passageway, another cloaked figure approached, also wearing black armor. He looked like a male version of Nikira, with a pale face, delicate features, and webbed fingers.

"Ah, Sinkhar," said Nikira, glancing at the approaching figure. "Bring Arcvon immediately. We may want his help."

As Nikira spoke to the other soldier, Jariel seized the distraction. Diving forward, she drove her knife into Nikira's foot. Nikira screamed in pain and backed away. Ignoring orders, the second soldier, Sinkhar, drew his own pair of swordbreakers and charged. Jariel rolled away, but one of the swordbreakers slashed her left arm. She cried out.

Suddenly an arrow sprouted from Sinkhar's leg. Finn crouched a few yards away, already nocking another arrow to his bow. Sinkhar roared. He advanced on Finn, deflecting another arrow with one of his swordbreakers.

Connor seized the opportunity. He dashed forward. Sinkhar wheeled around, but before the soldier could regain his balance, Connor leaped. Balling his fingers into a fist, he punched the soldier's exposed throat, the points of his tiger claws sinking into the pale flesh. Sinkhar lurched backward with a horrible gurgle, and the two fighters tumbled to the ground. When Connor pulled his weapon free, Sinkhar was writhing on the ground, his lips bubbling black foam. His skin turned a waxy yellow, his hair became a mat of seaweed, and his legs fused together into a scaly tail with a barbed end that thrashed violently. Connor jumped out of the way, but not fast enough. One of the spikes caught his right leg just below the knee, and he sucked in air.

"Let's end this," Connor said between gritted teeth. Grabbing one of Sinkhar's fallen swordbreakers, he raised the sharp edge over his head. There was a sickening *smack* as the monster's head rolled free. The tail thrashed for a moment more, then lay still. Black blood oozed onto the sandy ground.

Connor pulled in a shaky breath, trying not to throw up. Nikira was nowhere to be seen. She must have slipped away during the fight. Connor turned to Jariel, who was pulling herself to a sitting position.

"You okay?"

She twisted, trying to see the gash in her upper left arm, near the shoulder. Connor tore a strip off the bottom of his shirt, tying it tightly around the wound.

"Here. That should help stop the bleeding. Jude can look at it later."

"Thanks. How's your leg?"

Connor looked down. Blood streaked his pants where the spike had stabbed him. "I...kind of forgot about it, actually."

"Here." Jariel tore a strip off the bottom of her shirt and tied it around his leg. "Now we're even." She glanced at the headless sea monster, then back at Connor. "That was really brave."

Connor shook his head. "I would have been a goner if it hadn't been for you. Nikira almost had me. The things she said, they just sounded so...good. When you distracted her, it was like you broke some sort of spell."

Jariel smiled at him. "You're welcome."

Finn retrieved his spent arrows, giving a low whistle as he looked at the dead creature. "That was amazing. You're a good fighter, Connor."

"You too," said Connor. It was the first sincere compliment he'd ever given the Innish boy. A lot had changed since they'd climbed the Red Horn. "Thanks for the backup."

Finn nodded and was about to say something else, but he looked up. Connor followed his gaze and saw Nikira returning down the passageway. She limped slightly from the injury to her foot, but she was accompanied by another cloaked figure, armed with swordbreakers. Connor's heart sank.

"We have to get out of here. We can't fight two of them with our injuries. Run toward the main battle." Connor staggered to his feet, now feeling the stab of pain in his right leg. He could stand, but not run. "Go ahead. I'll catch up."

"I'm not leaving you!" insisted Jariel.

"Someone has to get help. Finn, please go."

Finn nodded and sprinted away.

Jariel picked up her short sword with her good hand, and Connor took one of Sinkhar's fallen swordbreakers. The two cloaked figures advanced.

When they were only about five yards away, Jariel charged. She slashed at Nikira with her sword, but Nikira sidestepped. She trapped Jariel's blade with her swordbreaker and wrenched sharply. Jariel's sword didn't break, but it flew out of her hand, and Nikira shoved her backward. Jariel hit a rock and lay there, stunned. With a yell, Connor aimed a swing at the other cloaked soldier. He caught the enemy's swordbreaker with his own and tried to twist it out of his grip. But the stranger was ready. Not even trying to disengage his weapon, the cloaked figure shoved Connor down, then knelt down on top of his injured leg. Connor bit back a scream of pain. His vision swam as the tip of a swordbreaker hovered in front of his face. Would it hurt to die?

But the cloaked figure did not strike. Instead, Nikira knelt down on Connor's other side and held a silky black handkerchief over his mouth and nose. He inhaled a foul smell and struggled, trying to pull away. But his leg was pinned and he couldn't move. Suddenly a wave of sleepiness washed over him. He lay back wearily. He felt tired enough to sleep for a hundred years. What was happening?

From a great distance, he heard someone calling his name. He forced his eyes open, caught a glimpse of feet running toward him…and then he remembered nothing more.

Chapter 22
Dawn Rises

That night, Ellie awoke to Vivian shaking her shoulder.

"Ellie. Wake up."

Ellie blinked and rubbed her eyes in the darkness. "Vivian? What's the matter?"

"I'm sorry to wake you. Only...I think I need you to call for Mukkech's doctor."

"The doctor?" Ellie sat up. "What's wrong?"

"The baby...I think it's coming."

Ellie tumbled out of bed and lit a candle with shaking fingers. For an instant, the bright flame reminded her of Rua. *Rua, please be here now,* she thought, flinging open the door.

Ellie ran to the great, locked gates that barred the starlit courtyard. Who would be listening now? She knocked on the doors, the noise loud in the stillness of night.

"Hello?" she ventured. No one answered. More boldly, she knocked again, louder this time. "Is anyone there? We need your help!"

Still no answer. Ellie pounded on the door with all her might.

"Help!" she shouted. "We need a doctor!"

Now candles appeared in a few doorways around the courtyard, and there was a rustling on the other side of the gates. Ellie kept banging until the bolt was drawn back and a guard's face appeared in the crack.

"Help!" Ellie said breathlessly. "My friend—she's having a baby. Please send for the doctor right away!"

Ellie ran back to Vivian, who was sitting up, her eyebrows puckered with pain, her skin glistening with sweat.

"Ellie, I don't want you to watch this. Go to Laralyn's," Vivian ground out between her teeth.

"I can't leave you!" Ellie exclaimed.

The door opened, and Laralyn came in, awakened by the noise.

"I'll manage until the doctor comes," said Laralyn, quickly taking in the situation. "Ellie, would you go and watch Gresha for me? Give her breakfast if I'm not back?"

"Are you sure?" Ellie looked at Vivian in panic. But there was no panic in Vivian's eyes.

"I'm...sure." She squeezed Ellie's hand. "Go."

Ellie felt a mixture of guilt and relief as she closed the door behind her. She wanted to be there for Vivian, but at the same time she was only too glad to escape. Quietly she let herself into Laralyn's room, where Gresha's even breathing calmed Ellie's nerves. Once she heard a piercing scream across the courtyard, and Ellie scooted closer to Gresha, trying to focus on the little girl's soft, warm breaths. *Oh Ishua, take care of Vivian tonight, and the baby, and...and Jude, wherever he is.*

It seemed to Ellie that she lay awake all night. But bright sunlight was coming through the windows when Gresha whimpered and Ellie opened her eyes. The little girl's bottom lip trembled as she saw a face that wasn't her mother's. Ellie smiled reassuringly.

"Hi, Gresha. Remember me?"

Gresha's whimpers turned into a howl, and Ellie picked her up. The little girl had gotten a lot heavier in the nearly ten months since they'd first met on Rhynlyr. Ellie wondered yet again where Deniev was—if he was even still alive. The rearguard mission should have arrived by now. She tried to distract herself by soothing Gresha.

"It's okay. Your mama will be back soon. Shhh."

Gresha's howling soon subsided into sniffles, then the soft sound of thumb-sucking. When Gresha was quiet, Ellie set her down. "Let's get you dressed and fed, and then we'll go see if your mama's still busy, okay?"

Gresha looked at Ellie with big, serious brown eyes, thumb firmly planted in her mouth. Ellie smiled. "I'll take that as a yes."

Feeding and dressing such a small person took a surprisingly long time, but finally Ellie let Gresha run outside into the sunshine. The little girl almost crashed into Laralyn, who was crossing the courtyard with Anaya, both carrying armloads of laundry.

"Mama!' Gresha shrieked, throwing her arms around Laralyn's legs.

"Good morning, baby," said Laralyn, her eyes underlined with deep shadows. Ellie hurried up anxiously, searching Laralyn's face for a sign.

"You can go in now," Anaya said kindly.

"Thank you for watching Gresha," said Laralyn.

Ellie, too distracted to answer, turned and ran toward the door of Vivian's room. Swallowing hard, she lifted the latch.

Vivian was sitting up in bed, propped against pillows. In her arms she held a small white bundle. She looked up as she saw Ellie. Though

Vivian's face looked pale and exhausted, her eyes twinkled with a deep and mysterious joy. It reminded Ellie of a look she had once seen in Ishua's eyes.

Tiptoeing through the quiet room, Ellie approached the bedside. Vivian tilted the bundle gently toward her. Half-lost in the white wrappings was a tiny face—a person's face, with a nose and a mouth and ears, and tiny closed eyes with even tinier eyelashes. Ellie had never thought a person could be so small.

"Ellie, I'd like you to meet my son," Vivian murmured, her voice thick with joy and pride.

"It's a boy?" Ellie asked, unable to take her eyes off the baby. She wanted to reach out and touch his red face, but at the same time she was afraid he'd pop like a soap bubble.

Vivian smiled. "Go ahead. Say hello."

Just then, the baby's mouth opened in a shapeless yawn that distorted the rest of his face, and one tiny fist peeked out of the blanket. Each of the five curled fingers was perfectly formed, complete with joints and wrinkled knuckles and even miniature fingernails. Ellie reached out her own finger to touch the tiny fist. The baby's skin was the softest thing she'd ever touched. Before she could draw her hand back, the baby's fingers curled around hers in a grip surprisingly strong for someone so small. He smacked his lips.

"Isn't he perfect?" Vivian whispered.

Ellie nodded, already completely convinced. Her heart was full. She already felt like this baby was her little brother. She wanted to keep him close, protect him, see that no harm ever came to him. "His grip is so strong," she whispered back.

The door opened, and Anaya came back in with a stack of fresh linens. Owen was right behind her.

"Isn't he a precious little thing?" Anaya clucked. She looked tired, but her gaze was full of love for the baby. Owen stood beside her, cocking his head to one side.

"Wow. It's so small. Is it a boy or girl?"

"Boy," said Ellie. "You guessed right all that time ago."

Owen smiled, adjusting his glasses. "Did you name him yet?"

Vivian shook her head. "Jude deserves to have a say in that."

Anaya finished hanging up clean towels and shooed Ellie and Owen out. "Her ladyship has had a long night. She needs her rest."

Ellie glanced back. "I'll see you both later."

Vivian just smiled.

Over the next several days, Ellie did everything she could to help with the new baby. She hung up a sheet that rocked like a cradle between the two chairs, and she made a nest of extra pillows and blankets for herself right beside it. She held the baby when Vivian was resting, helped change his diapers, and tried to make him smile when he cried. She'd never especially liked babies—she'd had to watch too many of them when she'd lived in the orphanages—but this one was special. She wondered how the world had ever existed without him.

They had a lot of visitors, too. Laralyn brought Gresha, who looked at the baby as if he were some sort of strange animal. Owen came often, though Vivian asked him to leave his animals outside for now. And Anaya was in and out every day. She always had some sort of housekeeping task, but Ellie knew she was just looking for excuses to cuddle the baby. She rocked him back and forth and talked to him in coos and gurgles.

"Such a fine little man. You're just perfect. Yes you are," Anaya clucked over the baby. He stared up at her, his big eyes following her every motion. "He's got your long eyelashes, your ladyship. A lucky thing, that is. But some features aren't like yours at all—I'll wager that nose is his father's. He must be a handsome man."

Vivian smiled. "He is."

"The master ought to come and see the little fellow. It'd put him in a good state of mind. He's been awfully busy lately, always closeted up with his advisers. I have to remind him to eat. He's fretting over something with the court astronomers…something about stars changing places. I don't understand it, but they don't ask me."

Vivian and Ellie exchanged a glance. If the court astronomers were noticing changes in star positions, that could only mean one thing: the island had broken free from its coral and was moving toward the Edge.

"I…don't know if the First Minister will be coming to see the baby, Anaya," Vivian said slowly. "You do know that we're here under house arrest, don't you?"

"Oh, I knew there'd been some sort of political scuffle," said Anaya, not taking her eyes from the baby's face. "The master's always negotiating politics back and forth, but the discussions don't usually last long."

Vivian cleared her throat delicately. "Your master told me exactly how long this one will last. He promised to keep all these people here until I agree to marry him."

Anaya looked up. "What?"

"He assumes my husband is not coming back and insists that I marry him in order for my people to go free."

"And…what do you say, your ladyship?"

Vivian chose her words carefully. "I am confident my husband will return, and I remain loyal to him."

Anaya nodded. "As well you may, your ladyship. It's well said. I'll not say I'm not sorry, for I'd like to keep this little one here always. But I'll have a word with my master. I've known him since he was a boy. He can be impulsive and rash at times, but he's a good man beneath it all."

That night, a note arrived for Vivian. She read it aloud to Ellie.

"I have reconsidered our position. While I will not retract my previous conditions for the Vestigians' release, I do apologize if my manner of speaking was unduly harsh. Please send word if there is anything I can do to make your stay more comfortable. Ahlmet."

Vivian sighed. "This must be all that came of Anaya's conversation with him. I'd hoped for a greater change of heart."

"Still, it's something," Ellie said. "Hold on to it. We might think of something useful he can do."

The next afternoon, Vivian was taking a bath, and Ellie sprawled on a blanket next to the baby. She waved the coral paperweight in slow circles over his face, smiling as he flailed his tiny arms and legs and made gurgling sounds. His eyes were a glassy dark blue color, but Vivian said that would probably change in a few weeks. Then they'd know if he'd have her brown eyes or Jude's light blue ones. Ellie brought the coral closer and closer until it touched the baby's fingers and he grabbed it.

"Got it!' Ellie exclaimed. "Good job! You're gonna learn to…" She stopped. From around the baby's tiny grip, streaks of pink were spreading over the brittle, gray piece of coral. Ellie quickly pried it out of his hand. He started to cry at having his toy taken away, but all Ellie could see was the pink flush on the coral, starting in the shape of a handprint, but already spreading out from there. Her eyes widened.

"Vivian!" she shrieked. She scooped up the baby, who had started to scream. Vivian, wrapped in a towel, opened the washroom door, her hair dripping wet.

"What happened? Is he all right?" Vivian held out one arm for the baby. Ellie handed him over and held up the piece of coral.

"He was playing with this a moment ago. Look!"

Vivian quieted the baby's screams, then looked at the coral. By now the pink had spread to a giant blob that had begun to glow faintly.

"Where did you get this? I thought there wasn't any healthy coral left on the island."

"There wasn't," Ellie blurted, her words tumbling over one another. "That was dead coral—the paperweight from the desk. I was playing with the baby, and he grabbed onto it. Then...that's what happened."

Vivian looked into the baby's tiny face. "*You* did this?"

Ellie remembered the visions she'd seen before the baby's birth. The growing roses. The glowing coral. And before that, the strange dreams and gifts her crewmates had received. The new Song music. The words.

Dawn rises,

new life from fire!

Ishua was making a way.

"Vivian," Ellie said slowly. "I think the baby needs to take a trip to the island core."

Chapter 23
Rua's Work

Ellie ran to tell the Council about the baby's gift. If it was true that his touch could heal coral, then there might still be a chance to save the island, even without caris powder. They did not know if he could repair a coral branch that had already broken loose from its tree, but it was certainly worth a try. The biggest problem was how to get to the core.

"One of us could take the baby and sneak out at night," Meggie suggested.

"I don't think you'll talk Vivian into that," said Ellie. Suddenly she remembered Mukkech's note. *Anything I can do to make your stay more comfortable.* She smiled. "I have an idea."

Vivian agreed to the plan. She sent a note with Anaya that evening, asking Mukkech to take her on an outing to the island core. His response came later that night. The carriages would be ready in the morning.

Ellie stood with Vivian and the baby outside the front gate the next morning. Vivian had wrapped her son carefully in warm blankets. Beneath a cloak, she wore the rose-patterned gown from their first evening here. Ellie shifted nervously. There were so many things that could go wrong, and they needed this to work.

Mukkech joined them, along with Anaya. The First Minister's eyes traveled slowly from Vivian's face to the baby sleeping in her arms. He bowed his head slightly, and they all got into a carriage and set out. A second carriage, carrying advisers and a few guards, followed them. Ellie remembered the first outing to the marketplace and thought about how much had happened since then.

"Have you...given the child a name?" Mukkech asked at last.

Vivian shook her head. "His father should have a say. I'm waiting for him to return."

Mukkech nodded. That was the end of the conversation.

It took nearly an hour to reach the island core. A wooden ladder lay beside the stone well. Ellie, Vivian, Anaya, and Mukkech looked down into the shaft, and Mukkech's eyes widened.

"The coral—it's broken," he said slowly. His advisers gathered around him, muttering to each other.

"It is as the astronomers said!"

"We are no longer anchored down!"

"The island *is* moving!"

Ellie looked at the cracked and ragged stumps of gray coral. If only Mukkech had believed them sooner. Would even the baby's astonishing gift be able to save coral that was already broken?

Vivian took a deep breath and turned toward the First Minister.

"Ahlmet, would you be good enough to lower the ladder into the water?"

"Why? Surely you're not thinking of..."

"I certainly am. Please move the ladder or I will do it myself."

266

Mukkech signaled to his guards, and two of them lowered the ladder, two hooks fitting snugly over the top of the stone wall. Meanwhile, Vivian laid the baby down on a blanket and undressed him, setting aside a towel and dry clothes for later. She took off her own cloak and bound the baby to her chest with a sling.

"Ellie, perhaps you would sing for us as I take him down?" said Vivian, the slightest bruise of worry in her voice. Ellie nodded.

Vivian climbed over the wall and began to descend the ladder. Ellie started to sing the new music that Alyce had dreamed and the words that went with it.

Come awake, O sleepers,
from the silence of night.

The warm seawater touched the hem of Vivian's dress, which instantly soaked and pooled out around her. As Ellie's vision changed, Vivian looked like a single rose with a golden center growing from the island core.

Dawn rises,
new life from fire!

Vivian slowly climbed down. As the baby's feet touched the water, he gurgled happily.

Rise up, O golden ones,
keep time with the music.

Keeping the tiny head above the water, Vivian guided the baby's hand to a twig of dead coral. His fist closed around it.

Come follow the kingdom

to its glorious day.

Golden tendrils began to swirl out from the rose. The gray coral began to glow from deep within. Veins of light ran down the branch, curling over it, wrapping around it. Then, like fireworks underwater, the whole coral tree lit up in bursts of gold. Ellie stopped singing as she helped Vivian climb back over the wall. Even with her ordinary sight, she could see the underwater coral recovering its healthy pink glow.

Ellie, Mukkech, Anaya, and the advisers and guards kept staring into the water as Vivian changed the baby into dry clothes. Ellie held her breath. The coral seemed to be recovering, but she wondered if it would re-anchor to the ocean floor.

Vivian had just finished wrapping the baby back up in blankets when there was a rumble and the earth began to shake. The baby started to scream, and Vivian clung to him tightly. The horses reared, and the guards held on to the carriages. Ellie grabbed the wall of the island core for support. When the shaking stopped, she looked back into the water.

All the coral branches were now a healthy, vibrant pink. But more importantly, the jagged ends that had snapped when the island broke loose were *growing.* Ellie could see a pink glimmer as the restored coral branch plunged downward, toward a new root at the bottom of the sea.

"It's working!" she cried.

Vivian held up the baby, kissing him on the nose. "You did it!"

Ellie sat down, her knees weak with relief. This war was big and their enemies were strong, but Rua's gifts were flowing out all around them, giving them what they needed to fight back.

The Vahyans stared into the water, spellbound.

"Well, I'll be," muttered Anaya.

"The coral is...*growing!*" breathed Mukkech. "How...?"

"The science of coral is a long story for another day," said Vivian. "But the earthquake must have struck when the branches began to grow again. If indeed the new tree attaches to the sea floor, Vahye is saved." Her gaze was level, but held no accusation. "Now do you believe I was telling you the truth?"

Mukkech sighed. "It seems I no longer have any other choice. Your story agrees with what my astronomers have observed. And I can see the coral growing for myself." He bowed his head. "I apologize for the ways I hindered you. I see now that the Vestigians did not intend to rebel, but to help. How can I make amends?"

"Well, you can lift the house arrest, for one," said Vivian. "And you can accept the fact that, while you have some good and generous qualities and I hope we will always be friends, I will never marry you."

Mukkech nodded slowly. "I had hoped you would reconsider. But I see now that your mind is made up. Very well. You and your friends are free. I will give the order as soon as we return to the palace."

The Vestigians were overjoyed to hear the double good news that the island was saved and the house arrest was lifted. They had to remain on Vahye until news came from Lady Lilia, but Ellie, Vivian, and Owen took advantage of their freedom to walk the garden's neat gravel paths. Sunny trotted in front of them, sniffing every bush they passed.

Owen had sewn a special pocket into his shirt for Pinta, and as they walked, he picked leaves to feed her. Moby's head poked up from his shirt collar, taking in the view and the fresh air.

The trees laden with fruit and trellises of flowers were beautiful, but Ellie couldn't help feeling sad. Of course she was overjoyed that Vivian and the baby were safe and that the island wasn't going to fall over the Edge. But now that the danger was past, all she could think about was how much she missed her friends from the *Legend*. Finn's harp leaned silently against a wall, and Ellie longed for one of Jariel's bone-crushing hugs. Most of all, she missed Connor. Something felt wrong when she thought about her twin, and she was worried about him. She glanced over at Owen, who was absently staring up at the sky as Pinta nibbled on a leaf.

"Are you thinking about them too?"

He nodded. "I hope they're all right."

Ellie sighed. "And that they'll hurry up and get here soon."

The next morning, Ellie and Vivian were walking in the garden, giving the baby some fresh air. He was restless, punching his little fists in the air and whimpering. Vivian was trying to distract him when Ellie glanced upward. Two black spots swam in her vision. She tried to rub the floaters away, but they remained in place. Could it be...?

"Vivian...I think we should go down to the docks," Ellie said, not taking her eyes off the spots.

"The docks? Why?" Vivian followed Ellie's gaze. Her eyes widened. "Hurry, we have to tell the others!"

Guessing that the flying ships would make a water landing, all the Vestigians rushed down to the docks. Mukkech provided carts, but he rode separately in his litter. By the time they reached the docks, the ships were close enough for Ellie to recognize the *Legend* and the *Venture*. Hope and worry tumbled fiercely inside her until she could barely breathe. She gripped Vivian's and Owen's hands, trying to see over the crowd in front of them.

The ships slowly descended to the water, their lumenai humming with the effort. Vahyan islanders gawked at the whirring propellers and the graceful wing sails. As the Vestigian travelers furled their sails and tossed mooring lines to the pier, Ellie tried to identify her friends. She spotted Jariel's tuft of red hair, but she couldn't see Connor.

Suddenly Vivian's fingers clamped down on Ellie's. "There's Jude." She handed Ellie the baby and waved her arms. A distant figure vaulted over the *Legend's* railing and hit the pier at a run, pushing through the crowd. He and Vivian flew into each other's arms and held on tight, hugging and kissing and crying all at the same time. Finally Vivian pulled away, grabbing both of Jude's hands and leading him over to where Ellie stood. When Jude saw what Ellie was holding, he froze, blinking like he'd forgotten where he was going.

"Jude, my darling," said Vivian, "there's someone I'd like you to meet." She knelt down beside Ellie and loosened the blanket from around the baby's face. "Your son."

Jude's eyes swept from Ellie to the baby to Vivian and back to the baby again. He knelt down too, the hem of his nautical coat sweeping the dusty ground. The baby was awake, and Ellie carefully tilted him forward so he could see Jude. Their eyes met. The baby stared, his big eyes blinking curiously. Ellie thought Jude might have stared too, if his eyes hadn't kept filling up with tears.

"Hello," Jude croaked thickly. Ellie smiled and handed him the baby. Jude settled the small bundle in his arms as carefully as if the tiny, squirming boy were made of blown glass.

"There you are," Jude murmured, his big callused thumb stroking the downy fuzz on the side of the baby's head. "You perfect, precious creature."

Just then, Jariel came flying toward them.

"Ellie!" she shouted, and barreled into her. Ellie got the bone-crushing hug she'd wished for. Not far behind came Finn, Alyce, Aimee, Kai, and Korrina, plus all the Janaki coming off the *Venture*. At a distance, Ellie was surprised and relieved to see Deniev as he wrapped Laralyn and Gresha in a hug. But there was one face Ellie didn't see.

"Where's Connor?" she asked when Jariel let her go. No one answered. Ellie looked around at her friends, their eyes averted. "Jude? Jariel? Where's Connor?"

"And Makundo," said Vivian, frowning.

"We…need to find somewhere to talk," said Jude.

"Tell me now," Ellie insisted, her voice rising with panic. "Is he all right? He's not—" her breath caught in her throat.

"No, he's not dead—at least, not when we last saw him," said Jude. "But the truth may be still harder to hear. Are you sure you're ready?"

"Nothing could be worse than not knowing," said Ellie anxiously.

"He was captured by the Enemy," said Kai.

All Ellie's bones suddenly felt bendy and soft. Jariel put an arm around her shoulders.

"There's a lot to tell. I saw it happen," Jariel said. "But first let's find a quiet place to talk."

Just then, a man in white robes with a sharp, curved beard came toward them. Mukkech looked embarrassed and almost shy as he approached the group.

"Ahlmet, may I introduce my husband, Jude," Vivian said with a smile, slipping her arm around Jude's waist, his hands still full with the baby. "And these are our shipmates, the brave crews of the *Legend* and the *Venture*. Everyone, this is the First Minister of Vahye."

"It's an honor to meet you. Thank you for showing our loved ones such generous hospitality," Jude said with a respectful nod. "My wife has always spoken of this place with great fondness."

Ellie coughed into her hand. Vivian and Jude had a long conversation coming to them.

But Mukkech simply nodded back, his expression carefully controlled. "The honor is mine. You are…a lucky man."

"I couldn't agree more." Jude smiled down at Vivian.

"Come, be my guests, all of you," said the First Minister. "You are welcome to stay as long as you like. I will restock your ships with the supplies you need."

"Again, your generosity is great," said Jude. "We thank you."

The crew of the *Legend* gathered in what had been Ellie and Vivian's room in the palace. The children sprawled on the carpet. The falcon Zira perched on Aimee's shoulder, and Sunny curled up beside Owen. Vivian sat on the bed, holding the sleeping baby, with Jude's arm around her shoulders. Kai and Korrina both leaned against a wall. Ellie took a second look when she realized how close they were standing to one another.

"So tell us what happened on Nakuru," Ellie begged.

"You first," said Jude. "We followed your message here, Ellie. It said Vivian was ill—I was worried—"

"I *was* ill," said Vivian. "I had a relapse of the underground fever."

"The underground fever?" Jude paled a shade.

"I owe my life to Ellie's quick thinking—and her trust in Ishua's visions. She gave me the caris powder that healed me, even when the island was ready to break loose. We *both* owe her our lives." Vivian kissed the baby's forehead.

"Wait—*did* the island actually break loose?" said Alyce. "Then...how did you..."

"Turns out your son has a *very* interesting gift," said Ellie, pointing at the pink and faintly glowing paperweight that still rested on the desk. "That was a dead piece of coral two days ago—before he touched it."

"Jude, you should have seen it," said Vivian, her eyes lighting up. "I took him to the island core, and at one touch of his hand, the broken pieces of coral turned pink and began to *grow* again. He fused the coral back to the sea floor and stopped the island from drifting."

"So really, we're alive because of him," said Owen.

Jude raised his eyebrows, staring at the baby, who was deep in the limp and heavy slumber of infants. "I...don't know what to say. I'm...grateful, and amazed, and even a little afraid. How could a child of mine have such power?"

"How can any of us do what we do?" said Ellie. "I mean, we've seen amazing things happen—Aimee speaking with the falcon, Vivian understanding Janaki, Alyce and Meggie's dreams. Or even the things we do all the time—Finn's storytelling, Owen's care for animals, Connor's leadership…" she trailed off.

"We're up against a lot. I should know," said Owen quietly. "Maybe this is Rua's work inside us—Ishua's way of balancing the scales."

"And an amazing balance it is," said Jude, touching the baby's soft cheek with one finger. "This could change everything for the Vestigia Roi."

"Now will you please tell us about your mission? I'm dying to know about Connor," Ellie pleaded.

Taking turns, the Nakuru crew told their story from the beginning: the great mirrors that had nearly shot them out of the sky, the diplomatic mission to reunite the Vestigians and Nakurans, and the scaling of the Red Horn. Ellie went cold as Jariel described the battle with Nikira.

"She tried to tempt Connor over to the Enemy's side," said Jariel. "He started to fight her, but she had backup."

"It took all three of us to bring down her partner," said Finn. "But by then she had brought another creature like her."

"Finn ran for help while Connor and I stayed to fight," said Jariel. "But we were already injured. Connor took a spike in the leg, and my arm was hurt. I got thrown against a wall and couldn't move, but I saw them knock Connor down and put a handkerchief over his mouth. They must have drugged him, because he'd never have gone with them willingly."

"I was running back toward the cave with reinforcements when we saw them board a flying ship and take off," said Finn. "We tried to catch up, but we were too late."

"So he's been captured by the Enemy," Ellie muttered numbly. "Where would they take him? What are they going to do to him?"

Kai shrugged. "If only we knew. Connor is a Vestigian ship captain and your brother. I fear they'll try to squeeze him for information about our plans."

"But Connor would never—"

"Not willingly," agreed Kai. "But the Enemy has terrible ways of making people see his side."

Ellie jumped to her feet. "We have to go after him! We can't let him be tortured!"

Jariel grabbed Ellie's hand and pulled her back to the floor. "We won't abandon Connor, I promise. We will find a way to save him. But first we have to figure out where he is."

"If it hadn't been for his bravery and cleverness, we might never have won the battle or gotten off Nakuru," said Kai. "Connor was— is—a very fine sailor."

The accidental word *was* froze Ellie's heart. Connor wasn't dead. He couldn't be dead.

"He's still alive—or was, when I last saw him," said Jariel, as if reading Ellie's thoughts. "That means there's still hope for him. Makundo and Markos weren't so lucky."

"They fell bravely," said Kai.

"I'm so sorry," said Vivian, looking at Korrina.

Korrina shook her head. "Makundo with his family now," she said. "He is happy."

"Zira isn't happy," said Aimee, stroking the bird's feathers. "She misses him. But I'll take care of her."

"And Korrina will take care of the *Venture*," said Kai. "She inherited Makundo's command."

"We owe Makundo our gratitude for many reasons," said Jude. "Not least that he died defending Omondi, the Nakuran prince, in battle. It is because of Makundo's sacrifice that Omondi is leading a force of Nakurans to help us take back Rhynlyr. The Nakurans have joined the Vestigian fleet under Vice Admiral Trull and will meet us when we identify a rendezvous island."

"That's wonderful news," said Vivian.

The crew shared their stories all afternoon, including the tale of how the *Legend* had found Deniev and the rearguard mission adrift on the ocean, their ship's lumena disabled. All had survived the mission except the young sentry Ravago. He had given his life to help the others escape. Ellie was sorry to hear it, but she was only half listening. All she could think about was Connor. Was he dead too?

Chapter 24
Following the Kingdom

When the sun went down, the crew went out to the gardens for the feast Mukkech's household had prepared. On the way out, Ellie handed Tangwystl to Finn.

"I kept her for you," she said. "I'm glad you came back for her."

"Thanks," said Finn, stroking the harp's smooth wood lovingly. "I...I'm glad you're okay too. And...I really am sorry about Connor. I wish you could've seen the way he fought. He was braver than any of us, and cleverer too. He's the one who killed that...that thing like Nikira, even though it was bigger than him and had better weapons. I wish I could have stopped him from being captured. If there's...anything I can do to help find him, I will."

"Thank you," said Ellie. She didn't know how Finn could help save Connor from the Enemy's clutches, but the sincerity in the Innish boy's gray eyes made the task seem a little less hopeless.

Lights and pavilions had been set up in the gardens. Vivian took great pleasure in introducing her shipmates to traditional Vahyan delicacies. Owen gagged on the pickled snails still in their shells, but there were plenty of other delicious things: small, sweet *kiryss* fruits stuffed with soft cheese and rolled in a spicy powder; at least a dozen types of olives; sweet, flaky pastries oozing layers of olive oil and honey.

Mukkech sat at a separate table with his advisers. Ellie hummed a few bars of the Song and was pleased to see that the black cloak he had worn before was now a rich red, studded with golden stars. The First Minister had found a way to make amends.

Anaya was overseeing the serving staff, but she still managed to slip over and hold the baby for a few minutes between dinner and dessert.

"I see the resemblance," she said, looking from the baby's face to Jude's. "It's the nose."

Vivian laughed. "I told you he was handsome."

The environment was festive, and Ellie saw Kai take Korrina's hand under the table. But though she was glad to have her shipmates back, part of Ellie's mind was still on Connor. Where was he? Was he being tortured? Could he be dead?

Alyce got into a debate with Finn about the phrasing of the new Song music. As she sang a few bars, Ellie's vision changed for just a moment. She glimpsed a boy with blue eyes, eyes that were like looking in a mirror. *Connor.* The blue eyes blinked. Then the music ended and the vision was gone.

Connor's alive. Ellie couldn't say how she knew it, but she did. Connor was her twin brother. It was as if an invisible string ran between them, and she had just felt a gentle tug on the other end. He was alive. And she was going to find him.

Servants were clearing away the dishes when three majestic figures descended from the sky, alighting in the middle of the feasting pavilions. One of them was Lady Lilia. On her left side was a male Alirya with jet-black hair, almond-shaped eyes, and deep red wings, the tips edged in orange and gold like the heart of a flame. Shimmering orange tattoos scrolled up the left side of his bare chest, neck, and face. On Lilia's other side was a blue-winged Alirya Ellie recognized.

"Kiaran!" she cried out.

The solemn Alirya, his blue tattoos curling over skin dark as walnut wood, gave her a grave and respectful nod. *Three* Alirya in one place!

Serle, Phylla, Katha, Meggie, and Ellie quickly rose to greet the messengers.

"We are grateful for your return," said Councilwoman Phylla.

Lilia nodded. "We come bearing urgent news for the Vestigia Roi."

"You may speak freely," said Councilman Serle, glancing at Mukkech's table, where the Vahyans wore awestruck expressions at the sight of the Alirya. "We are among friends now."

"My companions, Hoyan and Kiaran, assisted me in the scouting mission," Lilia explained.

"Gwalior has fallen in the east," reported Hoyan, the red-winged Alirya.

"To the south, Amalpura still stands, though it is besieged," said Kiaran.

"Ajmer, too, has fallen to the Enemy," said Lilia. "But Dhar is safe. It is under attack, but a hundred rescue ships returned from Nakuru some months ago, and they have helped hold the island. The terrain is mountainous and defensible, and it is near Rhynlyr."

Meggie nodded. "Then it sounds like we've found our base."

"There is more," said Lilia. "Lord Ishua has sent Kiaran, Hoyan, and myself to assist the Vestigia Roi in its war against the Enemy. We cannot fight the entire war for you. But against Draaken's creatures of darkness, we may be of some help."

"Thank you," said Ellie sincerely.

"We must dispatch eyret messages at once," said Councilman Serle. "We will direct the mission crews to meet at the Haven of Dhar, along with the troops they have rallied. As for us, we can set sail tomorrow."

The Council immediately dispersed. Serle and Phylla went to send the eyret messages, while Ellie, Katha, and Meggie stayed behind with the Alirya, distributing the news and giving instructions to the ship captains. The Vestigians thanked their host and began to scatter, packing and preparing for their journey to Dhar. Ellie stood beside Jude and Vivian as Mukkech approached them.

"I wish to send soldiers to aid the Vestigian efforts," he said. "One hundred men from my personal guard. They have all gone through elite training and can be ready to leave in the morning."

"Ahlmet...that's very generous, but are you sure?" said Vivian. "Just a few days ago, our cause was distasteful to you."

Mukkech nodded. "Much has changed since then. Not only have I seen flying ships and growing coral with my own eyes, but I have also seen the purpose and courage you have because of your devotion to Ishua. I hindered that cause before, but now I wish to help. Anything that inspires such loyalty, such...love, is worth being part of."

Vivian smiled. "You've shown yourself to be a fine person, Ahlmet. I wish you well."

He bowed. "And I you."

The next morning, the *Legend*, the *Venture*, and the three convoy ships took to the skies. As the *Legend* gained altitude, Ellie watched the waving islanders beneath them shrink and blend into Vahye's tropical landscape, then into the larger archipelago of Arjun Mador. Kai, the acting captain, was at the ship's helm, but he frowned as the *Venture* pulled ahead of them.

"Trim the sails! Heave!" he called. Ellie, Owen, Jariel, Alyce, Finn, Jude, Aimee, and the new Vahyan soldiers aboard scuttled to obey, and once again the *Legend* pulled even. From aboard the *Venture,* Korrina waved and applied more pressure to her ship's propellers for even greater speed. Ellie smiled. If they kept up this contest, it would be just a few days before they reached Dhar.

The day passed quickly, and the sun sank below the Edge of the world, turning the clouds brilliant shades of orange and gold. The crew was on deck, taking advantage of the warm evening and the last bit of light. Jariel was up in the rigging, while Finn taught the Vahyans some sailors' knotwork. Jude and Vivian sat together on a crate, Jude holding the sleeping baby. Alyce shooed Aimee and Sunny off the sail she was mending, and Owen picked up Pinta before Sunny could sniff at her too roughly. Ellie stood at the railing, watching stars come out in the sky and lights appear on the islands below. She remembered her long-ago dream of Ishua, when she'd wondered if the *Legend* was the last Vestigian ship left in the whole world. So much had changed since then. The Vestigia Roi had risen up. On Dhar, they would meet allies who came from every archipelago in Aletheia. They were not alone.

Ellie could hear Jude and Vivian talking behind her.

"Have you thought of any names for the baby?" Vivian asked.

"What? You didn't give him a Knerusse name no one can pronounce?" Jude teased.

"I will if you don't help me come up with something soon," said Vivian mischievously.

They were quiet for a moment.

"Talmai," murmured Jude.

"What?"

"Oron Talmai. Wasn't that the name of the seer who pushed Draaken back and led the Vestigia Roi to victory?"

Ellie turned, recognizing the name.

"Yes," Vivian answered. "Talmai received Canto Twelve of the Song and was strengthened by the power of the new music."

Jude slipped his free arm around Vivian's shoulders. "Then I think that's what we should name our son. Talmai once came as Ishua's gift to help the Vestigia Roi survive and overcome the Enemy. The times are as dark now as they were then, and yet Ishua does not leave us without hope."

"But isn't that a bit presumptuous? Choosing the name of such a famous person?"

"For a child whose hands can regrow a broken coral tree?"

Vivian chuckled. "I suppose we could shorten it to Tal."

"Talmai. Tal." Jude kissed the sleeping baby's forehead. "Ishua's new Song in the world."

Ellie smiled in the dark. She'd never thought of a person as a part of the Song before. But maybe, in a way, they all were—Jariel and Owen, Tal and Jude and Vivian, Finn and Alyce and Aimee, Kai and Korrina, herself. And Connor, especially Connor, alive and fighting for the One Kingdom somewhere in a dungeon far away. But not too far away to find. Not for her. Not for Ishua.

Dawn rises.

I'm coming, Connor.

Epilogue
Not Alone

C onnor struggled to come awake. Sleep sucked him down like mud at the bottom of a lake. He could just stay down here, let the deep water claim him. No—he needed air, needed light. He opened his eyes.

He was lying in a dim room, lit only by yellow and red glimmers that wavered somewhere overhead. The walls looked strangely wet and smelled like spoiled meat. He was cold. Lifting his head slightly, he saw that he was lying on a stone slab. When he tried to move his hands, he found that they were strapped down. Panic washed over him. *I'm trapped. I'm a prisoner.* Connor's heart thudded wildly and his mind raced, trying to come up with a plan. First he needed to find out if he was alone.

"Hello?" He willed his voice to sound confident. "Is anyone here?"

There was a long moment of silence. *Just as I feared. I am alone,* Connor thought.

Then there was a dry rustling sound, like the whisper of rough hands being rubbed together. It was hard to tell where the sound was coming from. Connor frowned, trying to identify it. Was it snake scales? A silken gown slipping across a stone floor? It sent shivers down his back.

Gulping down his fear, Connor shouted, "I said, is anyone there?"

In the dimness above him, two glowing yellow eyes opened. Their vertical black pupil slits were like windows into a world where light had never existed.

"Yesss."

The adventure continues...

Stay tuned for Book 4!

Glossary

A

Academy, the: School on <u>Rhynlyr</u>, comprised of <u>Administrative</u>, <u>Scholastic</u>, <u>Nautical</u>, and <u>Occupational</u> Houses, that trains future members of the <u>Vestigia Roi</u>.

Administrative House: <u>Academy</u> House focusing on <u>Vestigian</u> business, political leadership, and diplomacy. Its emblem is a ten-pointed star.

Adona Roi (uh-DOE-nah roh-EE): "The Good King"; the immortal and supernatural ruler of <u>The One Kingdom</u>.

Ahearn (AH-hern): Chieftain of the <u>Innish.</u>

Ahlmet Mukkech (ALL-met MOOK-etch): First Minister on <u>Vahye</u>, former suitor of <u>Vivian Sterlen</u>.

Aimee Kellar (KELL-ahr): Five-year-old daughter of <u>Estir Kellar</u>; younger sister of <u>Alyce Kellar</u>.

Al-akalea (AL ah-kah-LAY-ah): Nakuran name for the Red Horn plateau.

Aletheia (ah-LEE-thee-ah): The known world, home to the Four Archipelagos. Its surface is covered with ocean and dotted with islands.

Alirya (ull-EER-yah): Supernatural winged beings, servants and messengers of <u>Ishua</u>, <u>Rua</u>, and <u>Adona Roi</u>.

Alston, Pa, Ma, Samanta, and Robert (ALL-stun): <u>Ellie's</u> second adoptive family.

Alyce Kellar (AL-iss KELL-ahr): An eleven-year-old <u>Scholastic</u> student with an exceptional singing voice. Accompanist to <u>Ellie,</u> daughter of <u>Estir Kellar</u>, older sister of <u>Aimee Kellar.</u>

Amalia, Miss: Art teacher at the <u>Academy.</u>

Amalpura (ah-mall-PUR-ah): Southernmost of the <u>Vestigian Havens.</u>

Amra, Provost: <u>Scholastic</u> member of the <u>Council</u> on <u>Rhynlyr</u>.

Anadyr (ANN-ah-deer): <u>Newdonian</u> island; <u>Jude Sterlen</u>'s home island.

Anaya (an-EYE-ah): Housekeeper to Ahlmet Mukkech.

Archipelago (ARK-i-PELL-ah-go): A group of islands connected to a single coral tree. Four archipelagos survive in Aletheia.

Arcvon (ARK-vonn): A Lagorite agent and servant of Draaken.

Arjun Mador (ARR-jen mah-DORE): One of the Four Archipelagos.

Asthmenos (ASTH-men-ows): A poison deadly to island-supporting coral. Its only antidote is caris powder.

Aton (AH-tawn): Fever-reducing plant.

Ayva (AY-vah): A native dialect spoken on Vahye.

B

Basilean (bah-sill-AY-en): Term of contempt for a member of the Vestigia Roi, most commonly used in Newdonia.

Beswick, Nevin and Darling (NEH-vinn BEZ-wick): Ellie's first adoptive family.

Black borrage root (BLACK BORE-udge ROOT): Antidote for helkath poison.

Bramborough: A Newdonian island.

C

Caris (CARE-iss): Powder made from the leaves of the stellaria tree, used to feed and restore coral sickened by asthmenos poison.

Cloud trout: A type of fish native to clouds; common food source for Vestigian ship crews.

Connor Reid: Thirteen-year-old captain of the *Legend*, twin brother to Ellie.

Cooley, Horaffe, Loretha, and Ewart Horaffe Theodemir (YOO-art HOR-aff thee-AWE-deh-meer COO-lee): Ellie's third adoptive family.

Coquin (COKE-win): Vestigian currency.

Council, The: The highest human authority over Rhynlyr and the Vestigia Roi. Made up of four elected members, one from each House, plus an Alirya adviser.

Cygnera (sig-NER-ah): Swan-like bird; figurehead of the *Legend*.

D

Daevin Blenrudd (DAY-vinn BLEN-rudd): Deceased Vestigian sailor and former captain of the _Legend_.

Defiance: A Vestigian ship commandeered by urken.

Deniev (DEN-ee-ev): Vestigian shipwright, husband to Laralyn and father of Gresha.

Draaken (DRAY-ken): "The Enemy," the supernatural being served by believers in Khum Lagor. Occasionally takes physical form as a great sea serpent.

Draaken's Eye: The ring of ocean spray at the bottom end of a waterspout. An indication of Draaken's interference with the natural world.

Draos, draoi (DRAH-ows, DRAH-oy): Innish seers and priests of Mor Nathar.

Dshinn (JINN): A powerful servant of Draaken that inhabits a human's mind and communicates what it learns to its master.

E

Edge, the: The boundary of Aletheia, where the waterfall at the rim of the world flows upward. The ultimate fate of islands that break free from their coral trees. None who go over it ever return.

Elbarra Cluster (ell-BAR-ah): The fifth archipelago of Aletheia, destroyed by asthmenos during Thelipsa's Rebellion. See Lost Archipelago.

E'liahnea (eh-lee-AH-nyah): Innish word meaning _light_.

Ellianea Reid (ell-ee-an-AY-ah REED): A thirteen-year-old girl with the gifts of a seer and an illuminator. Daughter to Kiria Reid and Gavin Reid, sister to Connor Reid. Her name means _light_.

Ellie Altess (ALL-tess): See Ellianea Reid.

Estir Kellar: Late mother of Alyce and Aimee Kellar.

Eyret (EYE-ret): Heron-like messenger bird used by the Vestigia Roi.

Elgin, Master (ELL-jinn): Master at the Mundarva Library.

F

Finn: An Innish orphan boy and shanachai, now a sailor aboard the _Legend_.

Firestars: Missiles that fall, blazing bright trails, then explode on impact.

Freith (FREETH): Newdonian island; Ellie's home island.

Furleti (fur-LEH-tee): Innish for *welcome*.

G

Glimmerstone: A small black pebble that glows after being struck on a hard surface.

Gresha: Daughter to Deniev and Laralyn.

Guduk: A language of Aletheia.

H

Hakara/hakaran (HAH-kah-rah): Literally, "fire mountain"; Numbani for *volcano*.

Hasheya (ha-SHAY-ah): Nakuran leader, mother of Omondi.

Havens: Vestigian flying islands; outposts of refuge and sources of lumenai for the One Kingdom.

Helkath (HELL-kath): Butterfly-like creatures of Draaken whose bites cause a loss of hope in their victims.

I

Ilorin Reformatory: A flying island prison for violent or traitorous Vestigian criminals. Rehabilitation is encouraged, but some prisoners remain on the island for life.

Innish: An island in the Orkent Isles. The word is also used as an adjective for the island's inhabitants.

Intrepid: A Vestigian ship commanded by Vice Admiral Trull.

Ishua (ISH-oo-ah): Son of Adona Roi, Commander of the Winged Armies, bringer of caris to the islands, and founder of the Vestigia Roi.

Ithrom Jaron (ITH-rum JARE-un): A regent in the Second Age who first began to record the Song.

J

Janaki (jah-NAH-kee): An island in the <u>Numed Archipelago</u>, formerly the home island of <u>Makundo</u> and <u>Korrina</u>. Also an adjective used for residents of the island.

Jariel Kirke (jare-ee-ELL KIRK): Spunky thirteen-year-old girl with an interest in navigation; <u>Ellie's</u> best friend.

Hoyan (ho-YAHN): One of the <u>Alirya</u>; a winged messenger of <u>Ishua</u>, <u>Rua</u>, and <u>Adona Roi</u>.

Jude Sterlen (JOOD STIR-lenn): <u>Vestigian</u> doctor and second mate aboard the <u>*Legend*</u>, husband to <u>Vivian Edrei</u>.

K

Kai: First mate aboard the <u>*Legend*</u>, formerly bodyguard to <u>Ellianea Reid</u>.

Kaspar (KASS-par): Early <u>Lagorite</u>, servant of <u>Draaken</u>, deceiver of <u>Thelipsa</u>, and first known source of <u>asthmenos</u>.

Katha Radburne: Elder daughter of <u>Consul Radburne</u>.

Kentish: A family of dialects spoken in the <u>Orkent Isles</u>.

Khum Lagor (KOOM la-GORE): The ultimate goal of all Lagorites: to subjugate or destroy all land-walkers until the whole world serves Draaken.

Kiaran (kee-ARR-un): One of the <u>Alirya</u>; a winged messenger of <u>Ishua</u>, <u>Rua</u>, and <u>Adona Roi</u>.

Kingdom Bridge: An iconic <u>Rhynlyr</u> monument formed from the living roots of the original <u>stellaria</u> tree, reportedly planted by <u>Ishua</u> himself.

Kiryss (KEY-riss): small, sweet fruit native to <u>Vahye</u>.

Knerusse (neh-ROOS): A long-dead language of <u>Aletheia</u>, original language of lyrics to the <u>Song</u>.

Korrina (corr-INN-ah): A <u>Janaki</u> warrior.

Kucha: <u>Janaki</u> for *stop*.

L

Lagorites (LAH-gore-ites): Followers of <u>Draaken</u> and believers in <u>Khum Lagor</u>.

Laralyn (LEH-rah-linn): Wife to <u>Deniev</u> and mother of <u>Gresha</u>.

Legend, **The**: A Vestigian ship commanded by Connor Reid.

Lilia, Lady (LILL-ee-ah): Alirya adviser to the Council on Rhynlyr.

Lost Archipelago, The: Modern name for the Elbarra Cluster, believed to have been destroyed during Thelipsa's Rebellion.

Lumena, lumenai (LOO-men-ah, LOO-men-eye): Water ferns whose fronds carry electrical current. Cultivated at Havens, they are transported to Rhynlyr to power Vestigian flying ships and islands.

M

Makundo (mah-KOON-doe): A Janaki warrior.

Mapepo: Literally, "demon spawn." Janaki word for *urken*.

Marafi: Janaki for *friends*.

Markos (MAR-kose): Former lookout and navigator aboard the *Legend*.

Meggie Radburne: Younger daughter of Consul Radburne.

Merai flowers (MEH-rye): Small orange flowers on Rhynlyr whose seeds add a spicy flavor to food.

Mharra (MAR-ah): A volcanic island in the Numed Archipelago.

Minaria tree (min-ARE-ee-ah): A small Rhynlyr tree with low-growing branches.

Mirin te (MEER-in TAY): An Ayvan phrase that can mean *hello, goodbye,* or *welcome*.

Moby: A Mundarvan bluestripe ribbon snake owned by Owen Mardel.

Mor Nathar (MORE nah-THAR): "The Great Serpent," Innish manifestation of Draaken worshiped as a deity.

Mordaz (MORE-dazz): A powerful dshinn.

Mundarva (mun-DARR-vuh): An island, now destroyed, from the south of Newdonia; a renowned center of learning and home of the Mundarva Library.

N

Nakuru (nah-KOO-roo): An island in the Numed Archipelago.

Nautical House: Academy House focusing on training members of the Vestigian fleet. Its symbol is a four-pronged propeller.

Navir (nah-VEER): Suor term of respect meaning *teacher*.

Newdonia (noo-DOE-nee-ah): One of the Four Archipelagos.

Nikira (ni-KEER-ah): A high-ranking <u>Lagorite</u> agent and servant of <u>Draaken</u>.

Numbani: A family of dialects spoken in the <u>Numed Archipelago</u>; also an adjective used for residents of that archipelago.

Numed Archipelago (NOO-med): One of the Four Archipelagos.

O

Occupational House: <u>Academy</u> House focusing on teaching skilled trades. Its emblem is a wheel.

Ojen (OH-jenn): Unscrupulous <u>Vestigian</u> dockhand.

Omondi (oh-MOAN-dee): <u>Nakuran</u> cliff climber, son of <u>Hasheya</u>.

One Kingdom, the: The original state of <u>Aletheia;</u> all the archipelagos unified under the governance of <u>Adona Roi</u>. Its restoration is the goal of the <u>Vestigia Roi</u>.

Onot/onotes (OH-not/oh-NOTE-es): Rock shafts on the island of <u>Mharra</u> with freshwater pools inside.

Orkent Isles (OR-kent): One of the Four Archipelagos.

Oron Talmai (OR-on TAL-mye): A historical <u>Vestigian</u> seer and warrior whose military victory ended <u>Lagorite</u> violence for three hundred years.

Owen Mardel (MAR-dell): A nine-year-old boy with an interest in animals and science.

P

Phylla (FILL-ah): Acting Councilwoman for the <u>Vestigians</u>.

Pinta: Miniature tortoise owned by <u>Owen Mardel</u>.

R

Radburne, Consul: Former <u>Administrative</u> member of the <u>Council</u> on <u>Rhynlyr</u> and father to <u>Katha</u> and <u>Meggie Radburne</u>. After he betrayed the <u>Vestigia Roi</u> to <u>Draaken</u>, he disappeared.

Ravago (rah-VAH-go): A <u>Vestigian</u> sentry on the island of <u>Mharra</u>.

Regents: Caretakers of the islands appointed by <u>Adona Roi</u> during the Second Age. Some, however, became hungry for more power, leading to revolts like <u>Thelipsa's Rebellion</u>.

Reid, Gavin and Kiria: <u>Vestigian</u> agents, late parents of <u>Ellie</u> and <u>Connor Reid</u>.

Reinholdt, Brother (RINE-holt): Brother and head illuminator at the <u>Vestigian</u> <u>Haven</u> at <u>Amalpura</u>.

Rhynlyr (RINN-leer): Historical headquarters of the <u>Vestigia Roi</u> and home to the <u>Academy</u>; the largest and most central flying island, currently under the control of <u>Draaken</u>.

Rilia (RILL-ee-ah): Plants commonly known as "falling stars." Its berries are used for relief of stomach pain.

Rua (ROO-ah): A supernatural presence equal to Adona Roi and Ishua. Invisible and mysterious, it offers Vestigians a source of power, guidance, and inspiration.

S

Sai (SIGH): Long, slender daggers.

Scholastic House: <u>Academy</u> House focusing on the three branches of academics: the languages, the sciences, and the arts. Its emblem is a <u>triskele</u>.

Scorpionflies: Creatures of Draaken whose stings cause temporary, localized paralysis.

Serle (SURL): Acting Councilman for the <u>Vestigians</u>.

Shanachai (SHAHN-ah-hai): <u>Innish</u> for *bard* or *storyteller*.

Sidra (SID-rah): A hard-shelled <u>Vahyan</u> fruit with sweet juice inside.

Sinkhar (SIN-car): A <u>Lagorite</u> agent and servant of <u>Draaken</u>.

Sketpoole (SKET-pool): A coastal city on <u>Freith</u>.

Song of Ishua, The: The powerful, neverending melody used by <u>Adona Roi</u> to create life and sustain the universe. Also the anthem of the <u>Vestigia Roi</u> and the basis of <u>Ellie's</u> visions.

Spark: A <u>Vestigian</u> ship carrying passengers to <u>Vahye</u>.

Steele, Dr.: Professor of <u>Aletheian</u> History at the <u>Academy</u>.

Stellaria (stell-AH-ree-ah): Tree native to the City of Adona Roi, transplanted to Rhynlyr by Ishua. Later clippings were planted on other Havens. Stellaria leaves are used to make caris powder.

Sunny: A shaggy golden dog belonging to Owen Mardel.

Suor (soo-OR): An island, now destroyed, in the south of Arjun Mador.

Sylvia Galen (GAY-len): A Vestigian agent and keeper of the Sketpoole Home for Boys and Girls.

T

Talia (TAL-ee-ah): Maid in Ahlmet Mukkech's palace.

Tangwystl (tang-GWI-stul): Finn's harp.

Tarlbayrn (TARL-bay-ern): Home of Chieftain Ahearn and seat of Innish government.

Tehber (teh-BARE): A dead language of Aletheia.

Temkal (TEM-call): A Nakuran juice derived from cactus plants.

Thelipsa (thell-IPS-uh): Regent and later queen of Vansuil, instigator of Thelipsa's Rebellion, and destroyer of the Elbarra Cluster.

Thelipsa's Rebellion: The first large-scale show of disloyalty to the One Kingdom. Thelipsa gave in to Lagorite advice and used asthmenos to break up the Elbarra Cluster.

Tixra (TEESH-rah): A small farming village on Vahye.

Tobin, Councilman (TOE-binn): Occupational member of the Council on Rhynlyr.

Triskele (TRISS-kell): A design made up of three intersecting spirals. Used as the emblem of Scholastic House.

Trull, Vice Admiral: Vestigian leader grounded on Nakuru after the tidal wave.

Twyrild (TWEER-illd): A Newdonian island; Owen Mardel's home island.

U

Ulfurssh (ULL-fursh): Contemptuous Lagorite term for the Vestigia Roi.

Ujuba (oo-joo-bah): Waxy berries whose oil burns slowly and is suitable for use in lanterns.

Urian (yoo-RYE-ann): Captain of the Vestigian ship *Spark*.

Urken (URR-ken): Cruel and brutal creatures of Draaken; souls plundered from falling islands and attached to deformed bodies.

℧

Vahye (VA-yay): An island in Arjun Mador; Vivian Sterlen's home island.

Vansuil (VAHN-soo-ill): Island governed by Thelipsa in the lost Elbarra Cluster.

Venture: A Vestigian ship commanded by Makundo.

Verana (vehr-AH-nah): The original Aletheian continent, which was later broken into the Five Archipelagos.

Vestigia Roi (ves-TI-jee-ah roh-EE): A secret organization following Ishua, Adona Roi, and Rua, whose goal is to restore the One Kingdom. They use land-based agents as well as flying ships and islands to counter the effects of asthmenos with caris powder and rescue people from falling islands. Members are known as Vestigians, but are sometimes called Basileans as a term of contempt.

Vestigian (ves-TI-jee-an): A member of the Vestigia Roi.

Vivian Sterlen (STIR-lenn): Scholar and linguist, wife to Jude Sterlen.

ℨ

Zarifah (zarr-EE-fah): A blind seer from the island of Suor, late mentor to Ellianea Reid.

Zelfmyr (ZELF-meer): A leaf that purportedly cures bruises.

Zira (ZEER-ah): Falcon belonging to Makundo.

Discussion Questions

1. Why doesn't Connor think he has a gift? Why does Ellie think he does? What do you think it means to be gifted? (51)

2. When Ellie finds the Vestigia Roi again, she thinks it will be like going home. Instead, what does she find? (67)

3. Why doesn't the Council listen to Ellie about the new Song music and words at first? (99)

4. What does it mean for new life to rise from fire? Can you think of some examples where this happens in *The Illuminator Rising*? In nature? In the world around you? (108)

5. Why don't the Vestigians and Nakurans get along at first? (173)

6. Why does Owen allow the dshinn to come inside him? (199)

7. Kai says, "People fear things that are different. They hate what they don't understand. Trouble is, hate never got anything new off the ground. Only faith can do that" (203). Do you agree? Can you think of an example of this in the real world?

8. Why do the Nakurans eventually agree to help the Vestigians? (216)

9. Why does the Council decide to use the single pouch of caris powder to save Vivian's life? (233)

10. How does Nikira tempt Connor? (252)

11. What are some ways Ishua gives the crew of the *Legend* the strength to fight back against Draaken? (274-275)

12. By the end of the book, how have the Vestigia Roi risen up? How has Ellie?

Project Ideas

1. The crew of the *Legend* must solve a riddle in order to find the Vestigia Roi (9). Find a book of riddles and try to solve them without looking at the answers. Then test your friends!

2. The crew of the *Legend* uses different kinds of knots for sailing as well as for rock climbing on Nakuru (20, 204). Look up instructions and learn to tie at least three types of knots.

3. Ellie's friends teach her how to swim in the *onot* (109). Think of something you know how to do, then try teaching it to your friends.

4. On Nakuru, Alyce cooks rattlesnake stew (174). You may not be able to find rattlesnake, but find a recipe and try cooking a food you've never tasted before (ask an adult for help). Serve it up and see if you like it!

5. Finn uses ventriloquism to make his voice sound like it's coming from other places (117, 245). Watch some videos on ventriloquism and give it a try!

Acknowledgments

To Mama, my PR manager, best cheerleader, and partner in crime: You work for the world's worst salary, yet never quit believing in me. Thank you for everything—from respecting the DO NOT DISTURB sign on the writing cave, to listening to me talk endlessly about fictional people, to painting readers' hands, to proofreading, to chatting at a bazillion sales tables, to getting up at 6 AM to help me lug boxes of books across town. You're the best. That's all there is to say.

To Daniel: The readers of this book thank you that there are action scenes in it. Without ten-minute pauses for conversation. Thank you for test reading, for helping me choose chapter names, and for challenging me to keep at it until the characters worked and the physics...well, sort of worked.

I'd like to thank Pilgrim Tours and our immensely knowledgeable guide Ilhami for introducing me to the rich and beautiful landscape of Turkey.

Thank you to all the educators who have worked with me to arrange author presentations in your classrooms and homeschool groups. You go above and beyond to give your students enriching educational experiences. The young minds in your care may not understand your dedication just yet, but I do, and I thank you for it.

Thank you to Jenny Zemanek of Seedlings Design Studio for another absolutely stunning cover.

Thank you to Angela Wallace for the beautifully formatted e-book (and the pep talks).

Thank you to Caleb Fong for your genius tech support on my website, for answering even my stupidest questions, and for staying calm when I thought I'd broken the Internet.

My immense gratitude goes to Ruth Wakefield, inventor of the chocolate chip cookie.

Thank you to my amazing team of test readers: Amy and Sarah B., Tom, Tammy, and Michael C., Kalyn M., Daniel S., Zoe S., and Kristin S. You guys are fast, thorough, imaginative, and responsible for the fact that the final draft of this book looks nothing like the one you read!

And last but not least—to Adona Roi, to Ishua, to Rua—for the gift, for the joy, for the journey. Alleluia, alleluia.

About The Author

Alina Sayre began her literary career chewing on board books and has been in love with words ever since. Now she gets to work with them every day as an author, educator, editor, and speaker. Her first novel, *The Illuminator's Gift*, won a silver medal in the Moonbeam Children's Book Awards, and all three books in *The Voyages of the Legend* series have received 5-star reviews from Readers' Favorite. When she's not writing, Alina enjoys hiking, crazy socks, and reading under blankets. She does not enjoy algebra or wasabi. When she grows up, she would like to live in a castle with a large library.

If you enjoyed this book, please help spread the word by sharing a review on Amazon.com!

Connect with Alina online!

Website: alinasayre.com

E-mail: alinasayreauthor@gmail.com

Facebook: www.facebook.com/alinasayreauthor

Twitter: @AlinaSayre

Made in the USA
Middletown, DE
11 June 2016